South

Tomorrow will be a better day

Lindsay Anderson-Faulkner

Copyright © Lindsay Anderson-Faulkner 2022

Lindsay Anderson-Faulkner has asserted her rights under the Copyright, Designs and Patent Act 1988 to be identified as the author of the work. All Characters and Places in this Publication are fictitious and any resemblance to real persons living or dead is purely coincidental.

A CIP catalogue record for this book is available from the British Library

ISBN

978-1-913369-11-8

For my husband Terry and my girls Emily and Annie, loved always and appreciated forever.

And for Roxy who is always at my side.

With my thanks to the following companies without whom this book would never have been possible.

Artwork by Printspot
Berwick-Upon-Tweed (01289) 309217

Printed by Martin the Printers
Berwick-Upon-Tweed (01289) 306006

SOUTHLANDS

Chapter 1

The view from the kitchen window was perfect. Blue sky, bright sun, long shadows falling from brightly dressed people who were laughing and joking, smiling and drinking. But now she knew that she wasn't part of the festivities at Hudson Hall Farm.

Robert Bucannon was tall, dark and handsome. He was witty, fun and the most popular boy at Young Farmers, so when he begged her to come to his farm for the Summer Solstice party, Frances had accepted with just a little bit of hesitation. It had been nearly one and half years since she had been out socially and she couldn't remember the last time she'd not worn jeans or baggy pyjamas. Frances had spent three frustrating days trying to decide what to wear. It wasn't because she had a lot of clothes, one thing for certain she didn't, it was just trying to decide what was the right thing to wear! Three pairs of working jeans, one pair of best jeans and one pair of bottle green cords for really cold snowy days. Her only other choice was a pair of faded grey linen trousers that she had bought for her holiday to France with the school when she was sixteen. She had a lovely pale pink cotton blouse that freshened up the trousers and her once white trainers still looked smart enough to be seen in public. Decision made.

Robert as promised had picked her up in his battered 4 x 4 at 1.00pm prompt. When she opened the front door to him she was met with a brilliant white smile.

"Ready." he said.

"Yes nearly, I just need to get my bag and give the dogs a drink."

Frances settled into the shabby, worn seats of the truck. They were soft and cool to the touch on such a hot day. "Sorry Frances but air conditioning wasn't invented when this girl was built, you will need to open your window and stick your head out like a dog if it gets too hot." She giggled. Frances rolled down the window and felt the cool breeze of air slide over her skin. Today was a good day. Today the sun was out, the sky was blue and there was not one cloud in the sky or in her head. She turned and smiled at Robert. He gave a quick smile back and said a quick pleasantry about how she looked. Robert was the same age as her and he had just come back from University in Edinburgh where he was training to be a vet. He was full of stories about it, he was always happy and bubbly. She liked that about him most, he seemed happy and content. His blue skinny jeans hugged his legs and the oversized white linen shirt rippled in the breeze in the truck. His thick, curly, brown hair just touched the collar of the shirt and reminded Frances of a lion's mane. Frances smiled inside to herself. Yes, today was a good day.

They were the first to arrive at Hudson Hall Farm. Robert had said that about twenty people had been invited but he wasn't really sure how many would turn up as his mum just kept adding to the list. Robert drove down the long, tarmacked drive pointing out the cattle, the sheep and the new combine harvester which was parked near the entrance to the farm. When they arrived at the farm house Frances just stared open mouthed at the view. It wasn't a quaint, shabby farm house as she had imagined but an imposing, almost stately manor house. It was huge. Row upon row of windows with perfect white shutters endorsed the front of the house. A large wooden front door could just be seen behind the four large pillars holding up an equally large portico, she was impressed to say the least.

"Nice house Robert!" She said whilst staring in awe at the imposing building.

"Yes, it's what we farmers call home." His jovial reply made Frances smile as he drove round the side of it, through an arch and into a large courtyard area surrounded by stables and outbuilding. In the distance, the hills rolled on as far as the eye could see, only interrupted by a large wooden barn which also stood quite majestically against the stunning backdrop.

They came to a stop in the yard and both got out of the truck. Frances stood on the large flagstone courtyard which was surrounded on two sides by stables and other outbuildings. All the doors that opened onto the yard were painted in a dark green paint, all newly painted by the look of them. Large old troughs lay against the solid walls brimming with the brightest coloured flowers.

"It's been in the family yonks, dad's, dad's, dad I think bought it and one day poor Marcus will be landed with the place. Don't get me wrong I love this place, the farm, the fields and the views but it's a lot to take on and I just don't think it's me. I think I'm more of a city boy at heart, I think I'll live in London or stay in Edinburgh if I can get a job. Come and meet mum and dad they'll be in the kitchen and both will be pleased to see you."

They grabbed some shopping bags out of the back of the truck and carried them towards an already open back door. "Great, look the tables are already set and all the chairs and benches are out too, saves me a job!" Frances followed Robert past the biggest table she had ever seen in her life, it looked like it was set for about fifty never mind twenty. It looked so pretty covered in red gingham table cloths and white china. Vases full of local wild flowers and grasses made it look homely and perfect. A very brave decision too, to have a dinner party outside in June in Northumberland! She was determined to enjoy herself today.

"Hello Frances it's nice to meet you, thank you for coming up. Right let's get started then, can you wash and prick the potatoes and then pop them in the Aga and then can you help chop up that lot," pointing at a pile of cabbages "and make a huge bowl of coleslaw. Then you need to keep on top of the washing up. Great. Thanks. Do you want a drink before we start, water or tea?" Frances looked at the pile of potatoes and the sink that was already full of pots. "Just water please."

Two hours later she had washed all the pots up, cleaned and pricked all the potatoes, made five bowls of coleslaw, made a hundred homemade burgers and hardly said a word to anyone or even seen Robert. Family and friends were all arriving now. All were offered champagne or beer. Everyone knew each other but none of them had come into the kitchen and worked. None of them had been offered tea or water. All were outside in the late afternoon sun drinking and laughing. Some were being shown to their seats and all looked happy. She stared out of the window wondering where Robert was. She glanced at her watch, she'd been in the hot kitchen for nearly two and half hours! She felt hot and sticky and her appearance in the mirror reflected her new opinion of herself. Behind her, one of the oak chairs scraped across the floor. Startled she turned around to see a man about thirty slumping into one of the chairs.

"Sorry I didn't mean to scare you but I'm so knackered I just needed to sit down, get a drink of water and brace myself before I go outside and pretend I want to be here. Sorry I'm Marcus, number one son and you are?"

"Hi, yes I'm Frances I'm Robert's... friend. I came to the party with Robert, your brother, but I haven't seen him since I got here about two and a half hours ago, I'm not sure where he is really. I've just been helping your mum in the kitchen since I got here and not had a chance to go out and find him," she said awkwardly. Marcus stood and was about to say something when his mum walked into the kitchen and gave him a great big hug and lots of kisses.

"Hello my darling. I'm so glad you managed to get away from the hospital in time. Felicity and her parents are already here so pop upstairs and get yourself ready dear."

"Frances, how can I ever thank you, you have been a complete marvel, Robert said you knew your way around a kitchen. I think we can manage from now on, the barbecue is well alight and all the salads are ready to go out. Right, here's thirty pounds for your time and I will be sure to call on your services again the next time I need a kitchen help." She left the money on the table, picked up more wine and left the room with a flurry. Frances looked at the money and then Marcus. Shock was etched all over her face.

"I think I need to go." Frances walked swiftly over to the chair by the door and picked up her bag and was about to leave the kitchen when she hesitated, turned and spoke to Robert's brother.

"I'm not sure what's happened but I think there has been a mistake, I thought I was Robert's friend for the party not the 'kitchen help', I don't know what to say really, to you or your mum. Can you tell Robert that I've gone home!" She put the tea towel down which was in her hand. She noticed that her hand was shaking. As she walked towards the door she looked at the money but didn't pick it up, then she left the room.

Marcus stood up and watched her run across the courtyard towards the big barn which was just outside the yard. She went inside. Marcus watched and waited for her to come out, hopefully accompanied by his brother who should be begging the poor girl's forgiveness. But instead of Robert and the girl walking out together, he saw the girl run out as swiftly as she had gone in but as she left the barn she leant against the wooden door briefly before running down the dirt track that led to the main drive. "That bloody sod, he's done it again". Marcus slammed down the glass of water which was in his hand and ran out of the kitchen in the direction of the barn using the side path.

Minutes later he was inside the barn shouting out Robert's name. "Robert, Robert you bloody idiot, where are you?" Seconds later, Robert walked towards his brother tucking his shirt quickly into his trousers and doing up his shirt buttons. Miles Jeffries followed him tucking himself in just as quickly as Robert and trying in vain to tidy his mop of blond hair. "You bloody idiot, doing it with your boyfriend in the barn with all of mum and dad's friends and family only a hundred yards away. You bloody, bloody idiot. And what about that girl, she thought she was your date and not a maid to mum and certainly not a cover story for you. How could you treat her like that you fool and she obviously saw you two together? What are you going to do about her? She left the money mum gave her on the table you know. She had absolutely no idea that she was here only to work". Rage could be heard in Marcus's voice as he stared at his brother

Marcus struggled to breathe , he was so angry he noticed that he was sweating profusely. Robert pushed passed him and growled at him. "It's nothing to do with you, we can't all be perfect like you, the perfect doctor, the perfect farmer, the perfect son and heir." With that he left the barn with Miles trotting behind him sheepishly. Marcus sat down on one of the bales and pushed his hands through his hair and breathed a very heavy sigh, he was tired and he didn't feel in the mood for a party, his mother or even Felicity. The last thing he needed was more trouble with Robert. He stood up and walked out of the barn towards the house, but in the distance, he caught sight of the girl walking down the drive. The drive was a mile long and Alnton was at least three miles away.

"OMG,OMG!" Frances could not believe what she had just seen in the barn. Shocked at what she'd just watched and also shocked that Robert was definitely into boys and definitely not girls and definitely not her. God what an idiot she had been. Tears trickled down her face, she'd not cried in ages. She thought she had no tears left. How could he treat her like that, to use her so badly and why hadn't she seen him for what he was. She felt broken again. How had she been so foolish and not seen that he was into boys, only she deserved to be fooled by someone like him. "Frances, you are a complete idiot." She said out loud.

Marcus ran into the house and picked up his car keys and then ran over to his dad in the yard and told him briefly that he had to do a quick errand and that he'd be back soon. Without even looking up at his son, Richard Bucannon continued to turn the beefburgers on the large American style barbecue. 'Don't be too long son or all the burgers may be gone and they look rather tasty."

"They will be great this time dad, mum didn't make them!" He said with a smile. He ran over to his car which he'd parked at the side of the house and was thankful that he hadn't been blocked in by anyone. He jumped into the car and reversed it out and sped off down the drive. Moments later he slowly passed Frances and gently pulled up in his sleek, black BMW and rolled down the window.

"I think you need a lift home. I'm sorry about my stupid brother and my selfish mother. I'm afraid neither of them would ever offer an apology to you in person as they both think they are right all the time. But I do think after the day you've had, the very least I can do is offer you a lift home." Frances looked at the long drive and then at her dusty trainers. She was tired and emotional and most of all ashamed. She hesitated before she spoke.

"Thanks for the offer, it's very kind but I think it's best if I just carry on by myself, you have a party to go to and you wouldn't want the downstairs staff to be seen in the master's car, would you?" She said with a slight smile.

"I'll risk it if you dare to risk it, jump in."

Frances walked slowly around the back of the BMW and looked back at the farm. Today had started off well, really well but now it was a disaster. If he gave her a lift home it would enable her to get home faster, lock the doors, take a shower and console herself in the fur of Max and Bert. She didn't need to speak to him. It was just a lift. She didn't want to accept the lift but it was the means to an end, the end of a very long and sad day. Frances opened the door hesitantly, scared not to mark the expensive paintwork and slid into the front passenger seat and buckled up. She felt out of place, the car still had that new car smell and it was so clean and lavishly luxurious. She felt dusty and dirty and very out of her depth. The drive home took about ten minutes, much better than a hot and sticky two hour walk. Considering she didn't know him, the trip wasn't stressful or awkward as both seemed in their own worlds, thinking their own thoughts. She wondered if he knew about Robert. He spoke once, only to ask her where she lived. She gave him the directions and pointed to her house as they pulled up. It suddenly became an awkward silence. Frances's mind raced.

They had stopped outside a pretty little terrace house in the middle of a row. There was a black metal gate leading to a small garden which was full of roses, lupins and poppies. Three shallow steps lead up to a painted mottled green front door where a large hanging basket hung on either side, displaying copious amounts of summer flowers. The windows were painted white and it was kept very clean and tidy. Frances loved this house especially as it was where her grandparents had lived. The house was full of warmth and memories and it was the best place in the world to live, much nicer then Hudson Hall Farm. Here she could just close the front door and lock out the rest of the world and be safe and quiet. It may not be big and it certainly didn't have acres of park and farm land but it was home.

"Thank you for driving me home, I hope you enjoy the party." Frances opened the car door and got out and walked to the gate, behind her she heard the electric window lowering.

"Are you sure you're OK, you were lost in your thoughts on the way home."

"I'm fine, it's just been a strange day where things were not as I thought they were. I'll be better when I get a drink and something to eat." She fumbled in her pocket to find her keys and then quickly unlocked the door pushed it open and then gave a quick smile and nod to the man in the car before diving in and closing the door behind her. She leant back on the door and slowly slid to the floor, the tears flowing easily now that she was alone.

Marcus pressed the window button and the car window slowly moved up and closed. It felt wrong to just drive off and leave her. She looked upset and seemed lonely. He knew that she'd had a really bad day, first as a kitchen porter and then she had caught her so called date at it with a boy in the barn. How was she to know that Robert was in a relationship with Miles. Everyone knew Robert loved Miles and they were together, apart from his mum and dad. Robert, as brash and aggressive as he could be, still hadn't had the courage to tell his mum and dad about Miles or the fact that he was homosexual. If he was Miles, he would've been off months ago and let Robert stew! He turned the car engine off and just sat in the car trying to decide what to do. Go home and endure a party with all the local gentry and his parents nearest and dearest friends and pretend to be part of it, laughing and drinking till the sun went down or go up those three steps and ask a very simple question?

"Are you okay?" He could tell she'd been crying, the streaks still visible across her face. "If I'm intruding just tell me, I'm just so angry at my mum and Robert for what they have done to you and just wanted to see that you're okay." He paused before he spoke again. "Who do you live with? Will they be back soon, it just doesn't seem right leaving you alone in the house? And I'm not really in a hurry to get home and face them all. I've had a long and difficult day at work myself and I wondered if you wanted some company and maybe talk things through, I mean what you saw, what he did to you?" God, he couldn't stop mumbling on, he sounded more like a shrink than a doctor he thought as he looked away from her back towards his car.

"I'm alright honest, I'm tougher than I look, really, I was just caught off guard, twice!" She tried to smile at her own joke. "I was making some tea, you are welcome to have quick drink before you have to go back. But it's fine if you have to get off, I've got Bert and Max with me so I'm not on my own." On cue, two black Labradors waddled down the hall with their tails beating against each other. Both had grey beards and slightly arthritic gaits. Marcus bent down immediately and gave both dogs a good pat and ruffled them around their ears. Both dogs jostled together to get the most attention, loving every minute of the pleasure this new person was giving them.

"Tea please, just with milk." She stood to one side closed her eyes as he passed and gritted her teeth in exasperation at her own stupidity. She let him pass followed by Bert and Max who definitely enjoyed all the attention that this new person was showering down on them. He stood back as she closed the door and then followed her along the hall and into the lounge, kept company by the dogs. The room was quaint, as if it was still stuck in the 1960s. A heavily patterned carpet dominated the room which he hoped she had inherited with the house as the gold and cream swirls were definitely an acquired taste. The sofa and two armchairs were a shade of red or maybe maroon, they were leather and very retro with large broad arms and low seats. All the seats were covered with blankets for the dogs to sit on. The TV sat on an old wooden trolley. It was the oldest TV he seen for years outside of a museum. It had a twelve-inch screen and it was decorated with a faux wooden material around it and had knobs on the left hand side of the screen. He wondered if it was black and white. The curtains were a heavy cream velvet and touched the ground. The room was full of ornaments and pictures, it seemed too old for her he thought.

Frances went into the kitchen and filled the old whistling kettle up with water, turned the gas on, lit it with a match and put the kettle on to heat up. She got two cups and saucers down and placed them on a small wooden tray, took the lid off the teapot and popped in two teabags. Two teabags! It had been a while since she had made tea for someone else, she leant against the cooker as she waited for the kettle to boil just pondering the one or two teabag rule for two people. As the kettle started to whistle she opened the fridge to fetch the milk.

"Is that all you've got in your fridge just milk and butter?" Frances turned around quickly and shut the fridge door with a slam.

"I thought I was eating out tonight and I've not had chance to go to the shops yet so it's a little empty!" Her voice was squeaky and high.

"No, I mean there's nothing in your fridge no jams, pickles, jars, plastic containers filled with old rotting veggies, it's the tidiest fridge or the emptiest fridge in the world. What do you normally like to eat?"

"I eat very well and very healthily normally." She opened the door and replaced the milk quickly.

"I'm sorry, I didn't mean to offend you. I suppose I'm used to a massive double American style fridge full to bursting usually. That's what my mum's and Felicity's fridges are like anyway." Marcus knew that he was mumbling again. He felt embarrassed which was a new feeling for him but he guessed he wasn't as embarrassed as she felt. He was annoyed at himself too, she'd had a bad day and didn't need him making her feel worse.

She poured the tea without speaking and wished that she hadn't asked him in after all. This was just all too unsettling for her. She liked being on her own, she wasn't sure if she really needed his company but he seemed to need a reason to delay going back home. If only she had a packet of biscuits or some cake she could just get out and place on the tray to show him that her cupboards weren't completely empty. Mental note to self, buy emergency biscuits for such an occasion. What did the contents of her house have to do with him anyway she decided, annoyed at her own previous thoughts. She picked up the tray and beckoned him to follow her through to the lounge and he followed. She sat in one of the armchairs and placed the tea tray on the table.

"It's been a while since I've had tea in a teacup and saucer, it reminds me of when I was small at my grandparent's house." Marcus sat down on the old leather sofa where the two dogs quickly accompanied him.

"Me too, I like old things and family things. These were my nana's, I use them every day and sometimes I even raise my little finger and feel all together rather superior." She laughed a small shy laugh. A laugh that Marcus noticed, it was the first time he'd heard her laugh. She smiled too. It was a beautiful smile it made her look younger and even carefree but he knew at this moment she was anything but carefree.

"I'm so sorry about my stupid brother, he's so selfish and immature. If he's into boys that's fine but to run around the County the way he does, causing trouble and mayhem, one day mum and dad will find out and it would be far better coming from him than the butcher or the gamekeeper." Frances smiled again and Marcus realised that she was laughing at him. Gamekeeper, how pretentious did he sound, he laughed at himself. He took a drink from his cup and relaxed back into the sofa and closed his eyes, it had been a strange twenty-four hours to say the least. He was tired, he'd not been to sleep for so long and all he wanted to do was close his eyes and catch up on desperately needed sleep and to try and put his thoughts in order. God, he needed a break and he didn't need his parents or Felicity piling on anymore of anything on his shoulders, especially wedding talk or empire building!

Frances slowly took the cup and saucer from his hands and replaced them quietly on the table. He was fast asleep. She sat down and looked at him not quite sure what to do, to wake him or let him sleep. He needed to get back to the party but he did look exhausted, she hadn't noticed that before, she hadn't really studied his face before like she did now. He looked peaceful and younger in his sleep only twenty-six or twenty-seven, he looked handsome. She smiled to herself, she'd never really thought of boys in that way not even Robert who, after much harassment, had finally forced her into agreeing to go to the party with him. Marcus looked calm and the wonderfully white blond hair which had been slicked back perfectly before gently rested on his left eye. He looked slightly tanned but his eyelids were still pale, his hair was perfectly cut and shaved round the sides and he only had slight hint of stubble. He looked like Thor in a film she had recently watched. He had a similar build, tall, athletic, broad but not overweight. I bet Thor never wore a suit and tie to battle for the defence of Planet Earth, she smiled.

He stirred and started to move in his seat. Frances looked away feeling guilty that she'd analysed him so closely whilst he was sleeping. She could feel herself going red and shifted uncomfortably in her chair. He settled again and she looked at the clock and let her face cool down. It was 7.45 now and she had noticed the glow of his phone in his shirt pocket a couple of times. His family and friends would be wondering where he was so she decided to wake him.

"Marcus." She paused. "Marcus," she said a little bit louder. "It's time for you to wake up and go back home."
He stirred and slowly opened his eyes, rubbing them gently and then slowly he realised where he was and sat up.

"Oh god I'm so sorry, how rude of me to fall asleep on you whilst you were talking to me, I'm so, so, sorry I bet you think I'm just another rude Bucannon."
She smiled, she didn't think that at all, he wasn't like the rest of his family. He jumped up and patted the dogs quickly and then walked out of the room towards the front door followed by Frances.

"Thanks for the tea and the respite. I think it's time that I left and faced the party and the family. It's been really nice to meet you and Robert's a complete idiot for not whisking you off your feet when he had the chance. I'm so sorry that I fell asleep when you were talking but I felt like I was sort of at home in your house, on your sofa......... it's a really lovely, homely home you have and I'm sorry about 'Fridgegate', I shouldn't have said anything." He stopped talking abruptly realising that he was now waffling.

Frances opened the front door and stood back to let him pass. He smiled down at her with his mouth and his sky blue eyes, Frances returned his easy smile with a more awkward smile in response. Neither seemed to know what to say to bid each other goodbye. He walked down the steps and slowly turned around.

"Bye."

"Bye and thanks for the lift." With that, Frances closed the door and went back into the lounge and picked up the cups and saucers and replaced them on the tray. She tidied the cushions and the blankets and then walked into the kitchen and placed the tray near the sink and opened the fridge door. Nothing to eat she thought. I'm surprised he hadn't passed comment about how old her kitchen was. It seemed like he liked to voice his opinion about a lot of things. His home was amazing, stately, traditional, contemporary, immaculate and expensive, very expensive! Thinking about it as she tidied she looked around her kitchen and her lounge, her house must've been quite a shock to him so he'd actually been quite polite.

She opened a cupboard and got out a tin of tomato soup. She opened the drawer and took out the tin opener. She opened the tin and poured half of the contents into a pan and put it on the cooker, turned on the gas and lit it. She put the pan on the flame and looked inside the other cupboards to see what she could find. Her lucky day, a box of water biscuits only a few months out of date! She poured the hot soup into the bowl and carried the box of biscuits over to the old tiny Formica topped kitchen table and chair. She slowly swirled the soup round in the bowl waiting for it to cool down again. She wondered what they would be eating up at the party right now. They would be tucking into a banquet with only the best champagne and wines flowing freely. The burgers had looked absolutely amazing, they should do, she'd made them, and so did the sausages. The salmon looked too good to cook on a barbecue, what a waste, the smoke smell would overpower the fresh salmon. All the salads, at least five different varieties, presented beautifully. The coleslaws were homemade and looked fabulous, made with the best and freshest ingredients. She loved salad. The coronation chicken smelt divine and she imagined the butter melting in the hot jacket potatoes. The cakes and large bowls of fruit salads were to die for, fresh strawberries as far as the eye could see. She suddenly stopped and forced her thoughts back to the task in question. "Don't worry Frances, tomorrow will be a better day," she said aloud as if trying to convince herself. She looked at the boring bowl of soup and the dry biscuit and slowly started to force it down.

The drive back home to Hudson Hall Farm had been quick, he turned the music up in the car as he drove, he was into loud Rock music which helped to keep him awake and focused. Guns 'n' Roses at full volume, nothing better and he always knew it had the extra benefit of usually annoying Felicity. His mind wasn't on work, the hospital, his parents, the farm, Felicity or even her ever so annoying meddling family. His thoughts were slow and simple tonight, a refreshing change for him. He thought about Frances. He'd never met her before and had a strange feeling about her. She was quiet, kind, uncomplicated, gentle, delicate and beautiful. He thought if she was a friend of Roberts she would be about twenty or so but she looked much younger than the other girls that were in Robert's friendship groups. She had dressed simply, comfortably and hadn't slapped on an inch of make up or thrown on a gallon of perfume. She had smelt just, he pondered, natural. But she seemed lonely and lost in that house. That house seemed to suit her in lots of ways but in other ways it felt like it wasn't hers, as if she rented it and all the belongings inside too. But the quaintness suited her very well, it was a peaceful and serene home and he decided he liked it very much.

"Marcus, Marcus where on earth have you been you've been gone over two hours and I've been getting really worried about you and so has Felicity, why didn't you answer your phone," gushed his mother as she wrapped her arms around him. Marcus noticed that her perfectly made up face showed signs of distress and she had at least one hair out of place which was most unusual for her as she was always immaculately dressed and always wore full make up and perfectly styled hair.

"Sorry mum it's been a long day, I took that girl home, and then had to deal with a few matters which were easier to do in the car than in a house full of people. I'll just nip upstairs to freshen up and put my phone away. I'll be down in five minutes and mine is a cold beer from the fridge please," he said as he walked out of the kitchen.

Chapter 2

Frances finished the washing up and gave Bert and Max their evening meal which they both ate eagerly. She opened the back door and walked up the small garden path to the wooden gate in the fence. She opened it and called for the dogs to come out and have a stroll with her. They obliged and waddled up the path sniffing the garden as they went. The gate opened onto a farmer's field that just had grass in it this year. It took about fifteen minutes for the three of them to slowly walk the perimeter. They were getting older now. Bert and Max were fourteen years old, they were brothers but the two Labradors now showed their age with every step. They sniffed and did their business and were both ready for their beds when they got back. Frances locked the back gate and door and settled herself on the sofa with Bert and Max on either side ready for a night in front of the TV. She only had three channels but she wasn't fussy what she watched and finally decided to watch the end of an old black and white film. It was nearly nine now and she had her usual Sunday off so she could watch the film to the end.

She woke up the next morning with the sun streaming in and warming the room. Bert and Max were still asleep in their beds at the side of hers, Max as usual snoring. She turned over and looked at the clock, 7.32am perfect, she thought, a lovely lie in. She jumped off the bed and nipped to the loo. Neither dog stirred as their eyes followed her. Five minutes later she returned to the bed with a hot mug of tea and settled herself down into bed and picked up her book. The shabby red covered book had been neglected for long enough and she hoped to finish Pride and Prejudice today before she did anything else. Shopping, gardening and cleaning could all wait for just a few more hours.

Monday morning always arrived far too soon she thought to herself as she rolled over to switch off the alarm. 6.00am Monday morning was the worst time of the week, it signalled the start of yet another gruelling week for her. She got out of bed and slipped her feet into her slippers before shuffling off to the bathroom. Twenty minutes later she was showered and dressed with her long blond hair left to dry naturally . She ran down stairs to prepare breakfast for Bert and Max who obligingly waddled into the kitchen and a bowl of granola for herself. Kettle on, she leaned against the counter eating the granola, watching her boys wolf down the chappie breakfast she had bought for them as a treat. The dried food the dogs had eaten for so many years just seemed too much like hard work for them to chew and swallow these days.

Breakfasts eaten she quickly put on her boots and coat and took the dogs out for a walk around the perimeter of the field. Both enjoyed a good sniff and a little explore before they all headed home. She made a thermos flask of hot tea, pushed some fruit and some crisps in a lunch box and put them in her work rucksack. She ran upstairs and quickly made her bed and straightened the room before cleaning her teeth in the tiny sink.

Frances looked in the mirror and sighed. The week hadn't started yet and she looked tired. She ran the brush through her hair then nimbly divided her hair and plaited it. Today was a definite lip gloss day she thought as she opened her old and fairly empty make up bag. She took out the fuchsia pink lip gloss and ran the applicator around her lips. She did it several times squeezing the last bit out of the applicator. Tomorrow she would finally find time to invest in a new one, she'd pop it on her shopping list. It was amazing what a bit of colour could do to a tired looking face as she studied herself in the mirror. With a last look she turned and ran down the stairs. She went into the lounge and gave both boys who were now settled on the sofa with the radio on a farewell kiss, "see you later, don't do anything I wouldn't." She checked their water bowls as she put her boots back on and minutes later she was sat in her Defender driving to work.

Grovewood Stables were only about ten minutes away located on the Grovewood Hall Estate. She loved her job and didn't mind being in work first at 7.00 to get things started. The roads were always quiet and it gave Esme, her boss, a chance to get her kids up and get them off to school. Esme was a great boss and also a great friend. They had worked together for about a year now and they did work well together. Esme wasn't her actual boss, Arabella Forster-Smythe was or Bella as she was known. Her father, Mr Xavier Forster-Smythe owned the Hall but she oversaw the stables whilst Esme was the everyday stable manager. The stables were private and only the family's horses were stabled there. They had nineteen horses in total, a range of thoroughbreds, one very black stallion, six breeding mares, two foals, a couple of old family ponies and Hector, the most demanding Shetland pony in the world whom she loved most. She always smiled when she thought of Hector. He was ten years old now, solid black and had been bought as a companion for Hero, the fabulous black stallion that the family had invested in two years ago. Hero was seventeen hands of pure muscle, placid and very calm. He shared the paddock with Hector. Hector was always up to no good getting caught on the fence, always trying to escape to try to get to greener grass and he always tried to eat Hero's breakfast before he could finish it. He successfully ate his companions breakfast most days and thankfully a solution was eventually found. Now the two friends were fed on opposite sides of the paddock during the summer months. They had tried to part them but both would get upset and pace around until reunited. Frances often wondered about their relationship. She used to think it was a love hate thing but now she realised it was just a love love thing and annoying as they found each other at times they were just two soul mates who couldn't stand to be parted.

She drove up the drive towards the stables and parked up. She turned up the radio and caught the headlines on the news before jumping out of the Defender. As she locked it up she had a good look at her Defender and wiped some mud off. She was three years old now and looked in great condition. Burgundy defenders, long wheel base, were quite uncommon but her dad had just fallen in love with the colour when he had bought it, and now it was her's and she just loved her. The black top and mud guards just finished off the whole look. She was glad she'd washed and polished her yesterday, she was gleaming in the early morning sun, she really was her pride and joy.

Mornings were the busiest time of day at the stables. All the horses needed to be checked, given breakfast and then taken out to the paddocks for some grass and fresh air. Some horses stayed in the paddocks all day at this time of the year, feeding on soft green grass and frolicking in the warm sun. Once the horses had all been moved to the paddocks the stables then all needed to be mucked out and fresh bedding put down, the water troughs all cleaned and the water supplies checked. When the horses had all been seen too and their stables cleaned, Frances managed a sit down in the office for a morning tea from her flask. It was gone 10.00, where was Esme? She got her old phone out and checked to see if she had missed any calls. Just one from Esme. She listened to the message which Esme had left just over an hour ago to say she was running late. As she finished listening to the message her boss walked into the office.

"Sorry Frances, sorry I'm so late. Jed woke up with an awfully high temperature, the doctor has checked him over and thinks it's just a virus. I was lucky to get him an appointment for the doctor to see him so quickly. Mum's a life saver and she's got him now. Poor thing he'll have to watch day time TV all day over the sound of mum's knitting needles. All okay?" She swiftly took off her coat and piled it onto a chair with her bag and lunchbox.

"Yep, everything here is fine. How's Jed feeling now? How's Gabe, he hasn't caught it has he, these virus's do like to spread themselves around."

"So far, it's just Jed, touch wood," she leant over to touch the wooden desk.

"I'm hoping it stays only with him. It's a busy week this week. We've got a party of six on Wednesday out riding with Arabella and then we have those prospective buyers coming to look at the new foals on Thursday so the stables need to be spick and span and she wants all the horses washed, groomed and looking their best. It's a big day. Hero's first foals are due to be sold and hopefully we can get good prices. If it goes well there will be a lot more foals around this place. I really just don't have the time to be off ill or have to deal with sick boys. Right, finish your tea and let's get started on checking all the paddocks for ragwort

and then we can start to wash down the stable yards ready for inspection. You get the barrow and I'll nip and get the spades. Are you at the ball this weekend Fran?"
They left the office and started to walk towards a store room to get the equipment.

"Yes, Paul's asked me to go in for 6pm to help set up the tables and then I'm serving till one. He said it's a sell out so it will be really busy and hot in the marquee and loads of drunks as usual."

"Why don't you ever just get a ticket and actually come to a ball. You could have fun, get drunk, dance, endure the food, laugh, sit with us, please." She smiled with begging eyes .

"Thanks Esme for the invite as always but I can't. The money is too good to miss. I get to enjoy the music, eat left overs for free and I don't have to pay for a ticket or buy a new ball gown or shoes. So, I see it as a win win for me. It will cost most people including new outfit, ticket, drinks and a taxi about £250, I'll walk away with £80.00 and I'll have been to the same event." Frances smiled.
As they picked up the barrow and shovels they chatted again.

"But it's not the same Frances. You don't have the same fun having to work and be polite to a room full of selfish and over inflated idiots. You said yourself some of them barely talk to you. Come with us, just once. Pleeaase...... The summer Ball is always the best Ball, and the longest day too, they've got a live rock band and the disco. It's on till 2.00am now and there's a midnight buffet. Just wear any old dress you've got. I know monies tight babe but I've never seen you in a dress ever or even at a social event. No one will know that it's not a new dress, come on at least just think about it."

Frances nodded but she knew she couldn't go, she needed the money and she didn't own any dresses not even an old one.

They started to tidy up the paddocks, clearing up after the horses as they went and checking no new ragwort has grown. Frances did think about the ball. She really needed the money, the TV was on its last legs, even Marcus had laughed at it. It was nearly thirty years old according to the receipt in the kitchen drawer, it had served the family well. The new flat screens were so expensive. She liked the one she had seen at Electricland, it was only small, 22" and had Freeview *and* a remote with it. How she'd missed a remote. It was in the sale at the moment at £250, from £350, it was a good price and if she got the extra money from waitressing on Saturday night, that's what she was going to put it towards. She had already agreed with Gino that she would waitress for him Tuesday to Friday and that would also go towards the new TV too. It was going to be a tough week, forty hours at the stable this week, seven hours at the ball and another twenty hours at the Italian restaurant. Hopefully she would be able to buy the new TV in a couple of weeks if she was careful.

"Are you okay Esme, you look very pale" Frances asked as she peeled an orange at lunch break.

"I think I'm ok, I've just got a bit of a headache. It's warm out today and I don't think I've had enough to drink. I don't have time to be ill this week anyway," she smiled.

Tuesday morning the phone sprang in to life on the dot of 6.00am Frances jumped out of bed to turn the alarm off only to realise it wasn't actually ringing. It was Esme. She listened to her friend on the phone, "You sound rough, no you stay in bed get some sleep and I'll see you when you feel better." She listened and affirmed the instructions that Esme had passed on to her. "I'll do the horses, stables and paddocks in that order and then I'll concentrate on the office and store rooms later today. Tomorrow will be ok, Arabella can do her own horse and then that just leaves the others for me to do. Have two days off please, doctor's orders. I don't want to be there on my own on Thursday so you must do your best to get better for then or I'll not talk to you again...ever." They both laughed and Esme promised she would be in for Thursday even if she arrived accompanied by two undertakers. Frances laughed and put the phone down and started her morning routine and then headed off for work.

Later that day, just after 5.30pm she arrived at No 64, the Italian restaurant in town where she generally worked Thursday, Fridays and occasionally Saturday evening. Gino and his wife Laila had run the place for about twenty years, very successfully. It served good, wholesome Italian food, pizza being by far the most popular. It was always full and such a happy place to work. She loved this little job and they always gave her something to eat as an extra perk. Gino had asked her to do some extra shifts to cover while his daughter, Sofia, was away on holiday for two weeks. Frances had jumped at the opportunity to get some extra cash but did feel very guilty that Max and Bert would have to spend so much time on their own this week. No 64 like most Italian restaurants which she had ever been in was strongly decorated in a red, white and green colour scheme. Flags were draped all around the room and old faded posters of Italian beauty spots adorned the walls. There were seventeen tables and when full the room could hold forty people. Tonight, there were twenty eight bookings which was a nice number, busy but it gave

Frances the opportunity to chat with the customers and not feel too pressured. She had waitressed for Gino for about ten months now and really enjoyed working for him. They were a nice family. Gino and Laila laughed and smiled all the time and seemed so in love, genuinely in love. They had four children Sofia was the youngest and still lived at home, the others, Melanie, Edwardo and Matteo were all at university and always helped out when they were at home for the holidays. Frances loved it when they were all in the restaurant, it was always a wonder that anyone ever got any food as the family argued, shouted, loved and hugged each other all the time. No 64 was a great job with great perks and Frances was happy to have this little job.

Wednesday started just like any other day at work for Frances at the stables. She'd arrived at 7.00 and had spent the morning doing all the routine jobs for the horses. In addition, this morning she needed to get ready the six horses that Arabella had asked for so that she could take her friends out for a ride. She was planning to take them over to Rothington where the horses could be tied up and they could all nip in for lunch at the aptly named Horseshoes Pub. Someone in the group was celebrating their birthday and Arabella had planned the day down to the very last detail.

"Morning Frances, are they all saddled up and ready to go?" Arabella's voice echoed around the stable yard.

"Morning Bella. Yes, all washed, groomed and saddled up ready for their adventure." Frances stopped as she looked at the group of friends. She knew Arabella and her fiancé Bill, Olivia and Jack were friends and she also knew Marcus! They all said hello and thank you as they took control of their horses. Frances helped some of them mount and checked the saddles and stirrups. The only person who didn't speak to her directly was the red headed woman who she knew to be a friend of Marcus. This must be the famous Felicity who Marcus had told her about, she hadn't met her before. She was absolutely stunning and looked like a goddess sitting high on the back of Della, her chestnut mare for the day. She was tall and slim, dressed in a black tweed jacket and jodhpurs with a thick mass of red curls that cascaded down her back and gentle brushed the saddle. She never spoke or looked at Frances as she settled herself into the saddle and adjusted the reins.

"Bells, you keep your horses in such perfect condition, they all look fab darling, thank you so much for arranging this birthday treat for me, it's fabulous." Felicity didn't wait for any answer from Arabella.

"How are you doing darling?" She spoke to Marcus.
"I know horses aren't really your thing babe but when we fill Hudson Hall with horses again I know you'll learn to love them as much as I do." Marcus did look quite uncomfortable on his mount, Woodward or Woody as he was known was seventeen hands and twenty two years old. He was a very well trained and a slightly lazy boy who plodded along happily and generally kept up with the other horses as long as cantering wasn't required. Marcus stroked his mane and comforted himself in the saddle.

"I like horses." He spoke to Felicity but looked at Frances as she adjusted his stirrups. "You forget that I've been riding since I was five years old. I'm not at a standard where I could enter at Badminton but I'm more than capable to trot over to Rothington and back. So, don't worry about Woody and me and if you all feel the need to canter off ahead into the sunset, please feel free. Woody and I have a plan to have a relaxing, not too stressed or fast paced day together, don't we boy." Marcus gently patted his new found, best friend and winked at Frances.

"He likes it nice and slow Marcus and here's a few treats for him if you find he's taking too many little rests, he can be a bit of a tinker if he's not bribed!" she smiled. She handed him the treats and their hands touched briefly. They both stopped for a moment, both aware that they had touched each other. No one else noticed. They all said goodbye to Frances and thanked her again, apart from the stunning Felicity. Marcus looked back and smiled at her. Bella shouted out a few last minute instructions to Frances and then there was silence in the yard once more. Frances carried on doing all the tasks she'd been set in the peace and serenity of the empty stables. As she worked her mind wandered and she found herself thinking about Marcus, he did have a nice smile she thought as she walked into the office.

Thursday came and went and was a massive success. Esme had arrived as promised, minus the undertakers, and looked tired but she said she was over the worse. She had dealt with the buyers and had managed to obtain the best prices possible for the two young foals. Bella was thrilled. Her new life as a horse breeder seemed to be more established now. The two boys were loaded up in the back of the horse box and then went off with their new owner to start their new lives. Frances hated to see any horses leave the yard for any reason, it made her sad. They all seemed like family to her. She waved to them as the horsebox left the yard and then took a few moments for herself in the office on her own.

Frances didn't often work Saturdays at the stables but Arabella had arranged for some old school friends who had come up for the Ball to go riding. She'd been happy to do the seven hours extra overtime helping Bella out and she had even been offered some extra pay. Esme had declined the offer as she wanted to have a pamper day getting ready for the ball and spending time with her boys. Even though she was already exhausted, Frances had agreed to do the day but told Bella that she needed to be gone by 4.15 pm at the latest. She needed to race home then, grab a shower, take the boys out for a walk and be at the marquee for Paul at 6.00 ready to help lay the tables. And somewhere in her plan she needed to fit in something to eat and drink.

Chapter 3

When she eventually arrived home, it was 5.00pm. She was angry with herself for allowing Bella to manipulate her into staying later. Bella had known she needed to go and get ready, as she needed to be at the ball for 6.00pm. She would have someone to walk her dogs, make her tea, run her bath and help get her ready. Then someone would drive her, in all her splendour, to the ball for the 8.00pm start. Frances was in a mad panic trying to grab something to eat, say hello and feed the boys who jostled around her for some affection. She felt bad that she needed to leave them alone again. She didn't compromise on the walk around the field though. They had been on their own all day and both dogs needed some time to sniff and enjoy the fresh green grass. It gave her time to reflect and do some sums in her head. This time next week she would have enough money to go and buy that new TV. She smiled to herself, how lucky was she, a new TV, with a remote and Freeview.

She changed quickly into the black jeans, black T Shirt and black boots. She brushed her hair back and pulled it into a bunch, pulled on the black bobble and looked at her appearance in the mirror. Perfect attire for the county ball. "You look absolutely stunning darling, loving the new hairstyle, did Jean-Pierre do it for you darling." She laughed at her put on posh voice. She tried in vain to put some of the pink lip gloss on but it was now totally and utterly empty. She made another mental note to buy a new one the next time she went shopping.

She gave the dogs a last kiss and hug, checked the water bowls and left the radio on for them. She raced to her Defender and drove off down the road in a mad rush. She had five minutes to get to the marquee, she hated being late. She didn't like letting Paul down, he always offered her work and was really kind to her. Paul met her at the entrance of the large marquee that was in the Middle of the Field at Meadows Farm.

"Hi, cutting it a bit fine there, I've never known you to be late or let me down Frances, I wouldn't know what I'd do without you." He gave her a quick embrace and grabbed her hand pulling her behind him towards a large group that had gathered, all of whom, were dressed in black.

"Right, girls and boys we are gathered here today to wait hand and foot on everyone who is here to have fun. Twelve people seated at each table, each one of you gets two tables apart from you Fran, can you manage three for me?" He asked but didn't wait for a reply. "That is twenty four happy customers each, and thirty six for you Fran and I'll help when I can. I want quick efficient service from you all, hot meals delivered in front of them and not on them please!" The group laughed. "You say yes sir and no sir and even three bags full sir. Keep their wine glasses full and be respectful at all time. And if all else fails think of the tips! You will have no time to stand and natter and those of you going to the disco later you are free from 11.00pm onwards. All tables need to be cleared of tableware by then, supper is served from 12.00am but that's a self- service arrangement with paper plates. The caterers will put the supper out and replenish it as needed. Those working till 2.00am please make sure that every table is clear of debris and take the table clothes over to the large laundry bags by the end of the night so everything is ready for the dismantlers to come in at seven tomorrow morning, okay gang. Drunks and silly people are not your concern we have security to deal with them this year. Have a good night everyone, be careful and you can keep any tips that your tables give you and we'll share the rest out later."

Thirty six people, thirty six places to cover. I'm so tired and he gives me extra thought Frances. But she didn't moan or say anything to Paul, she just put on the supplied white cotton apron and got on with it. She was here to work and work is what she did. She felt sad and tired and in desperate need of her bed. She smoothed the apron down with her hands and tied the bow tighter at the back and shook her head. Only seven more hours to go Frances Eliza and then you can dive into bed and not get up till Monday morning. "Think of the TV, Think of the TV," was her new Mantra.

The large marquee started to fill up after 7.30pm. The girls all looked fabulous in their ball gowns of every colour and every style. The ladies had obviously been busy at the hairdressers today! Long hair, short hair, all perfectly styled hair. Men in dinner jackets, grey suits, blue suits, even tweed suits. Everyone had made a real effort to look the part. As Frances moved through the room she took in all the sights and tried decide which kind of dress she would wear if ever got to go to a ball rather than just work at one. Red, she liked red, it was such a vibrant colour. Yep, she would definitely wear red but which style, full on Cinderella ball gown or a stylish sleek little number which would show off her petite frame the best. Decisions, decisions she thought. She negotiated her way through the growing crowds in the bar area and made her way down to her tables to check that they had been perfectly laid out and nothing was missing. The theme was green this year. Green decorations, green table cloths, gold cutlery and porcelain white plates. White candles bobbed in the little tray of water on each table and a small bunch of white and green flowers in a gold vase finished each and every table. Frances thought the tables and the room looked fabulous this year, the Summer Ball was always her favourite ball too.

Her tables were beginning to fill up now. Name cards indicated where everyone should sit. Some people picked up the cards, read their own names and still asked if that was the correct place to sit. Frances rolled her eyes in her mind but smiled outwardly and helped them take their seats. Everyone seemed to have full glasses already from the bar but she started to walk around each table offering and pouring either red or white wine and telling everyone water was to be placed on the table shortly and to let her know if or when the wine bottles run out. All wine was included with this meal which Frances thought was a little bit silly as some people drank far too much just because it was free. Bar staff placed large glass jugs of cold water and ice on the tables and took orders for other drinks. Paul waved at her and this was the signal to let all the waiting staff know that the starters were ready. She collected her first tray and walked over to her first table and started offering the guests a choice of game pate and toast or vegetable soup. Decisions were made quickly and she was soon on her third table. She stopped. It was the Bucannon family, Felicity and her family, Bella and family and Miles, Roberts 'friend'. She took a deep breath and put the smile back on her face. This must be the worst table here she thought to herself. A table full of people who look down on me and will only ever look down at me. Her heart had dropped even more and she suddenly felt ten times more exhausted. "Pate or soup sir," she said to Mr Bucannon senior.

"Well hello there, it's our little kitchen maid. How are you my dear? I must say the beefburgers you made were an absolute triumph, loved them and all the salads were marvellous too, how you can make something like coleslaw taste so tasty, was just beyond me my dear. I think my wife could learn a thing or two from you my dear, I'm having the soup." Frances smiled at him as she placed the hot soup down in front of him. Mrs Bucannon scowled at her husband and then at Frances. Frances continued round the table offering the starters to the guests. Felicity just waved her away and didn't speak or acknowledge her. Robert and Miles grunted the word 'pate' to her in unison. She served them as she would've served everyone else, professionally.

"And you sir, pate or soup?"

"Which do you recommend?" Marcus asked.

"Err, I'm not sure as I've not tasted them."

"Okay then I'll go for the pate and if you have any extra toast I'd appreciate it."

Frances placed the plate of food down in front of him and said she would just nip off and see if she could get some extra toast for him and the table. She raced back to the kitchen filled her tray again and added a plate full of toast. Passing table number 3 she stopped and handed Marcus the toast and carried on to serve table number 1.

When all the starters where finished, Frances went around her three tables gathering the used plates, knives, forks and spoons. Almost no one spoke to her. Marcus did, he said it was lovely, a good choice and thanked her.

Next was the mains course. The dinner plates were larger on the tray and she could only carry six at a time. She served the plates of either beef roast dinner, vegetarian curry or salmon to the guests as each one offered her a request. As she finished each table she carried out large bowls of rice and vegetables to be placed in the middle of the table for the guests to share. She reached table 3 again and offered them each a choice. Requests were asked for and promptly served. Felicity ignored her again and asked Marcus to order her the salmon. Marcus asked for the salmon, as requested and the beef for himself.

"Sorry about that, the beef looks great, Yorkshire puddings are my favourite, it all looks so tasty." He smiled as he spoke to her, Frances noted that he had a lovely smile that always spoke volumes to her. She simply smiled and carried on serving people from the heavy tray. Marcus suddenly felt very sorry for her, an overwhelming sorry for her. He knew she'd had a bad few weeks with his mum and brother both being awful to her. He now knew that she worked full time at Bella's stable and he'd also seen her on Friday night going into No 64 with their uniform on. She'd been at the stables all day today again helping Bella out and here she was serving tables, to people who barely spoke to her or just totally ignored her like his own mum, brother and girlfriend. God, she must be tired, he examined her face. She looked tired and if he wasn't mistaken a little tearful. He felt for her. She carried on delivering plates of food from the heavy tray talking and smiling to everyone. Marcus noticed no one spoke to her apart from one word answers or requests for more food or drink.

After the plates from the main meal were collected and the tables tidied, Frances moved the fork and spoon from the top of the placemat and placed them either side. She did it elegantly with her left arm resting gently behind her. Marcus watched her as she seemed to glide around the tables. He had no interest in the gossip on the table. He could hear Felicity and his mother talking again and the only word he heard was wedding. His heart sank, now he was in for it, 'both barrels' as his grandpa used to say. A whole table desperate for him to propose. He had no more arguments left him in, he had achieved everything he had set his heart on and so had she. He was a Cardiac Consultant now, doing quite well and she was a partner in a law firm, De La Valle's of Newcastle. They were the perfect high flying, achieving couple from old influential Northumberland land owners. Their fathers had planned their union since they were born and he'd been happy to go along with it. But now it felt, uncomfortable. Marcus now knew that his fate was sealed and he would have to propose.

"Christmas day Felicity, let's get engaged on Christmas day as you have always dreamed of, have a big party and an even bigger ring!" It just rose in his stomach and blurted out, a bit like vomit he thought ashamedly. The table stopped and stared at him. It was as if the world had suddenly stopped spinning on its axis. They all stared. Suddenly they all erupted and cheered, cried, and laughed. They congratulated the happy couple and eventually Marcus leaned into Felicity and said

"That okay with you?"

"Yes," she said abruptly. "I was beginning to think you'd never ask. We then need to plan for a summer wedding and start as family as soon as we can. Neither of us are getting any younger." Marcus smiled at her and stroked her ring finger. That was it, his life was now a done deal.

It was nearly midnight before Frances had a chance to sit down and grab something to eat. She tucked into a leftover cold beef dinner, she was famished and hadn't eaten since 5.30. She'd now been on the go for seventeen hours and her body was beginning to ache. She still had two more hours to go. She had been due to finish at 1.00am but a very persuasive Paul had asked her to finish at 2.00 as others had finished at 11.00 to enjoy the disco. She sighed at her own weakness. It had been a long day. She made a mental note to herself never to work so many hours again. Then she began to work out how much she had earnt today and she felt a little brighter when she realised that she would now have enough to purchase the television. She would go to the shops tomorrow and definitely buy that new TV.

Feeling more energised she left the kitchen and went into the main party area. The party was in full swing. She could see Esme on the dance floor with a large group of friends, hopefully she would have a chance to catch up with her before the end of the night. Most people had left the tables area and were either on the dance floor or just mingling around the bar area. People were laughing, drinking, smiling, yawning, some were just falling over and thankfully some had already left. She set about emptying all the large tables removing any left glasses, plates, vases full of wilting flowers and anything else that had been left.

She worked swiftly and uninterrupted. She and two others had the task to empty the tables and put the laundry in the bags but she was the only one there doing the work as usual. She noticed the two other girls sitting on chairs near the dance floor wrapped around two young lads, kissing and fondling in public. She was annoyed that they weren't helping and then she was annoyed at the lads, the wealthy sons of gentleman farmers, the 'users and dump them' types. But they were all old enough to know what they were doing. She returned to carrying out the job which she was being paid to do. The quicker she worked the quicker she could get home.

The Ball was due to finish at 2.00am and then there would be just the final clean-up which would be quick as it mainly comprised of throwing everything into black bags.

When she was at the very back of the marquee and lost in the darkness she allowed herself a five minute sit down, the tables had been cleared and her work was nearly finished. She looked at all the people laughing and having fun, drinking, hugging and kissing each other. They all looked as if they were having a good night. They all looked happy. The girls dresses sparkled on the dance floor and some of the men held their girl close, held them lovingly just swaying slowly to the music, the girls gently and lovingly stroking the back of their partners necks with their fingertips. Frances watched those couples intently. How long had it been since someone had touched her or kissed her or loved her? In that instance, she longed for her mum to stroke her hair and gently kiss her on the brow, a soft kiss that always meant she was safe, loved and wanted. Frances stared into the distance. She wiped a single tear and sat back into the chair.

"You must be tired, I'm exhausted and I've not done much today myself and compared to you, I have been in fact totally lazy." Startled and lost in her own thoughts Frances jumped up and off the chair in a second.

"Oh, I'm so sorry I didn't see you there in the dark. I only just sat down for a moment," stammered Frances. She felt instantly guilty.

"It's okay, it's just me, Marcus." He said in the half darkness. He leant forward in his chair to show his face in the light. "I only said you must be tired, I didn't mean to scare you. Sorry. You deserve a sit down, I know you were at the stables all day and then you must've rushed over here to help out. I also know that you worked Monday to Friday at Bella's and did four nights at the Restaurant. I have my spies watching you, you know." He laughed.

Frances looked confused.

"Don't look so worried I spoke to Arabella today and then Paul tonight and I saw you at the restaurant the other night when I picked up a pizza and Gino said you were covering for his daughter." He paused, Frances remained silence. "When do you get to go out and have fun if all you do is work?"

"Simple. I don't. I need a new TV as you saw when you popped in and so I need to work as much as I can to buy one. There's a sale on at Electricland, so I need the money quickly. If you remember, my TV is very old." Frances was annoyed at herself for mumbling.

"Why not just sell your old TV to a museum or antiques dealer as the oldest working TV in the world and they'd give you enough money to buy a new one and you wouldn't need to work all these hours," he smiled at her. "Do you mind me asking Frances but how many hours have you worked this week?"

Frances began to work out how many hours she'd worked this week, using her fingers to help her out. She sat back down into the chair and sighed when she'd finished the sum in her head. "I think I've worked for sixty eight hours this week, I need to recheck that, that can't be right." She did the sum again in her head, eight hours tonight, twelve at the Restaurant and forty eight hours at the stables. Yes, she really had done sixty eight hours. "Yep I've done sixty eight hours this week, no wonder I'm feeling so tired". She felt tearful, suddenly overcome with tiredness and emotion, she looked away from him.

"You've worked for sixty eight hours just to get a TV, wow. I don't really think about money, if I want it I just generally buy it." He hesitated and reflected on what he had just said. "I'm so sorry, that was really rude of me and very unkind, I'm sorry I just didn't realise how hard you, and others had to work for things." He stared into his glass of wine and swirled it around the glass deep in his own thoughts. Why did he always say the wrong thing to this girl. She got up and tidied her apron and watched the people on the dance floor. Marcus stood up too.

"I'd better go or Paul will give me the sack, can't be caught talking to the upstairs people you know." Marcus could hear the laughter in her voice as she pretended to imitate a cockney maid. Marcus watched her walk away. He suddenly felt emotional and frustrated. Sadness, yes, guilt definitely, sorry for her absolutely but something else that he couldn't quite put his finger on. He wished that she hadn't left him. She stopped, paused and slowly turned around to look at him

"I really do need the money, not just for a TV but for everything else as well, I only have what I earn. And in answer to your question, no, I don't go out, I don't dance or drink or have fun. I don't own a ball gown or any dress come to that. I don't need going out clothes cos I don't go out really. I just need casual and work clothes at the moment. But I do have a roof over my head, I have food on my table and I have my boys to snuggle up to and this time next week I'll have a new TV with a remote and Freeview. So, I'm good and have everything that I need. She started to walk away, but paused for a moment to end their conversation. "Congratulations by the way, I heard you were getting engaged and married next summer. I wish you both well. Bye." She turned and walked briskly away.

Marcus sat back in the chair and felt very uncomfortable. The three or four glasses of wine which usually made him feel relaxed suddenly vanished from his system. He felt ashamed of himself for prying into her business. He didn't really know her at all and he had just embarrassed her. He liked her, she was a nice girl, a hardworking, honest girl who was just trying to keep herself going. He and his family had treated her so bad, laughing at her, used her. He felt awful. He watched her as she continued to work, throwing the remains of the uneaten suppers into plastic bags. She seemed the only one who was actually working. He saw Paul who was manning the exit door saying goodbye to the crowd of party goers that were beginning to disburse. Yep. he felt crap as he sat there in his £1,000.00 suit, £250.00 shoes and £10,000 watch. He didn't realise how lucky he was most of the time. He also wondered why her congratulations to him made him feel even more uncomfortable.

    He wandered over to the dance floor and saw Felicity dancing with her mum and friends. His own mum and dad were deep in conversation with the Forster-Smyths and he didn't really care where his brother was! He saw that Paul was on his own so walked over to him.

    "Hi mate, how are you? Did you have a good night?" Said Paul.

"Yes, great, thanks Paul, perfectly organised as usual. I'm tired now and ready for the off as soon as those lot have finished, I'll be glad to get into the taxi and find my bed."

"Yep, I'm knackered too, I hate these late nights, we must be getting old," he smiled at his friend.

"It's a long time since we were at school having fun, without a care in the world but I hear you're soon to join the club, old married man, tied down with kids and commitments, congratulations mate." He shook his friend's hand and Marcus smiled in acknowledgment. The two men stood in silence, happy and content in each other's company, a mutual and an enduring friendship which didn't need words to hold it together.

"I'll need a best man next summer if you're not doing anything, I'd be grateful if you are up for it ?"

"Yes mate, I think I'm free." Nothing else needed to be said.

Marcus broke the silence. "I can't believe that girl over there, she served our table and all of the tables around us. She then cleaned and tidied all the tables on her own and she's now the only one sorting things out at the end of the night. She has the youthful energy that I want."

"Frances, yes she's great, a real worker, she's only nineteen mate that's why she has the stamina. She takes up the slack when all the others can't be bothered, I don't know what I'd do without her. I think she quite likes it though, being busy. She always asks for any jobs that are going and always happy to do extra hours. She's quiet, I don't know much about her only that I always know that she will get the job done for me."

"Hopefully you pay her accordingly and make sure you look after her."

"Err, I wouldn't go that far, I'll pay her what I promise to pay her." Paul walked off smiling and switched all the lights on to show the guests it was time to go.

Marcus waited at the exit for his family and friends to join him. The mini bus had been booked for 2.00am and he was desperate to get home. Frances walked past him as she was leaving and he noticed that she had a white envelope in her hand. She was just in the middle of putting her jacket on when Marcus walked over to her.

"Franny, I'm really sorry about earlier, I didn't mean to pry and I didn't mean to embarrass you." He hesitated. "I just wondered what you were doing on Saturday Night, next Saturday night I mean. I've got two tickets to a Ball, a Hospital ball and I'm expected to attend and Felicity can't. There'll be a three-course meal and a live band. I think you would enjoy it and you would be waited on hand and foot instead of you looking after everyone else." He managed to stop talking.

"Thanks for the invitation Marcus that's really kind of you and it sounds fab but I don't have anything suitable to wear for a pub let alone a Ball and I can't afford them at the moment as you know. I'm just not the kind of person who goes to balls anymore but thanks for the invitation, that was very kind of you to ask, night." She smiled and started to walk away knowing he had only invited her as he felt sorry for her.

"Okay then, I'll pick you up from your house next Saturday night at 6.00. I think Paul may have put a little extra in your white envelope," he knew his friend. "Night Franny, I hope you have a good rest tomorrow. I'll get your number off Paul and I'll send you a text with the details and the menu. And I won't take no for an answer." With that he turned and walked towards the waiting full taxi.

Marcus had called her Franny. Her dad used to call her Franny.

Chapter 4

Frances woke up to July sunshine flooding through the windows. The old pale yellow and white daisy curtains failing in their attempt to keep the light out of the bedroom. She rolled onto her back and gently started the process of opening her eyes. She felt the heat of the sun through the glass on her face. She rested her head gently on the feather pillow enjoying the sensation and resisting the urge to open her eyes. Her mind drifted off to the night before, she'd worked hard yesterday, in fact she had worked hard all week. She was tired and her body ached especially her feet. Not even the thought of going to the shops to get a new TV filled her with excitement this morning. She turned over and curled up in the soft, yellow cotton sheet and snuggled down again, she left only her eyes and nose in the bright sun. A lie in on a Sunday was the highlight of her week, the best part of the week. No one asked anything of her today, no please will you do this or that or table 3 needs cleaning, or the toilet's blocked, can you sort it out. She snuggled further down enjoying the sensation of freedom and laziness.

Last night had been a funny night, generally it had been hard and tiring, the Bucannon's had been really rude to her treating her like a servant, get this, get that and not a single please or thank you from the whole table or even a smile from any of them or anyone on the other tables she served. Only one person on all of the tables had spoken to her, one who had said please and thank you when she served him and he had actually been kind to her, not that the family noticed or cared. Marcus had spoken to her. He was a nice man, always kind and polite. I bet he's a great doctor she thought to herself. And she also thought that his family didn't deserve him and Felicity definitely didn't deserve him. She was awful. She treated everyone as if they were at her beck and call, telling everyone what to do. Even when she had overheard Marcus asking her to marry him she turned it into a set of instructions, to be done, to be dealt with. Didn't she realise that the nicest person that Frances had met in a very long time had just told her and the rest of the table how much he loved her, wanted her and needed to spend the rest of his life with her. She treated him as if it was just another business transaction. He was too nice for her and the rest of them too.

Frances fantasized about someday, someone asking her to marry them, to promise love and devotion for the rest of their lives. She was an old romantic at heart, too many Jane Austin books she surmised. She wanted to be swept off her feet, to be loved, cherished, honoured and adored. She wanted the full fairy tale. Him, down on one knee, opening a box to show her and the world that he couldn't live without her, that she was his world. She would obviously accept and fall into his arms and seal the engagement with a kiss and.....

But life wasn't like that. People didn't notice her, boys didn't notice her or talk to her. She had just turned into one of those people who was just around. Everyone knew she was there but no one bothered with her. Somehow in the last few years she had become invisible. No one noticed her, or cared about her. It hadn't always been this way, she reflected. Once she had been popular, she'd had loads of friends, boyfriends even. She went to pubs, cinema and shopping with friends, girls and boys. She was liked and loved. People asked to spend time with her, sleep overs and more. She had got really good grades at GCSE, all 9's, ten of them, she'd had dreams too, dreams of university. Dreams of a career, a life filled with friends and family, she had hoped to marry and have kids and be an auntie, a godmother, a friend. But that was all gone. It was then that she noticed, she was crying, she wiped a tear and tried not to think. Thinking was not good for her soul. Working and being constantly busy was good for her soul. She let the warm sun on her face dry up the tears. She lay still, her head on the pillow and didn't move until the sunshine had moved away from her face. She sat up on the edge of the bed quickly and opened her eyes.

Marcus had invited her to the Hospital Ball. That was sweet and kind. But she wouldn't be going. How could she, she had nothing to wear. Paul had given her an extra twenty pounds and her share of the tips was nearly twenty pounds but that wouldn't buy her a new dress, shoes, bag, makeup or a very much needed trip to the hairdressers. She looked at her hair in the dressing table mirror. It had been over two years since she had been to have her hair cut. It had always been long but now it tumbled down her back and sat in a clump on the bed, it was past her hips if she stood up. Most of the time it was just pulled back into a tight bun. Maybe a haircut was a priority for her to have, to spend the £40.00 on that rather than a dress.

She sat and worked out in her head her priorities. Should she save it or should she put it towards a dress, she wondered what kind of a dress £40.00 would buy? The two dogs disturbed by her started to wake up and shuffled towards her for a cuddle and a stroke, Frances obliged immediately.

"What should I do boys, should Cinderella go to the ball or save the £40.00 for a rainy day?" It's a chance for a nice dinner and a bop on the dancefloor, a chance to be young and to have some fun for a change. Just for one night. It was a chance to enjoy a nice meal with a kind man who she knew felt sorry for her but that was okay really because he didn't really know her or understand her. Her thoughts then changed their direction. Would she really be offending him if she said no after he had only ever been kind to her?

She dragged herself off the bed and opened the curtains onto the most beautiful day. The sun was shining and there were absolutely no clouds in the sky. It was 8.30 and time for her to get ready and to go and let the dogs out. Twenty minutes later she was showered and dressed. Her hair was washed and brushed and she was nimbly dividing it into 3 sections, plaiting it as she walked downstairs with dogs behind her.

"C'mon then boys and how are you this fine morning?" Bert and Max slowly walked towards the back door. Frances prepared breakfast for them both and set the table for herself.

"Boys, as it's a special day today, just a quick nip into the back field for you and then we are off to the beach for a nice walk and a swim, won't that be fun. The sun is shining and we are free all day, you've both been indoors far too much this week and it's all been my fault." As she spoke to the dogs they followed her out the back of the house and up into the field. Both had a good old sniff and then did their business as usual. Twenty minutes later they were back in the small kitchen. This time she put the dog bowls down and made herself a coffee. She opened a brown paper bag and took out two enormous croissants. She had walked passed the bakery on Friday as the lady had been arranging them in the window. Frances smiled at them, put them on a plate and got the butter out of the fridge.

She placed the coffee and croissants on the kitchen table, left the kitchen for a few moments and returned with a large brown envelope and a bright gift bag covered in balloons. There was also a pink envelope that had come in the post yesterday. She placed them all on the table and looked at them, quietly she stroked the brown envelope and lifted it to her nose and smelled the paper. She paused and then she took another breath. She put them to one side and tucked into the croissants smothering them with butter. She took a big bite and the butter just melted into her mouth. She couldn't remember the last time she'd had a croissant, maybe three years ago on the school trip to France. It tasted so good. She had promised herself that she would eat them slowly and enjoy every single bite but she couldn't resist and they were devoured in a few minutes. She licked her fingers and carefully swirled it around the plate picking up all the crumbs before licking them off too. She got up and washed her hands before returning to the table. This time she opened the brown envelope and took a deep breath, breathing in the smell of the cards inside. She placed it back on the table.

She started to sing. 'Happy birthday to you, happy birthday to you, happy birthday darling Frances happy birthday to you, love you.' Her voice began to break as she finished the words. She paused and closed her eyes for a few moments, deep in her own thoughts. She said thank you in a quiet voice and then opened the envelope and let the cards fall out. The cards didn't have envelopes and all looked slightly crumpled. She picked up the first one. 'Happy birthday to our darling daughter.' The card was covered in brightly coloured balloons and a little black Labrador was trying to burst the balloons. It made her smile. It made her smile every time she saw it. She opened it and read aloud the message inside.

"To our amazing, beautiful, kind, bonkers daughter, Happy Birthday. We love you to the moon and back and then some more, love and kisses mum and dad." She traced her finger over the words mum and dad and then lifted the card to her face, trying to smell the last traces of her mum's perfume. She closed her eyes and breathed in. It was gone. A single tear escaped from her eye which she didn't wipe away.

Next card she picked up was from her brother, Barns. He had made the card and hand painted himself and it was a cartoon of her sitting on a wooden fence. The likeness was amazing in the face but he had made her look very fat indeed. She opened the card and smelled the inside.

"To my fat grub sister, hope you have a great day and don't eat too much cake." If only he could see her now. The next card was also hand made. It was in the shape of a black puppy dog. She read it out loud. "Happy birthday to the best sister in the world love Clara, Bertie and Max." This card made her cry too as she pulled it into her chest. She opened the next card.

"To our little Frances, always be the star that you are and shine brightly every day, love nana and grandpa Tulip." Brightly coloured tulips covered this card, she loved tulips. The next card was a small gold card with black writing on it saying birthday girl on it from her auntie and uncle. Gold glitter still fell off from the words happy birthday as she touched it. "Have a great day and enjoy spending the money, love Auntie Rosie and Uncle Bob." She stood the cards up on the table.

She opened the brightly coloured gift bag that had been left on her bonnet and pulled out the card and the soft parcel wrapped in tissue paper. It was from Esme. She tore open the envelope and pulled out the card. It was a picture of a black Labrador holding a bunch of tulips in its mouth. She smiled. Esme knew her so well, dogs and tulips her favourite things. "To my amazeballs friend Frances who I couldn't live without, honestly and literally. Thanks for running the stables and letting me pretend to be your boss. Luv ya loads, Esme and the gang XXXXXXXXXX. A typical Esme birthday card! She hugged it and smelt it. The pale pink tissue paper tore easily in her hands and she opened it to reveal a pink and purple soft velvet scarf. She let it tumble out of its coil and drape over her knee. It was beautiful, she buried her face in the soft material and enjoyed the sensation of luxury. It was perfect, Esme did know her so well. The noise of the phone made her jump, she got up and picked up her mobile. It was Esme. She pressed on the green circle.

"Happy birthday to you, happy birthday to you, happy birthday dear Frances, happy birthday to youoooooooooo!" Esme and the boys shouted happy birthday in differing volumes. Frances giggled and laughed at the voices that arguing to hold the phone.

"Thank you, thank you all so much, you've made my day and such brilliant singing boys, Esme yours was out of key." she giggled.

"Sod off you, I'll have my card and scarf back now please." Everyone giggled and laughed and Esme was told off for swearing!

"Thank you so much I love my card and my scarf, both absolutely perfect, and very generous. I feel thoroughly spoilt thank you all so much."

"What you doing today babe?"

"I'm having a very lazy day today. I worked sixty eight hours this week, so croissants for breakfast, a walk on the beach with the boys, then a readymade Steak and Ale pie for tea and a film in front of the TV for me."

Esme didn't laugh. "You've worked sixty eight hours in one week babe, you shouldn't do that, that's not good for you." Frances hesitated, she had been off her guard for a moment. " I know, I know but it was a one off week doing some favours and it helped me out as I need a new TV and I'm going to treat myself to a new dress," she said thinking she had recovered the situation.

"If ever you need anything just ask us you know I'm always here for you." Frances noticed that Esme's voice had changed, it wasn't light and cheerful anymore.

"Thank you, Esme. You know you are the one person I can count on and that means the world to me. But I'm okay. You know if I needed help you are the one that I would come too right?"

"Of course, babe. I'm free if you need someone to go dress shopping with. Well I suppose I better herd this lot up and then we are off swimming and then the Plough for lunch with the outlaws which you are invited to as well but I respect your decision not to spend your one day off with my lot."

Frances giggled. "Thanks so much and have a great day all of you, I'll think of you Esme, bye." Frances disconnected the call and sat down again and looked at the unopened card in the pink envelope. She knew it was from her uncle, he was the only other person who knew it was her birthday. She decided to make another quick cup of coffee before she opened it.

She eventually picked up the card and slid the knife down the crease of the envelope. Slowly she pulled the card out. It was a pretty card with lots of flowers on it, it looked like an old oil painting. It said happy birthday niece in gold old fashioned writing. She opened the card and read the handwritten message.

"Happy Birthday Frances. I hope you have a lovely birthday. It would be lovely to see you, you know where I am or I could come down to you. You know that I'm always here for you and I'll do anything I can to help you. There is always a home here for you. I've enclosed a cheque so treat yourself to something nice and not something you need. I know you never cash any of the cheques I send to you but hopefully this one you will. I'm here always for you Uncle Bob. She briefly looked at the cheque. It was for £500.00. She folded it and put it back in the envelope. She picked up the card and smiled. It was a lovely card and a lovely message. Bob wasn't one for words and that was the longest note she had ever had from him. But he knew her well and he knew what would happen. She placed Bob's card on the mantle shelf next to the ones from her mum and dad, brother, sister, grandparents, auntie Rosie and Esme.

Half an hour later she was driving down to the beach at St Chads Head. It was her favourite beach and never really got too busy. When she arrived, she pulled into the little side track and parked up. She walked round to back of the Defender and opened the rear door to see two dogs with two very waggy tales. She lifted both of the boys out and followed Max and Bert as they waddled down the dusty track which lead to the beach. Her car was the only one there which meant hopefully she would have the whole beach to herself. The boys were on the beach within a few minutes and it was deserted, perfect. The sky was blue, the sea was blue and the sand looked whiter than normal. It looked like a tropical beach today. Her favourite beach day and she had it all to herself.

Max and Bert made their way down the beach to the sea which was at low tide. Max went in first eager to run in the waves and cool down, Max loved the sea and would spend hours just running up and down and would fetch a ball for as long as Frances could throw one. Bert walked into the frothy water slowly as if he was checking the temperature before he would go in any further. His face was funny she thought, as if he was thinking what he would do if Max splashed him. As if Max would care thought Frances. The bay was almost a quarter of a mile wide which both dogs could manage to walk. There was a time when she could walk all day and cover miles but they were older now and slower and more like two old men than two excited labs. She had some water in her backpack and a bowl so the boys could have a nice cool drink half way. It was about 22 degrees now and she could just feel the heat of the sun hitting her back. It was so relaxing. She closed her eyes and breathed in the warm air. Freedom she thought and it's all mine.

A few hours later she and the boys were travelling back home and her mind was wondering, thinking about the Hospital Ball. She was surprised by his invitation, she didn't really know him that well. He'd invited her only because he felt sorry for her she thought, and that didn't seem the right reason to be invited to a ball, a real Summers Night Ball. It was stupid even thinking about going. She didn't have a dress and definitely no shoes or appropriate handbag but she really felt that she wanted to go. She really wanted to go. Desperately wanted to dance and laugh and have fun like other people did. She knew it wasn't real, it was only for one night but just for a few hours she just wanted to be someone, not overlooked and ignored, to be served a meal and to dance the night away to a real live band. Not a lot to want for the average twenty year old was it?

She dropped the boys off at home and let them finish their naps off in the comfort of their own beds. A quick trip to the bathroom, hair combed and some clean jeans on and she was ready again to go out. She gave her trainers a quick shake to get rid of the last traces of sand. When she was presentable she put on the radio for the boys to keep them company, made sure they had plenty of water and then grabbed her bag. It had just gone 3'o'clock and if she ran she could be in the town in five minutes. With inspiration and high hopes in her thoughts she ran as fast as she could and arrived outside one of the two charity shops in the High Street. She had never been in a charity shop before and felt a little nervous on entering. Her mum used to drop bags off when she was younger saying how fortunate they were and had all that they needed and they had the chance and the ability to help people who may not be as lucky as them. Was she now one of the unfortunate people?

She pushed the door open and a bell rang. The shop was empty not surprising as it was nearly closing time on a Sunday afternoon.

"Hello my dear, can I help you?" said a voice from behind the counter. The lady who was probably in her 70's was sitting on a wooden bench knitting a blanket.

"I'm just looking around really, I need a dress and I thought I'd pop in to see if you have anything that would be suitable."

"Long, short, evening or day wear dear?"

"Long, I think, and definitely evening wear."

The lady put the knitting down when she finished the row and got up and beckoned Frances to follow her to the back of the long thin shop.

"This is the section that I think you need. We have loads on the rail and even more in the back. People these days are too scared to be seen at a dance twice in the same dress so we get loads in, some only worn once and loads that have still got the labels in. Have a good rummage through and see what you can find and you can try it on in the changing room. I'm actually being picked up at 5 by my friend so don't rush dear" With that she gave Frances space to look through the racks of dresses and she returned to her knitting.

Wow thought Frances as she looked at all the dresses on the rail. There must be about fifty ball gowns here in every size shape and colour and most still had labels on! She slowly started to look through the rail, beginning on the left side pushing the other dresses to the other side as she looked at each dress checking the style, the colour and the size. After about 10 minutes she had found three dresses that were suitable and all in her size, all still with their labels on and all designer dresses. She couldn't believe her luck. She lifted the dresses off the rail and shouted up to the lady knitting that she was going to try three dresses on if that was okay. The lady smiled and put her knitting down.

"Try them on dear and come out and show me what they look like, have a walk in them and make sure you can dance in them too."

Frances took off her jeans and tee shirt and shoes, she felt so excited. It was years since she'd had new clothes and she had never tried on such beautiful clothes ever. The first one was a Tod Draper evening dress, full length, slim fitting with spaghetti shoulder straps, dark purple at the top metamorphosing to an electric blue. It was covered in hundreds and hundreds of sequins. It fit her so well and the zip easily pulled up on her petite size 8 frame. She pulled the curtain open and walked out of the changing room to show the lady and look at the dress in the full size mirror.

"Stunning dear, absolutely stunning and fits you like a glove, you look lovely in that one!" Frances looked at her reflection in the mirror. She looked amazing in this dress! It was beautiful and fitted her perfectly.

" I love it, I really love it, I look so grown up in it. I'm going to my first ball on Saturday night and I've never had a ball gown before or even tried one on before. I haven't had a new dress in ages, sorry if I appear to be too excited." She giggled.

"Enjoy every minute of it my dear, a new dress is always an exciting purchase even at my time of life. Try the next one on for me, try the black one on next, that's a Jane Morcombe one isn't it?"

Frances took a long look at herself in the mirror and smiled. This dress was definitely a contender. The next dress, the Jane Morcombe dress, was a simple figure hugging satin black dress. It was quite plain compared to the first dress with spaghetti straps and a sweetheart top. Around the top of the dress were a small number of little crystals arranged in small discrete circles. This dress too fit her perfectly hugging her delicate figure where it should. She opened the curtain and walked out towards the mirror, to her surprise this dress had a slight train which slid across the wooden floor of the shop. She looked at her reflexion in the mirror again and stood open mouthed. OMG she thought to herself, I love this one as well! The slit on the side finished just above her knee and Frances thought that this was a dress that was made to impress. If possible, she loved this one more than the first. Two contenders.

"That dress looks beautiful on you dear, absolutely stunning. You really are a beautiful young lady. How would you wear your hair if you decided this was the one for you? Up I think like Audrey Hepburn like in the film 'Breakfast at Tiffany's."

Yes.... thought Frances, up and sophisticated. "Yes, I think your right, up and in a bun would set this dress off beautifully. I'll go and try the last one on, I can't believe people spend so much money on dresses and don't even wear them," she said heading back to the changing room.

"More money than sense my dear."

The third dress was her favourite one that she had picked off the rail and it was red, scarlet red to be precise. She'd always dreamed of having a red ball gown and now it was her chance to try one on. She just looked at herself in the mirror. She wished that her mum and dad could see her in this dress, even her brother wouldn't have called her a fat grub, she pushed the thoughts quickly away. It was the most beautiful dress that she had ever seen, ever! She had watched all the ladies in their ball gowns at the balls for the last few years and she had never seen such a beautiful dress in her life and it was brand new, the label tickled her back. She couldn't believe that someone had paid nearly £600.00 for this dress and never actually worn it. It was so beautiful it looked almost like a wedding dress. It was made out of scarlet red pure crushed silk , the top had two small shoulder sleeves that sat on the edges of her shoulder with a slightly lower sweetheart front and a slightly, corseted top.

Down the back ran about fifty small buttons covered in the same red silk material, but thankfully they sat on top of a hidden red zip. The skirt from the front looked simple and straight but on movement it showed that it had a full skirt that attached to the sides of the waistband and cascaded away at the back to form a full skirt with a slight train. She looked in the mirror. Her slightly bronzed skin looked glowing next to the red, her green eyes where transfixed on her reflexion. She loved this dress. She stepped outside to look at the dress in the full length mirror.

"Yes, that's a nice dress too dear but I'm not sure if it's just a bit too fancy for a ball, it's definitely a ball gown but if it was white it would be a wedding dress. What do you think?"

Frances looked at the dress again and knew it was the dress for her, she understood the lady's comments but she just had fallen totally in love with the dress. This was a dress for any occasion, balls, weddings and one which she would just be just happy sitting in all day long just watching TV. This was the dress for her. All she needed now was some simple silver or black evening shoes and a small clutch bag to finish the outfit. She took the dress off and hung it back on the hanger on the hooks in the changing room and pulled the zip up. She caught site of the price ticket and realised that she hadn't seen the price that the dress was actually up for sale for and not the just the original selling price. £60.00 was way over her budget, she only had £50.00 to spend on the shoes, the dress and the bag, her heart fell out of her chest. She couldn't afford the dress of her dreams. She quickly looked at the prices on the two other dresses that she had tried on. She couldn't believe that she hadn't looked at them before trying them all on, she was so annoyed at herself for getting carried away. The purple sequined dress was £40.00 marked down from £399.99 and the simple black dress was £20.00 marked down from the original selling price of £299.00. Sadly, that made the final decision quite easy for her, she couldn't afford the red dress or the purple dress so the black dress had chosen her! She suddenly felt sad and disappointed, her previous excitement had vanished with the red dress.

"I think I'm going to opt for the black one, I think your right its younger and less like a wedding dress style, so I'll have that one and I need to just have a look for some matching shoes and a bag if that's ok with you and you have time."

"The shoes are just over there dear and the bags are just above them. I think the black one was my favourite one, you looked beautiful in it." The lady left her knitting and followed Frances over to the shoe shelves.

"What size are you, about a 6?" Frances nodded and looked at all the unwanted shoes on the shelf nearly all with labels. "These are perfect, not too high and allow you to walk and dance in them." The lady handed Frances a pair of patent leather evening shoes with peep toes and a T-bar strap and low sides cut away nearly to the toes. On the T-Bar was a line of shiny paste diamonds that shone in the shop light. The shoes had a narrow heel, not quite a stiletto which was about two inches high, perfect for someone who had never warn high heels. She slipped off her own shoes and put them on, they fitted perfectly. These shoes were brand new, the label was still on the bottom, they were from Dowers and had originally cost £69.99 but now they were £10.00.

"Thank you I'll take these and can I have a look at that black patent leather bag behind you as well?" The lady got it down from the shelf and handed it to Frances who held it next to the shoes she had just taken off. The bag matched really well and no one else would notice the slight difference in the shades of black. It was a small cylindrical shaped clutch bag with no strap and only a small silver clasp at the top gave the bag any sense of decoration. It had a few scratches on it but no price tag.

" I think I'll take this too please but there isn't a price on it, do you know how much it is?"

"Let's go and have a look dear." The lady opened the purse and pulled out the price tag and dropped it into the bin as she walked behind the till.

"Okay my dear that will be £20.00 for the dress and £10.00 for the shoes and £2.00 for the bag which if my sums are correct gives a total of £32.00, do you agree?"

Frances opened her purse and took out the correct money and handed it to the lady with the biggest smile feeling excited again with her purchases. "Thank you so much, and thank you for helping me choose, I've had such a lovely time trying the dresses on and I'm really pleased with the one I've bought. Now I actually think I'm looking forward to the ball. I think I'll feel like a million dollars in my outfit now. I even have some money left over to buy some make-up which is another treat to look forward to."

She thanked the lady again for helping her choose the dress and accessories and left the shop feeling very content with her new purchases. Happy and excited, she couldn't help herself and ran all the way home eager to show Max and Bert her new clothes. Today had been a good day, a good birthday and now she had a pie and a DVD to watch. Tomorrow she would go and buy her TV and that would be a good day too.

Marcus lay on his bed re writing the text for the tenth time. He was annoyed with himself. He wrote hundreds of emails and texts ever week and he never re-read them or re-wrote them. Done once then sent, spelling mistakes included as well. He was composing a simple text to just a girl who he knew he was doing a favour for, to say sorry about his rudeness and yet it had taken him over an hour to complete the text message let alone send it. How hard was it to say he'd pick her up at 6.00pm in his car, that everything had already been paid for by him , it was just a simple thank you and an apology all rolled into one. That bit was okay, it was the bit about saying she could stay at his city flat for the night as it saved them getting a taxi and that they could just walk back to his flat afterwards. Every time he wrote that bit, it sounded so wrong.

'Hi Frances, I didn't mean to be bossy but I think you will have a fab time at the ball and it would help me out as I hate going to these things on my own. The band is called Purple Harmony, a six piece wedding band who are great and the meal is either melon or soup (Boring), Salmon or roast chicken and vegetables followed by limoncello mouse or banoffee pie for desert. Coffee and wine included. If you come it will also be a way for me to apologise to you on behalf of my bonkers family and obviously me. I'll pick you up at 6.00 and pack an overnight bag and we can stay over at my flat and I'll drop you back on Sunday morning.' He pressed the send button.

"Christ, what have I done." He stared at the phone panicked thoughts hurtling through his brain.

'You don't have to stay over I can drop you back off straight after, its fine I don't need to have a drink. I only really suggested it as it would make for a late night but it's fine, I can drive you home, Marcus." He pressed the send button again, this time the text only took seconds to write.

Bert and Max were fast asleep on the sofa next to Frances. All three of them were tired and full of steak and Ale pie with baked potato and gravy. She was watching a DVD on her laptop snuggled up to her boys when her phoned beeped in the kitchen, she never kept her phone near her as it almost never rang and she only ever got texts from work. She picked up the laptop and paused the film and gently slid off the sofa trying not to wake the boys up or disturb them too much. Both stretched out more and incorporated the warm patch of leather that she had left behind.

Two messages, she couldn't remember the last time that she had seen two messages in her inbox, she swiped her finger across and opened the messages, both from an unknown number. She read the first message and smiled to herself and then quickly opened and read the second message. The messages were from Marcus. It sounded amazing, a ball, a band, a meal, wine and coffee and she now had an absolutely beautiful dress that was just perfect. She felt excited, she felt warm and definitely excited for the first time in ages. She read the bit about staying at his flat for the night and thought it was a great idea, it would be like a little holiday for her. Mrs Brewis next door would pop in and check that the boys were okay as long as she wasn't too late back they would be fine. She didn't need to be invited twice she really wanted to go and have some fun, even if she would be the outsider, a charity project even.

'Hi, thanks for the texts. I would love to come to the ball with you, thank you. I had some extra money in my envelope from last night and some tips so I now have a fab dress and shoes perfect for balls and special occasions! I'm happy to stay over at your flat to save you driving (or me in a city I don't know), it will be like a little holiday for me and I'm already looking forward to it. I would need to be back in the morning so that I can let the boys out and give them breakfast if that is okay with you. See you Saturday 6.00pm." She pressed the send button and hugged the phone to her chest. A night out and a weekend away, winner winner chicken dinner than laughed at herself for thinking about such a childish rhyme. She ran a glass of water for herself and returned to her sofa to watch the end of her film and snuggled up with boys. Her dress was hanging from the curtain rail in the lounge and the diamonds sparkled in the light from the lamp. Today had been a good day, considering it had been her birthday.

Marcus was working at his desk in his flat reading patient's files and checking information on his laptop. He was staying at the flat for a week as it was his turn to be on call Sunday to Friday. He didn't mind being on call he actually quite liked it as it was a chance to have some peace and quiet on his own and it also gave him the opportunity to see some exciting and urgent cases. Somehow, life in the hospital always seemed more exciting in the middle of the night and as he had only been a Consultant at the hospital for a few months, everything was still exciting. He liked being a doctor and had wanted to be a doctor for as long as he could remember and had worked hard to get where he was. He wasn't sure if this was the life for him in the long run as he had always wanted to be a family GP in the community dealing with people who would eventually be his friends and his community. He loved being a cardiac doctor but it wouldn't fit in with his life as a gentleman farmer at Hudson Hall Farm, a GP would definitely be better placed to have the two roles. He loved the farm, it was a real family farm and he loved his family very much and normally did everything his mum and dad expected him to do. But today he was still feeling embarrassed by them and slightly ashamed of both his brother and his mum.

He had been going out with Felicity for as long as he could remember. They had been brought up together as their parents had been best friends since the four of them had all gone to school together in Newcastle. His mum and dad had facilitated lots of trips out and family holidays together as two families and his fate seemed to have been written twenty years ago. He thought the world of her, Felicity was stunning, beautiful, hardworking and totally driven to be the best lawyer she could be. She had a hard edge to her, a controlling streak to her and that was fine as she needed to be strong in her in line of work. She would be a good wife and partner, strong and would adapt to running Hudson Hall Farm easily as she also had been brought up on a large farming estate. He wasn't quite sure how he felt about starting a family yet, both families seemed desperate for grandchildren and Felicity also seemed really keen to start a family. She felt that she was now getting to an age where she needed to start a family. Christ she was only twenty eight which was no age at all. He now felt that he didn't really have much choice on that particular subject and suddenly had empathy for the bulls in his fields.

His phone suddenly lit up when a text arrived. It was from Frances. He smiled when he read the text. Only she could send such an excited text, telling him about her new dress and agreeing to a night away with such flare. She was a nice girl who needed a break and a night out apparently. He was pleased that she had agreed to go with him as he really did hate going to these things on his own. Felicity was going to York for the weekend shopping with girlfriends which he knew she would enjoy. Now all he needed to do was tell her that he was going to the ball with Frances whom he had already invited. He put the phone down and returned to his laptop, the call to Felicity was for another time.

Chapter 5

Frances stared at her reflexion in the long wardrobe mirror, she almost couldn't believe it was her. For years she had really only worn work clothes, jeans, joggers and pyjamas and it felt strange to feel so special, so clean and so girly. She had taken the day off work and spent most of the day with the boys taking them on long walks trying to tire them out as much as she could so that they slept well tonight. Mrs Brewis, her neighbour, had agreed to pop in at 9.00pm and then again in the morning to let them into the field. She was a nice lady who at eighty-five years old still lived at home and was still managing well despite the efforts of her four children who were constantly asking her to go and look around care homes but she was having none of that. The two neighbours were pleasant to each other and often had little chats but they rarely went in each other's homes. Mrs Brewis had been her grandparents neighbour and it was nice to occasionally reminisce about the past and her grandparents but that was really the extent of the friendship but she was pleased that she had agreed to let out the boys for her.

After a long and lazy bath filled with bubbles she had spent ages drying her long hair with the hair dryer. It normally was left to dry naturally and then plaited down the back but this time she wanted it to be as straight as possible. She had tried earlier in the week to put her hair up into an Audrey Hepburn style but the weight of her hair was too much for the clips and it just kept falling out. She had decided on trying to straighten it with the dryer and placed a simple diamond hair clip that had once belonged to her nana on one side. The clip matched the dress and just finished the outfit off. The dress hugged her petite figure in all the right places and she had even made the decision to not wear a bra as try as she might she couldn't hide the straps. She had also made the decision not to wear any pants or tights as the dress hugged her so tightly that all underwear could be seen under it. That decision had made her smile.

Her hair was so long now that when straightened it actually covered her bottom and finished at the top of her legs and may well have covered the pantie lines but she had decided the dress was too tight for any pants. 'Rebel' she thought as she smiled at her reflexion she moved sideways and opened the side slit fully to show off her strong, long legs and'to admire the shoes. Perfect! She had only a small amount of pale pink eyeshadow on and some pale pink lipstick that she had bought from the local supermarket. She had formulated a plan to try and keep her hands discretely hidden. She had cleaned them, brushed them, cut and shaped them and put on some clear nail varnish, they looked good for her but nothing like the beautifully manicured hands of the ladies who usually went to these balls. She worked in a stable and a restaurant day in and day out she had tried her best and they would just have to do!

Her overnight bag or trusted school rucksack was packed with everything she would need for a night away. The boys where fed and watered and had been out for a last walk. It was 5.45pm and soon Marcus would be arriving and taking her to her first ever ball. She was so nervous and she hadn't been able to eat all day so now her tummy rumbled and gurgled away in protest. She quickly ate a banana to try and quieten it down. The doorbell rang at exactly 6.00pm and Frances walked down the hallway to the front door to let Marcus in. She was met with a soft smile and a man in an expensive looking black tuxedo. He looked like James Bond.

"Hi Marcus I'm nearly ready I just need to lock the back door and grab my bags."

"Wow Frances you look amazing, that dress is beautiful. You look just, wow, and your hair is just so long...and shiny. I didn't know your hair was that long, it's incredible." Marcus knew he was talking too much but she looked so amazing, truly beautiful with a small amount of make up on and just natural, beautiful, shiny hair. She was the most beautiful woman he had ever seen, Robert was such a fool!

"Thank you so much, the dress is actually Chateau de Oxfam and the shoes and bag are from the same collection, you ought to visit their shop it's a quaint and secluded little shop on the high street next to the butchers. I spent my tip on it, a little birthday treat to myself." She smiled and giggled at the same time. She looked at Marcus in his black dinner suit and black bow tie. "You look great too, a bit like James Bond but without the gun."

"That's in the car my dear." He said in a mock posh Scottish accent. "I didn't want to scare the dogs or your neighbours, I'll show it to you later!" They laughed as they walked into the back of the house, she locked up and they both gave the boys strokes and pats. She hadn't left them before over night and suddenly felt a bit anxious but committed to having just one night all to herself.

"Be good boys and I'll see you both tomorrow and enjoy Radio Alnton. I love you both very much." Marcus noted the quiver in her voice.

Soon Marcus had loaded the bag into the boot, he was careful not to add any comment about the shabby rucksack and Frances was settled into the front seat of the sleek BMW. The leather seat was so comfortable and the leather so soft. "I love your car Marcus, it's really nice I didn't really notice it the last time I was in it."

"Thanks, she was my treat when I was got the Consultant's post, so she's only a few months old and I love her."

"Does she have a name if she's a she?"

"No, I just think of her as a she, it seems to suit the car better than a he, what car do you drive?

"I have a Burgundy Defender long wheel base, the one parked outside the house, I think you may have seen it at the stables too"

"Yes ,I have, she's nice , it seems a bit big for you?"

"Yes, it is a climb to get into her but she's easy to drive and I absolutely just love her. Burgundy Defenders are just so rare, she just seems so very special I call her Jilly coz she goes up hillys." They both burst out in laughter.

Conversation was easy between the two and flowed all the way down to Newcastle. They laughed and giggled at each other's stories and compared their present lives.

"I heard you say you had bought the dress as a birthday treat, when is it or was it your birthday?"

"It was last Sunday, the day after the ball. I had a great day, great walk on the beach with the boys, fun shopping for my ball outfit and a lovely meal at night. Perfect day."

"How old are you now?"

"Twenty."

"Twenty, the same as Robert. You seem so mature compared to him. Do you get to see your family much, you don't talk about them very much, are they local?" Frances looked out of the window, her mind frantic for an appropriate answer.

"Sadly, I don't visit as much as I should as I'm always so busy." She hoped that answer would placate him.

Marcus sensed that it was a subject which didn't want to expand on so switched the conversation quickly. "Do you have any holidays planned at all Franny, you seem to just work all the time, do you ever just get away from it all?"

"Tonight, is my holiday, one night in your flat and I'm so looking forward to it! Have you been on holiday this year or got any plans to go anywhere nice or on your honeymoon?"

Marcus felt himself tense up but he wasn't sure whether it was the mention of his honeymoon or the feeling that any disclosure about his holidays seemed like bragging. "Easter, we went to America for a couple of weeks and we had a week in Italy last month. I'm not sure where we are going on honeymoon as I've not been told yet by the boss but wherever it is it will be expensive."

He continued to drive and kept his attention on the road, a simple mention of Felicity had dampened the mood in the car. What the hell was he doing going to the ball with this girl pretending he was being very gallant taking her and offering it all to her in the form of any apology. This girl didn't need to be tangled up with him or his family and he suddenly felt guilty that he hadn't told Felicity this afternoon when they had chatted on the phone, that he was actually taking Frances to the Ball in her place. The guilt suddenly consumed him and he really didn't want to acknowledge why he hadn't just been honest with her. The fact that he had told no one that he had invited Frances to the ball showed maybe that he actually didn't want anyone to know and he wasn't sure why.

They parked up in a small narrow street just off the road where the hospital was. The street was lined with lime trees and old terraced Victorians houses. "Here we are, I'll pop your bag in and you can freshen up, I'm on the second floor and be careful on the gravel, it's a hard to walk on in heels." Frances smiled to herself as he closed the car door behind her and she had an image of him walking in stilettos through the stones. The British Racing Green wooden door opened up and she was met by a colourful tiled floor, wooden staircase and the walls had been painted in a soft primrose yellow. She pushed the door behind her and started to walk upstairs behind him pulling up her dress as she ascended. The room was a large open plan lounge, kitchen, dining room and study all furnished in modern contemporary styles with a black glossy kitchen. The three enormous slate grey sofas dominated the room and as did the massive TV and gaming system that sat on the low wooden TV table.

"Wow this is so amazing, it's so modern now I can see why you were shocked at my house you must have thought that I lived in a museum compared to this." she said scanning the room.

"I had very little say in it sadly it is all Felicity's work but I did choose the TV. Right, come this way, this is your room sorry it's only a single bed and the door opposite is the bathroom and I have put out a couple of new towels in there for you as well. I'm across the hall there."

Frances looked in the small room that was all white, white walls, white wooden floor, white curtains, white bedding, white lamp, white rug and one plain sky blue cushion.

"Someone likes white, it feels very Mediterranean."

Marcus laughed. "We went to Rhodes last summer on holiday and the next thing is Rhodes is in my spare bedroom. Come on we better get a move on as its nearly 7.30. It's only a five minute walk up the road. Are you ready?"

"Yes, I've got everything I need, and just want to say thank you so much for inviting me to come to the ball. I'm so excited to see the room and the band. It just seems such a long time since I had a dance, it was at a friend's wedding a few years ago." She blushed and he smiled and they left the tiny room and their close proximity.

Within five minutes they had arrived at the Rocca Hotel and had been met by copious amounts of people all shaking his hand and patting him on the back and congratulating him. The hotel was very grand with high ceilings, velvet drapes and modern wooden floors. Contemporary art work mingled with plush leather sofas and Indian rugs. Some looked at Frances and said hello when he introduced her but most just glanced and then ignored her. Frances could feel that tingly excitement that had been in her tummy all day suddenly start to vanish, she was now starting to feel a little uncomfortable which was a much worse feeling.

Marcus steered her into the large dining room with his hand softly pushing her elbow in the direction of one of the large round tables. The room was amazing and overwhelming. The ceiling was gold, just gold with three massive gold chandeliers majestically hanging over the room. The walls were covered in green and gold patterned wallpapers, loud and proud her mum would have said. And a heavy walnut herringbone floor dominated the room. Gold chairs and large round tables covered in pristine white table clothes, with gold cutlery and gold rimmed glasses complemented the room. It reminded her of the summer ball in the marquee, similar colours but not much else. The room quickly filled with about two hundred people, men and women who all appeared to be dressed in the best and most expensive designer wear and jewellery. She felt rather plain now and a little under dressed or maybe a little too young to even be in this room. Marcus looked for their names on table 1 and guided her to her chair pulling it out for her allowing her to sit before he pushed it in slightly. They were the first to sit down

"Are you OK Franny, you looked slightly petrified in the foyer?"

"No, I'm fine. Why is everyone congratulating you Marcus?"

"Well actually I've just had an article published in a medical journal. A research article which I completed here at the hospital. It gives me and the hospital a bit of kudos so people are thanking me really. It's a bit of a fuss but we doctor's do like a good get together and to blow our own trumpets." He looked awkward.

"Well done and congratulations on your publication." She hesitated. "I feel awful now, it should be Felicity with you, celebrating with you and not me. Sorry."

"Don't be, she chose to go shopping with her friends and not come with me, so don't worry about it. She knows that I invited you and she's pleased that I'm not on my own." Marcus didn't tell her that he had only just texted her about 30 minutes ago. Marcus poured the wine, red for him and white for her and soon the table started to fill up with lots of other senior doctors and their wives. All met Marcus with handshakes and the women kissed his cheek, all obviously knew him well."

"Thank you all so much for coming and thank you George for organising everything I feel very grateful and lucky to have such wonderful colleagues. Can I introduce you all to a family friend Frances, she kindly agreed to accompany me tonight so that I am not here on my own. This is George and Freya, Rob and Linda and Bill and Grace." Pleasantries were exchanged between them all, the three men especially were very welcoming but the three women just acknowledged her. Frances felt a little better as Marcus seemed to be intent on making a fuss of her as it was her first ball and he was true to his word, he was making a real effort to make her feel special even for just one night. The waiting staff fussed around the tables pouring wines and taking additional orders from the bar, Marcus ordered two bottles of champagne for the table and asked for a particular brand which he liked, Moet. Her mum's favourite drink. It was the one that they had on all birthdays, wedding anniversaries, Christmas days and New Year's Eve. This was something she knew and she loved it almost as much as her mum. "Thank you, Marcus." she said as he poured the champagne eloquently into the champagne flute.

"You are very welcome Franny and thank you for coming tonight with me and I would also like to toast my three colleagues, and friends Rob, George and Bill whom I owe my position, my guidance and my friendship and success too. To my friends."

Everyone stood up at the table and clinked glasses and congratulated Marcus and drank the fine champagne. Frances felt really proud of him which was a strange feeling as she hardly knew him, didn't really know what his job was and she wasn't really even a friend of his or his family but she knew he was a good man, a nice man and she was really pleased for him. The table settled down into their seats and waiting staff arrived with the starters, a choice of either soup or Melon. Frances had chosen the melon starter which were drenched in a port sauce with raspberries and a raspberry coulis on the side. It was beautifully presented on a white porcelain plate with a gold line around the edge. "Wow thank you so much that looks amazing, almost too pretty to eat!" The waiter smiled and carried on asking the rest of the table their preference and serving them accordingly. The starter was amazing and the melon just melted in her mouth, she cleared her plate quickly. She didn't realise how hungry she was until she smelt the food. Marcus chatted away with the others at the table about work, their families and the latest cars that the wives had their eyes on.

"My dear Marcus, it is so sad that Felicity wasn't able to come tonight. It seems weeks since we last saw her, she must be really busy at work to miss such an important evening but work must come first for such influential women. Do give her my love when you see her and the sooner you set a wedding date the better. You need to put a ring on her as soon as possible or someone else might snap her up." said Grace in a smirky voice occasionally looking at Frances.

"Well actually I wasn't going to say anything as she's not here tonight with us but Felicity agreed last Saturday to be my wife and we are officially getting engaged on Christmas day, her choice, and getting married next summer, again her choice."

"Congratulations Marcus, well done Marcus, absolutely brilliant news, published Doctor and now a fiancée in one week." Grace gushed, endorsed by all the others at the table. The men shook his hand and joined him at his side of the table slapping him on the back and welcoming him to the married man's club. The women all smiled and congratulated him again individually wanting to know every detail of the proposal and asking about the ring. Marcus tried to fill in the details which the women were so eager to know but ended up just inviting them all up to the house for supper next Saturday with both him and Felicity and they would all have the chance to chat to Felicity directly. He hadn't really thought about the ring much but Felicity had said that whilst she was in York shopping with her friends that she would start to have a look in the shops to see what she liked and what she didn't like. He just assumed that one day this week they would go into Newcastle for lunch and then go and have a look around the Jewellery shops and choose the ring together. She had expensive tastes and if he knew one thing about Felicity the ring wasn't going to be simple or cheap.

Thankfully the main course arrived and the waiter swiftly moved around the table offering them all their choice for the main meal. All had chosen to have the roast chicken dinner. The plates were quickly placed in front of everyone again and copious amounts of vegetables in large bowls placed around the table. Frances spoke to the waiter. "Thank you that looks wonderful and steaming hot, thank you." Frances acknowledged the food presented to her and started to take a share from the large serving bowls on the table. Everything looked great, hot and still moist, often it wasn't at venues where there was mass catering. Marcus made sure that her wine and water glass were constantly topped up. He asked her if she was enjoying the meal and commented on how it must be a change for her not to be working. Grace, Bill's wife heard the last comment and picked up on it as soon as the conversation at the table allowed.

"Tell me Frances what is it that you do, are you a waitress or something?"

"No, I work in a private stable as a groom and then I work on the weekend as a waitress for a local restaurant, so I'm lucky I have two great jobs which I enjoy."

"So how do you know the Bucannon Family and Marcus, are you in the same set or are your parent's friends?"

Marcus answered quickly before she had a chance to respond. "No, she's a friend of my brother's really but we all just know her now don't we Franny?"

"Yes, that's right." Frances returned to eating her meal a little startled and Marcus successfully changed the subject on the table to Grace's new car which she was more than happy to discuss at great length. As she ate the lovely meal she noticed that Marcus kept looking at her even when he was talking to the others. When she met his stare he quietly asked her if she was alright. She smiled and nodded her head slightly and continued with her meal in silence enjoying every mouthful of the meal that had been prepared for her.

More wine and water were served all around the table into glasses that were never empty. The whole table were laughing and enjoying themselves when the waiting staff started to clear the tables and moved the dessert cutlery down to the sides of the placemat. Frances had chosen the Banoffee pie which arrived under a huge layer of cream covered in grated chocolate. The portion was large but Frances hoped she could manage it. She thanked the waiter again and waited for everyone else at the table to receive their plates. The pie was the nicest thing she had ever tasted, cream, caramel, banana and crushed biscuit what more could a girl ever want and she immersed herself in the luxury of the dessert. The others chatted away to each other but she felt she was not part of the table at all at this stage and she was very content on just enjoying the food and wine. Marcus seemed to be having a great time and she was pleased for him. He worked hard and he seemed very respected in the room. At that precise moment, George stood up with an empty glass in his hand and gently tapped the side of the glass with a tea spoon in an attempt to gain everyone's attention. Rob was way more successful when he stood up and told everyone to shut up. The room laughed. George began to speak. " As you all know we are all here enjoying the splendid hospitality of the Rocca Hotel for one reason and one person only. He is an inspiring and hard working doctor who I am also proud to call my friend and we are all here to raise our glass's to Marcus Bucannon, our newest and most accomplished Consultant." Everyone stood up and raised their glasses and toasted his new appointment and his Publication. Marcus stood up, he was slightly pink and slightly unsteady as he stood up resting one hand on Frances's shoulder.

He cleared his throat and began to speak. "What can I say but a massive thank you to you all especially all the doctors on the board, this motely group who I have the honour to call my friends and to each and every member of the team I want to say thank you, thank you for everything you have done for me, supported me and taught me. AND.... I would also like to say thank you to the nurses who have had to put up with me, endured me, protected and corrected me when I have made the odd mistake along the way. I raise my glass to every single member of the team, past and present. Thank you."

The crowd in the dining room all cheered and clapped him and then it was all over much to Marcus's relief as he hated making speeches, even short acceptance speeches.

" I didn't fluff it up too much did I Franny, I hate speaking in public, do you think it was okay?"

"Yes brilliant, loud, confident and short, a perfect speech I would say." Marcus noted the sparkle in her voice and the brightness of her eye's, she was teasing him but in the nicest way possible.

The table was cleared and large pots of coffee, tea and milk were placed in the centre of the tables so that those at the table could help themselves to hot drinks and the chocolate mints. The band who had quietly been setting up on the stage suddenly burst into life with a loud rendition of 'He's simply the best, adapted version of Tina Turner's big hit, Marcus groaned to himself as everyone else laughed and pointed at him. He sank back into his chair fending off the comments from George, Rob and Bill who had requested the ancient hit be played first. As if there was a hidden bell somewhere, the three ladies all stood up in unison gathered their bags and informed the table that they were off to the ladies room and then off for a little dance. Great timing thought Frances as she had planned to go to the loo as soon as the meal was over, but she didn't want to go when the others were there. She decided that she could hang on a bit longer.

About fifteen minutes later the three women returned to the table dropping their handbags down and danced off towards the dancefloor. Frances noted that they hadn't invited her to join them so she made her excuses to Marcus and left the table to nip to the loo. A few minutes later she was back in the dining room but didn't feel that she wanted to go back to the table and sit down. She wanted to dance. There was little space on the dancefloor and she thought that it might seem rude not to join the three women who were now dancing together. However, she saw a staircase at the end of the room that seemed to lead to an upper balcony area that overlooked the main function room. She glanced around and saw that no one was taking any interest in her so she walked up the narrow staircase. The room upstairs was about a quarter of the size of the room below and fully carpeted. All the tables and chairs had been stacked up on one side of the room. At the front was a wall about five foot high with a thick wooden rail on the top and bar stools pushed up to it.

Francis walked over and looked down at all the people below. She could see her table and the men chatting away with animated arm actions and she could see the women on the dance floor tottering away in shoes that were not made for dancing or maybe it was just the that wearers weren't made for dancing. She giggled out loud at her naughty thought.

The band was made up of eight men all in their forties and fifties playing drums, guitars, organs and one played a saxophone and they were good! The lead singer was singing La Bamba and he was brilliant singing in Spanish, Frances had no choice but to sway to the music. Before long she was full on dancing, playing air guitar and singing out loud to the brilliant catchy song. Everyone in the room was up dancing and joining in. Frances just spun round and round and relished the freedom the music gave. The band played brilliant songs one after another, all good songs that everyone could dance and sing too. Frances used the whole of her private dance floor, spinning and dancing to every corner. She was in heaven. The music changed and a slow romantic ballad started, showing the room just how good the lead singer was. Her heart started to slow down and her breathing started to settle, she was smiling like the proverbial Cheshire cat and she was feeling really happy and only slightly tipsy!

She hadn't realised that she had been joined in her special room by someone else who was leaning against the wall, drinking a mug of coffee watching her, it was the restaurant manager whom she had met when they had arrived.

"I'm so sorry to be here, if it's private, I just thought.."

"No, I think I should be the one apologising to you. You looked like you were having a wonderful time!" He hesitated. "This room is my favourite area, I like to come up here and watch when I am on a coffee break. It was nice to watch someone just having such an honest time, enjoying themselves without anyone else watching. And I also must offer my thanks and my serving staff's thanks as I think you were one of the only people in the room to be polite and courteous to them. Please's and thank you's are very basic words but most in this room tonight seemed to struggle with them."

Frances laughed and nodded her head. "I do agree with you, I didn't really hear many on my table, only a few from Marcus. I work in a restaurant and I hate it when people ignore me and the efforts of the chef, so rude. The meal tonight was amazing and the staff were just wonderful and I just can't begin to tell you how much I have enjoyed myself tonight, it's been brill, thank you."

"And yet here you are dancing on your own when you obviously came with people."

"Yes, I came as a companion to the doctor whose being celebrated tonight but I don't really know him that well, I'm a friend of his brother and I think he just felt sorry for me and hey, he had a spare ticket. I think the dancing up here on my own is much better, loads more space." she smiled widely.

"Well, I shall leave you to enjoy your private dance floor all to yourself and I hope you enjoy the rest of the night." He turned and walked down the stairs with the untouched mug still in his hand and joined the crowd below.

Frances didn't return to dancing, she stood at the top of the stairs and looked down at the table where Marcus was sitting. He was chatting to a group of men who had joined him at the table. Occasionally she noticed he would look around the room as if he was looking for someone. Could it be that he was actually looking for her? She felt guilty suddenly that she had been gone so long enjoying herself and not told Marcus where she was. She looked back at her 'private dance floor' and descended the stairs, making her way back eventually to Marcus and her seat. She smiled briefly at him as she took her seat not wanting to interrupt him as he seemed to be in deep conversation with his friends.

"Hello?" the voice hesitated. "Frances isn't it?" Her head bolted up. "How are you my dear, I have often wondered what happened to you and what you went on to do after you decided to defer?" Her eyes met the friendly smile of Professor Crowther. He had interviewed her for her place at medical school and he was the one who eventually offered her the scholarship to study medicine at the University. He was about sixty years old, small and portly in stature. He had a mass of curly grey hair and a smile that matched his kind eyes. She had liked him the moment she had met him. Marcus looked at the professor and then at Frances.

"How lovely to see you, you are looking so well. Tonight, has been such a lovely night, a night to enjoy the achievements of such a wonderful doctor, Marcus has done very well don't you agree?" Frances avoided Marcus's gaze. The Professor continued.

"Yes, my dear he has done very well indeed and we are all very proud of him, it shows what you can gain with hard work and in such a short time. Tell me are you thinking of starting your course soon, this September would be a great time as the money is allocated in this financial year and we may not be able to guarantee it for next year with all the cuts that are happening?"

"Hopefully I can, I just need to sort some things out before I confirm my place." She struggled to reply to him, she knew it was not quite true, she fiddled with her glass. She knew she couldn't leave the dogs and she knew she couldn't quite afford it yet, even if she had no tuition fees to pay, she still needed to save another £20,000 to secure her place for five years. "Well, we look forward to welcoming you very soon my dear."

The Professor and the other men said their goodbyes to Frances and Marcus and they were left alone on the table for the first time that evening. All the others had gone to dance or drink at the bar. Both remained quiet watching the band deep in their own thoughts. It was Marcus who broke the silence. " I didn't realise that you had applied to study Medicine here?"

Frances hesitated before she spoke, she put the empty wine glass down that she had been playing with in her hand and turned her head to face him. "It's a long story but yes I did apply and Professor Crowther was kind enough to offer me a full tuition scholarship but the timing was bad and I couldn't quite commit to five years. Hopefully soon

I'll be able to take up my place, maybe next year. As you know I work like mad, save like mad and there is an option that I could sell my car but that feels like a last option at this stage. I'm hoping that maybe a year in September I will have enough behind me and I can take up the scholarship. Fingers crossed." She felt flustered and wished that he would change the subject.

"I didn't realise that you fancied a career in Medicine. I thought you were horse mad. You should go as quick as possible, the longer you are out of education the harder it will be for you, try for this September if you can. If it's only the money stopping you, I'm sure I could help you out in some way, pay me back when you're a consultant or something." He smiled affirming his offer to her.

"Thank you that's really kind of you but one of my problems is Bert and Max, while they are still around I can't leave them, they are too old to be left any longer than I leave them now. Maybe next September." she said pessimistically. Thankfully he stopped asking her any more questions realising, maybe, it wasn't something that she wanted to talk about.

At 1.00 o'clock the band stopped playing and the remaining revellers started to leave the hotel. Marcus guided Frances through the noisy crowd to the front entrance saying good bye and thank you to friends and staff as he left. The warm July air was still hanging around in the night, they set off walking the short distance back to his flat. They chatted about the evening, the food, the champagne, the band and the other people on their table.

"I'm sorry about the women on the table tonight, the husbands are okay but the wives are such a shallow bunch of vain desperate examples of humans. I'm sure if their husbands all didn't have six figure salaries then none of them would stick around. Leaving you when they all went off to dance was so rude, I'm sorry I didn't say anything. I wasn't sure if you would've wanted me to cause a scene or not but I should have said something sorry."

"No, it's fine honestly, those people are yours and Felicity's friends, I doubt if I will ever see any of them again and if I did I am pretty sure that they would just ignore me anyway. Strange question but do you have anything in common with them apart from medicine, you seem very different from them all?" Frances regretted asking the question the minute it left her mouth, they were obviously his friends and colleagues. Marcus remained quiet whilst they walked home. The silence was only broken by her shoes tapping on the pavement as they walked.

"Actually, now you come to mention it, medicine is the only thing we have in common. They all live in the city and have city people's lives. I like the countryside and farming and animals and gardening and reading. I want children and a family and a farm house full of kids who I see every day and put to bed every night. None of them have children. Don't you think that's strange that none of my three colleagues have children? Do you want children?"

Frances smiled "I love children and hopefully when I've finished medical school I will be able to get a job as a GP and then I'm going to have at least four children, one their lonely, two they fight, three it's one sided and four it's alright. Yep, defo four, I even know the names I like Eliza, Fleur, Florence and Roxy for girls and Bertie, Rafe, Harvey and Jet for boys depending on what I have. Marcus noted that he liked all the names.

Well here we are, he opened the door for Frances and then stood back and allowed her to walk in past him. Door locked and bolted he followed her upstairs and headed for the kitchen. "A last night cap or a cup of tea?" He remembered she liked tea. Frances pointed at the bottle of brandy that he had in his hand. "I've never had brandy before, can I have a small taste please?" Marcus got two brandy crystal balloons down and poured two large glasses of the liquid and handed one to Frances. Instinctively she moved the brandy around the bottom of the glass and watched it slow down. She took a sip. "Mmmmm that's tasty, really nice and hot in my throat." She smiled at Marcus as she went over to join him on the sofa pulling her legs up underneath herself and relaxing into the leather sofa leaving her shoes on the floor.

"Like it?"

"I love it." She smiled back at him.

They chatted away on the sofa like two long lost friends talking about farming, horses, medicine and every other subject that they had in common. Conversation came so easily to both of them. They laughed and drank together for another hour or so before Marcus said he thought it was time that they turned in. He thanked her for a wonderful evening and then went to the kitchen to get them both glasses of cold water. He followed Frances as she walked to her bedroom door.

"Thank you for the best night of my life, I've had a wonderful evening." She looked up at him as he walked closer to her.

"You are very welcome, I've had a great night too and I feel so relaxed and happy, thank you." He looked at Frances, her smile was small and private and her tired eyes serene and beautiful in the half light of the room. Before he knew what he was doing his head was slowly moving down closer to hers, she kept still. He didn't hesitate and soon his lips were slowly and gently kissing hers. Both of them closed their eyes and fell gently and silently into each other's arms. He stroked the back of her head with one hand and held her around the waist with the other. Frances returned the kiss without thinking. All she knew was she had never felt like this, she had butterflies in her stomach and her body felt on fire. She wrapped her arms around his waist and pulled him into her. He responded and kissed her harder, his body and his hormones starting to take control of the situation. He wanted her, he needed her and he also he knew that in such a small amount of time he had fallen utterly and totally in love with this most amazing, beautiful, intelligent, humble woman and he wanted her to be his forever. He pulled back and looked into her face, she wanted him too, he could feel it.

He led her by the hand into her bedroom, the spare bedroom and sat her down on the bed. He took off his bow tie and undid his shirt, pulling it off and dropping them on the floor. She watched him with her eyes wide open as he embraced her gaze and joined her on the bed. His hands worked skilfully on her zip and he nudged the shoulder straps off her slim frame. Her dress dropped to her waist revealing her young body to him, he pulled her up to a standing position and allowed the dress to drop to the floor. She stood before him naked, so beautiful and perfect. He removed the rest of his clothes quickly and pulled back the quilt cover and allowed her to get in. He joined her. He held her and just stared at her momentarily lost in her overwhelming beauty and innocence.

"Where have you been all my life, I feel like you and I are one and the same and I need to be with you always, I ask you Franny, where have you been?"

"It doesn't matter where I've been Marcus, all that matters now is that I'm here now, with you." She moved to kiss him and they fell into each other. Moments later Marcus slid out of the bed and ran into his bedroom to fetch something to protect them both. He returned quickly to her and placed the protection on himself. Frances lay back on the bed watching him. She suddenly felt different, afraid and unsure. Should she say something. She felt he would know what to do and tried to relax back into the bed. He returned to kissing her, gentle and caring and softly caressed the tops of her legs with gentle fingertips. He started to join with her, slowly and carefully at first and then with a little more confidence and need.

Marcus could feel that she had changed, that she felt different and at first he didn't realise why. She started to relax a little and enjoy herself, she placed her hands on his waist but kept her eyes closed. Marcus realised with sudden and complete fear that she was a virgin, he had taken her virginity. He hadn't known but he couldn't stop. What man could stop at this stage. Frances groaned almost inaudibly to herself and was beginning to enjoy the things that Marcus was doing to her body. She started to respond and then, just as quickly as it had started it had finished. Marcus stilled for a few seconds and then slid off her to lie on his back, still panting. Frances remained still not sure what to do or what to say.

"OMG Franny you're a virgin, why the hell didn't you tell me, you are nearly twenty, I just thought." He stopped talking and covered his eyes with the back of his forearm. "What have I done, I'm so sorry, I should have stopped, you're a virgin, you were waiting for someone way better than me, god I'm sorry." Marcus jumped off the bed and went into the tiny bathroom to disregard the protection as quickly as he could into the bin. He quickly washed his hands and splashed his face with cold refreshing water and wrapped a bath towel around his waist. He starred at his reflexion in the mirror. He was a complete shit he thought. He'd betrayed Felicity, himself and god had he let Frances down, she was so young, he should've been the responsible one. "Dam, dam it you idiot."

Frances had pulled the quilt up around her neck. She wasn't sure what to do or what to think. Men didn't run out of the bedrooms after making love on the films that she had seen. She must have done something wrong. Had she really done it so wrong that he had run away from her without one word of kindness? Didn't he like her, had she upset him? Her mind was racing when he came back into the room and sat at the bottom of the bed. They were both quiet. Marcus lent down and picked up his shirt, trousers and underwear and stared at the wall. Frances stared at him saying nothing.

"I'm so sorry Franny I should never have done that to you. I didn't realise that you were a virgin. I'm so sorry, you're first time should've been with someone way better than me and with someone who deserves you. I'm getting married next year and my whole family needs me to do just that. He turned to face her. " It was all my fault and I take full responsibility, you never would have led me on, I kissed you and I was... selfish. You get some rest now and I'll drive you home in the morning". He stood up and walked towards the door. A small voice spoke.

"I wanted to Marcus, the whole of me wanted to and I'm not a kid I'm twenty now, I know what I want and I wanted you." Marcus closed the door as he left.

The next morning Marcus managed to get himself out of bed at 9.30pm. It had been a very late night and his head ached. He wished it was a hangover but he knew it was a pain that would take much longer to go. Guilt. He had tossed and turned all night debating whether he should go to her and see if she was alright but then she needed her sleep and she probably didn't want to be with him as he had been such a moron. He lay back down in his bed and relived the events of the night before in as much detail as he could. She had said she had wanted him as much as he had wanted her, right?

But he knew that he was the adult here, the older one, a doctor and farmer, land owner and future fiancé to Felicity. She was just an innocent naive girl who he had pounced on. He felt as if he had taken total advantage of her and he felt awful. But all the time he was giving himself a stern talking to, he kept remembering her. Her smile, her eyes, her smell, her laugh, her dancing when she thought no one was watching. She was like a drug and he needed her so much. Last night had happened because he not only wanted her but he knew that he needed her as much as she seemed to want and need him. The only thing that was different between the two of them was the fact that he knew he loved her.

With that resolve he jumped out of bed and pulled on old joggers and an old Ramones t-Shirt, bare foot he walked over to her bedroom door. He knocked quietly on the door in an attempt to wake her up gently. There was no sound from the room and he decided to knock on the door again, this time a little harder. Again, there was no sound from the room. He hesitated and turned the brass handle to open the door.

"Morning Franny, it's just me, it's nearly 10.00.am and I thought you might need to be up and about now. I can make breakfast and then I can drop you off at home, with Max and Bert." Still no noise so he poked his head around the door and saw that the bed was empty and already made. Her overnight backpack had gone and the only reminder of her was the evening gown, shoes, and bag which she had left on a chair. She had left a note attached to the dress. "Thank you but I don't think I'll be needing these again. Frances." His heart sank and broke. He had lost her, she knew she deserved better than him.

Frances had not had any sleep all night. She had tossed and turned and stared at the ceiling all night trying to figure out what she had done wrong. Her feelings for Marcus had been overwhelming and so exciting. She hadn't really known how much she liked him till the moment he had kissed her and then, in a moment it had all changed and she knew exactly how she felt about him. She had wanted and needed him so much, she felt safe and cared for when she was with him. Marcus had been very special to her and so kind and it was all gone and she didn't really know why. She had racked her brains all night. Was she really that bad in bed, obviously he had realised that she was a virgin so she wasn't experienced but didn't he feel how amazing they were together, how she responded when he touched her. She closed her eyes as tears escaped. He was Doctor Marcus Bucannon, land owner and farmer from one of the oldest and wealthiest families in Northumberland and he was due to marry the equally powerful, intelligent and beautiful Felicity. Frances realised the enormity of her mistake in a split second.

It was 6.00am and it was time for her to pack up and go. She quickly changed into jeans, a top and converses. Made her bed and pulled a brush through her hair before scraping it into a messy bun. She tore a piece of paper out of her diary in her bag and wrote Marcus a simple message. She had to be polite and she needed him to dispose of the clothes as she knew that she would never need them again. Then she left the flat being as quiet as she could as she didn't want to wake him and have any kind of a confrontation with him. This was the best way for her to leave, much better than a walk of shame and she certainly didn't want to get into the car with him to face an hour of silence or worse, a lecture. She left his flat closing the front door behind her and headed towards the hospital which dominated the sky line. She didn't know the area very well but she knew that she could get a bus home from the hospital, eventually.

It was almost 12.00pm when she had eventually got home. The bus had picked her up at 10.09 and due to delays in Newcastle and an accident on the A1 the trip had been long and slow. She tried to feel positive and that she hadn't been in the crash on the A1 and that she did have a home to go to unlike the people she had seen asleep in a doorway near the hospital, but she couldn't. She was famished and in desperate need of a cup of tea and she needed sleep not only to refresh her body but to stop her brain from thinking. She opened the door to be met by a pair of very excited dogs running up to her she fell to the ground and immersed herself in their fuss and licking. She had missed this pair and swore then and there she would never leave them overnight again. Eventually they allowed her to get up and they followed her into the kitchen where she treated them both to a dog treat which they both eagerly took from her to devour in the lounge.

She quickly called Mrs Brewis to let her know that she was home safe and sound and to thank her again for keeping her eye on the boys for her. Tomorrow, on the way back from work she would call in and buy her a nice bouquet of flowers as a proper thank you. Mrs Brewis hadn't asked if she'd had a nice time and Frances felt a sense of relief as she put the phone down. Last night was finished, she needed a bath to wash everything away and tomorrow thankfully, was a new day.

Chapter 6

August turned out to be a very long and hot month. Temperatures were in the twenties for almost 2 weeks at the end of the month which was great news for the farmers, but not great news for the horses who were not used to the heat. Frances kept herself very busy at work doing all the jobs that she needed to do on a daily basis but always she tried to find time in the day to give all the horses a quick hose down to help keep them cool. Bella had been away for most of August with friends on the family yacht which they kept in Nice, so she hadn't been down to the yard for ages. Esme had been on holiday to Spain for a couple of weeks with her family and in-laws and was due back at work on Monday. She had texted Frances most days to check that everything was okay and that Frances was managing but as yet Frances hadn't heard from Bella.

It had been a busy few weeks doing all the work on her own but it had worked out well for her. Summer's dry months meant the horses kept cleaner and spent most of their days in the paddocks grazing on the grass and free from humans wanting to take them for little treks. She had ridden them over the last few weeks but only gentle trots down a tree lined track which gave shade to them and Frances. Hero needed time with his saddle on otherwise he might forget what it was and try to throw it off. Hector just followed munching his way up the track but never straying too far from Hero. Frances tried to ride four or five horses a day and she in turn was beginning to look really toned but it was beginning to take its toll as she was starting to get tired in the evenings.

Esme would be back on Monday and her work would be return to normal. She had missed Esme. Frances missed her company and hearing about all the antics of her boys, all three of them and she was looking forward to hearing all about the holiday and what they had got up to. She liked that about Esme the most, she was happy to talk and chat all day but didn't ask too many questions about what she had done. The Monday after the Hospital Ball in Newcastle she had asked Frances a number of questions about how it had gone, if she had had a nice time and even jokingly asked if she had met anyone nice. Frances struggled to give her many answers that were not monotone so Esme realised that her friend hadn't had such good time and that she didn't really want to talk about it.

Frances had spent the whole of August trying not to think about that evening or even think about Marcus. But thinking about Marcus was her default thought. The Sunday after the ball he had sent her a text apologising for not seeing her and for sleeping in so late and thanking her for accompanying him and that he had enjoyed the ball. He was sorry that she had left so early and made her own way home and that could she please text him to let him know that she had arrived home. He also confirmed that he had disposed of the items of clothing that she had asked him to deal with. He finished the text with just Marcus. It had seemed such a cold text, like a work text that you would send a colleague, just words that confirmed actions. It wasn't the kind of text that a lover sent to a woman that he loved or even a woman that he had spent the night with. It was just a text and nothing more could be read into it. She had texted back eventually after three or four attempts. 'Hi home okay, thank you Frances' was all that she had managed to send in the end. Short and sweet as her mum used to say. She had not heard from him in over five weeks now but she knew that he and Felicity were on the yacht with Bella in the South of France at this exact moment. Bella was surprisingly really excited about going on holiday this year and had chatted copiously about her plans for the month- long holiday and who would be joining her. Felicity and Marcus seemed to be spending a lot more time with Bella over the last few months and Bella had even been asked to be one of the bridesmaids at Marcus's wedding. Frances had groaned inside when Bella had told her, she was so excited but Frances just didn't want to hear about the wedding at all and here she was stuck with one of the bridesmaids at work. She knew that she would know every little detail about the wedding probably even more than the groom!

As evening approached she started to settle the stables down for the night, water troughs checked and final feed given she started to shut and lock all the doors and gates. As she was walking over to her car she was met by Alfie the estate manager who had been living in the main house while the family were away for the summer. He was an older gentleman, about sixty or so and had worked on the estate since he was fifteen, just like his father before him. He was a nice jolly man who Frances liked . She always had a quiet joke in her head about Alfie, it was good that there was at least one gentleman on the Grovewood Estate and Alfie was definitely that gentleman. If only people knew the thoughts in her head sometimes!

"Hello Frances, you're a bit late setting off tonight everything alright?"

"Yes, thanks Alfie, everything is fine. I nipped home at lunch just to let my dogs out as it was so hot, so I was just catching up on my time."

"You are such a good girl, not many would be so honest. Night pet, I'll see thee the morrow."

Fifteen minutes later she pulled up outside her house and gathered up her belongings off the passenger seat. Even at 6.30 it was still warm and humid. She locked the car and went in to her home to be met by a Max with his tail wagging. Bert was lying in his bed with his tail wagging away but now he found it too difficult to get up and bounce around the same as Max. She bent down giving them both plenty of love and attention. She had cooked a chicken last night so tonight she was having cold roast chicken salad and the boys were going to share the rest of the chicken between themselves. Quickly she was showered and dressed in clean fresh clothes and started to prepare the meal for the night. The boys had both had a small walk in the back garden and were now eagerly waiting for the dinner to be dropped into their feeding bowls.

"Here you go boys, chicken avec gravy for dinner and accompanied by the best cold refreshing water that money can buy, dig in." She smiled as they both tucked in with their tails wagging. She loved these two more than she could ever say and it broke her heart that she had to leave them alone for such long periods of time. Both were getting older and slowing down in everything that they did, she quickly pushed those thoughts away. She tucked into her salad and her cup of tea, she was famished, she always was lately, all the work at the stables had given her a real appetite. The meal quickly devoured she went hunting in the fridge to find a yogurt and some grapes. She settled down on the sofa accompanied by Max and Bert to watch a DVD on her computer. Letters to New York, her favourite film, she'd watched it twice in the last month but it was an easy watch after a long day at work. The snacks were quickly eaten and the film started, Frances and her boys were soon all lying on the sofa, the boys asleep and Frances crying along to the film. She could never understand why she cried, she knew the film off by heart and the ending was always the same, the guy gets the girl!

At 9.30 she pulled herself off the sofa and persuaded the boys to have a final walk in the back field before they all went to bed for the night. The boys obliged eventually and Frances locked up, making sure that the water bowls were full. She dressed for bed and went to the bathroom to use the loo and clean her teeth. She remembered that she needed a new toothpaste so nipped to the airing cupboard at the top of the stairs to fetch it. She knew she had one hiding behind the boxes of Tampons. Eventually she found the red tube of paste and returned to clean her teeth and she let her mind wonder whilst she brushed, staring at her reflection. Shock and panic entered her mind rapidly as she suddenly realised that she hadn't been in that cupboard for ages and that she hadn't used a tampon for weeks.

She quickly finished cleaning her teeth and ran downstairs to look on the calendar in the kitchen. 17th August was her due day it was now the 1st September. She was late. She wasn't even sure if she had one in July. She wasn't sure if she was late or really, really late.

The panic set in, she started to shake and sweat and she could feel her heart beating in her chest. She couldn't be, she just couldn't be. They had only made love once and she was sure he had used protection. The word raced around in her head and then eventually the word pregnant tumbled out of her mouth. "I can't be, I just can't be," she sobbed "I can't be pregnant."

In almost an instant she knew that she was, she had a feeling she was. She had been eating more and there was no denying that she was late, very late. She tried to control her thoughts and her panic and an intense wishing that her mum was here with her now, oh god how she really needed her mum now. The tears cascaded from her eyes and the sobs hurt her chest, she struggled to breath and stay in control. Tomorrow she thought she would drive to a pharmacy in the next town, where no one would know her and she would buy a test. She collapsed on the floor and crawled over to the boy's beds and curled up with them hoping that they could give her the support and love that she was desperately craving.

Hours later she made her way to her own bed, she felt numb and exhausted. She had to be up at six to get to work but work was the last thing on her mind at the moment. She had formulated a plan. She would go to work, have a quick lunch break at home, let dogs out, leave early, tell Alfie, then go and get the test and do the test after work. Yes, that was a plan. She tried not to plan ahead, it may just be late as it was the first time and that may cause a slight delay, she didn't know, it may be the reason, maybe!

Eventually morning came and she got out of bed, dressed, used the bathroom and took Bert and Max out for a walk. Bert didn't seem keen to walk, he cleaned himself and waddled home leaving just Max at her side. Frances's mind was a million miles away from everything today, she was tired and way more than stressed. She grabbed some lunch, said her goodbyes and was away to work early, so she could leave early. The day was busy and hot. She dealt with all the horses quickly and cleaned the stables and paddocks as quickly as she could. Breakfasts were served and tack cleaned and checked. She raced home to see the dogs, eating in the car as she drove. After a quick fifteen minute walk she raced back to work to finish the day's final jobs. She called Alfie to tell him that she wasn't feeling great which wasn't a lie as she wasn't. He said that he was happy to do the evening jobs for her and to go home and get some rest.

Guiltily she put the phone down and raced out of the office and drove over to Trunington to pick up a pregnancy test. As she entered the pharmacy she felt as guilty as hell and uncomfortable as if people knew her secret and were staring at her. She kept her head down and found the correct section picking up one of the two kits that was for sale. She read the back of the package and decided it was the correct one for her, it frightened her to think that by just using this little box she would know within the hour if she was going to have a baby. She felt frightened just looking at the box but she knew she had to buy it and she had to use it. It was the only way she would know for certain. She bought the test quickly trying very hard not to look at the lady and concentrating on putting her pin code into the sales device. She left the shop quickly and jumped in her car. At least that was one part of the ordeal over, now just the worst part was left to do.

It didn't matter how many times she looked at the stick the result just didn't change. She read it over and over again and every time it said the same thing, pregnant. Frances was definitely pregnant. It even said she was six weeks pregnant. This stick didn't hold back anything. She lay on the bathroom floor and let the stick drop to the floor, she closed her eyes and laid completely still. She was pregnant and six weeks pregnant. What was she going to do? She had no family, no mum to help her, the father wasn't hers to have and she had no one in the world to help. For the first time in a long time she realised that she was completely on her own and not loved by another human being. The thought was too much and the tears and the sobbing started to erupt again. She knew she couldn't get rid of the baby but the thought of having a baby on her own was terrifying, she barely coped with everything at the moment just looking after herself. She felt scared. She felt alone.

Frances gave Bert and Max their evening meals but didn't bother with anything for dinner for herself. The last thing on her mind was food at the moment. She settled herself down on the sofa with a glass of water and her phone. She knew that the only person that she needed to talk to was Marcus. He was the father and he did need to know. She was only too aware that he was in the South of France on a luxury yacht, tanning himself, having fun and all with the love of his life, Felicity. She felt sick, really sick and she wasn't sure if it was the baby or because the knot that was in her stomach seemed to be crushing her from the inside out. She picked her phone up and scrolled down the short list of contacts. Marcus Bucannon. She had sent her last text over 6 weeks ago and nothing since. She opened up the message screen to him and started to text him:-

'Hi, it's Frances can you please call me at your earliest convenience Frances'.

Her fingers hoovered over the send button before she realised that she had told him twice that it was her and she realised that he would probably already know who the text was from, when it actually popped up on his phone. She deleted the message and started again.

'Hi can you give me a call please as soon as you can thanks Frances.' She re-read the text over and over again. It said what it needed to say, it was rather impersonal and short but what else did she need to put down, she was hoping to arrange a meeting with him and tell him in person or at least in person in a phone call. What to say and how to say it she wasn't quite sure about yet. Send. It was gone now, too late to change it and too late not to let him know what was happening. What a mess. She liked him a lot and she had thought he had felt the same way about her but she had got that wrong, looking back maybe he had just used her for a quick thrill. He was still with Felicity, obviously as they had still gone on holiday together and she had heard Bella on the phone talking to Felicity, before they had gone away, about house hunting in Newcastle for the newlyweds. Marcus's life still seemed on track to be the wonderful life that he and his family had planned. How would he feel about being a dad? He said he had wanted kids and that he couldn't wait for a house full of kids. Little did he know it but that wait wouldn't be much longer. Then reality stepped in. She was the outsider, the other woman, the tart and slut that he had slept with. He was going to marry Felicity and continue the line of Bucannon's in Hudson Hall Farm and be the land owner and country gent that everyone knew he was going to be. He would fill his house with their children not her children. She was the other woman.

Her phone lit up again as she opened it. He was reading her text. She could see he was reading it. The dots were pulsing. He was writing a reply, she waited, holding her breath. No reply came and the dots vanished, he had read it and ignored her.

'Please Marcus, please call me I need to talk to you, it's important, please. I won't ask again but please don't ignore me.' Before she knew what she was doing, the text was sent. The text sounded desperate and pleading. The thoughts in her head were desperate and she needed to talk to him and she needed his support. She needed him to tell her what to do and to tell her that everything was going to be okay. She waited for him to text back.

He read the second text. This time there were no pulsing dots. When she finally settled down in her bed she checked her phone for the last time, no message and still no pulsing dots. His answer was clear, he didn't want to speak to her. She closed her phone and turned the bed side light off. It was a warm night and she had left the window open. The thin cotton sheet rested gently over her legs. She watched the gentle rock of the ceiling light as it swayed in time to the slight breeze. She was on her own. Pregnant at twenty with not one single person to help her. Her hand rested on her tummy and she stroked the soft skin under her finger tips, she felt a sense of peace and calm. She was going to be a mum. She would have family now, one other person in this whole wide world would have the same blood as her. She was scared but she knew that she would be fine. Family, the only important thing in her world.

September continued to be warm and soon the leaves started to become dry. October was cooler and by the end all the trees were losing their leaves ready for the winter months ahead. December had eventually arrived and the coldness with it. She struggled to wake up on the dark December mornings but she now set her alarm five minutes earlier to do all the things she needed to do in the morning. Bert was getting older by the day and spent most of his time in his bed. He only ever ventured into the back yard now and didn't join Max and her on their daily walk around the field. She gave them both their breakfasts and actually handfed Bert with a tinned soft meat directly with a spoon. He seemed very tired today. She left their beds in the kitchen which seemed the warmest room and meant that Bert didn't have to walk far to get something to eat or drink. She didn't want to leave him but she didn't have a choice. She would pop back at dinner to see how he was. She kissed them both and held them both just for a few seconds longer than normal, inhaling and imprinting their smells to her memory.

On her drive to work she thought about her situation. Frances had never heard back from Marcus but she was now used to the idea of being a one parent family. She hadn't told anyone else yet that she was pregnant. She was twenty three weeks pregnant now but still very small and no one had noticed. She had plucked up the courage to go and see her doctor who had been great, she had said congratulations to Frances, the only person up until now, who had congratulated her. She had had one scan at the hospital and everything was going well. She loved that little black and white photo, the first one of her baby! She hadn't wanted to know the sex as she wanted it to be a surprise. The lady had asked her where her partner was when she had the scan but she said he was delayed. Now she felt sad that she had lied but she had felt embarrassed that she had no one to go with her which she guessed was quite unusual. She told herself that she needed to toughen up, loads of women did this on their own. But those women had friends and family she thought.

The baby was growing well and she was feeling great. She had suffered only a small amount of morning sickness and no other side effects or tiredness. If anything, she seemed to be flourishing whilst pregnant. She had raided her nana's old wardrobe and cobbled together a maternity wardrobe of sorts and had only needed to invest in a couple of pairs of maternity jeans. When she was in her jeans and knee length boots with a big coat on no one could see the bump. She was glad it was winter but she knew that she would need to tell people very soon. When she was working at the restaurant the uniform there was quite forgiving and she knew that after Christmas, after their busy period and after the Christmas parties for the farmers she would have to say something in the New Year. She needed the money, every single penny and was dreading telling Bella. She knew she would be finished immediately the minute Bella knew, stable girls just can't be six months pregnant. She suddenly felt panicky. Her baby was due at the end of March, what would she do for money for three months. She resolved not to say anything to anyone until she had too. She slipped her hand in her pocket and gently stroked her tummy telling Sploge that it all would be alright, trying to reassure herself at the same time. The morning jobs in the stables were finished just before 11.30 and Esme said that she could go home early and check on Bert. Esme was a dog person which was helpful as she understood how worried Frances was.

"I'll be back by 1.00, thanks for letting me pop off early see you later." And with a wave of her hand she was gone. She had a quick drive home and then she would be able to take the boys out for a quick walk. It looked and felt like snow, she loved snow and so did the dogs. She hoped it would snow. She let herself into the house and took off her coat and boots and went into the kitchen. She stopped in her tracks when she saw the boys. Bert was lying flat on his box and was breathing very slowly. Max had his head very close to Bert's and gently nuzzled him with his snout. Bert didn't respond. Frances dropped to the floor on her knees and stroked the back of Bert's head. "Hi my Berty Boy I'm here now, I'm here, sorry I had to leave you but it looks like your brother has been looking after you. I love you Bert so much, and I love you too Maxy moo." She gave both boys gentle and soothing kisses. The tears started to trickle out of her eyes. Frances didn't know what to do. She didn't want to call the vet and risk upsetting or parting the boys. Eventually after thinking about her limited options she decided the only thing she could do was to keep the three of them together and hold each other and keep Bert as comfortable as possible. She got up and walked into the lounge and picked up a selection of cushions and blankets which she arranged on the floor next to Bert. She picked up her phone and called Esme.

"Hi, it's just me," she said to the answer machine. "I'm really sorry but I need to be with Bert today, I think he's in the last few hours. I'll call you to let you know what's happening. Sorry." she sniffed. She placed the mobile phone back on the kitchen table and got down onto the floor next to her boys. They didn't make a sound. She could hear Bert's gentle breathing which seemed to get slower with every breath he took. Max never left his side and kept his snout within centimetres of Bert's snout. He let out a deep occasional sigh which was filled with such a deep pain that it was very tangible to Frances and broke her even more. Tears kept escaping from her eyes as she gently stroked the boys. Bert opened his eyes and looked at her briefly. "I love you Bert and thank you so much for all that you have done for me. I'll look after Max for you so don't worry about that. You need to sleep now, you've looked after me long enough now, its time for you to be with mum and dad." Max crawled closer and the three of them put their heads together needing to be as close as possible to each other.

It was 3.05 when Frances looked at the clock. Bert had passed away in the last ten minutes. She and Max had both just kept still holding Bert not bearing to move or loose that last connection. She was broken again, he had always been there for her, always kept close and loyal. She needed him to help her with the baby. She looked at Max, his eyes so very, very sad. He knew what had happened and she knew he would be heart broken that he had lost his brother, they had never been parted since birth, she gently stroked his head and nuzzled into his neck. "I'm so sorry, I know how much you loved him, I'm so sorry," she cried. "I'll call Uncle Bob and see if he can come down and help me to take Bert to the farm, I think he'd like to be in the woods near your mum and dad don't you Max." He didn't raise his head but just kept still. She stood up and picked up her mobile and looked for her uncle's number.

It rang a few times before Bob picked it up. "Hi Frances, is everything alright, can I help?"

"Hi. Can you help me?" she cried. "Bert has just passed away and wondered if you would help me to pick him up and bury him in the wood with his family."

"I'll be their as quick as I can, about an hour or so, don't worry I'll be there ASAP. I'm so sorry Frances I know how much those dogs mean to you."

"Thank you, uncle Bob, I'll be ready for you."

She gentle wrapped Bert in his blanket that he slept with in his bed. She cut some fur off the back of his neck as a small keepsake and removed his leather collar with his name tag on and placed them on the table. She had taken

Max into the back field to clean himself and picked a bouquet of holly leaves and laurel leaves which she secured together in a red ribbon.

She heard Bob's truck arrive outside her house before she saw him. She went to the front door to let him in. Max didn't follow her to see who it was he kept his silent vigil next to his brother.

"Hi, I'm so sorry love, glad you called me so I could help you. Where is the old chap? I'll take him in my truck, with you and Max and then I'll drop you both off. It will be easier that way and I don't really want you driving. Agreed?"

"Thanks uncle Bob that sounds like a plan. I've wrapped him in his blanket, he's in the kitchen. Thanks for coming and helping me, I just didn't know what to do." Bob gently patted Max on the back and almost telepathically passed on his condolences to him for the loss of his brother. Max managed to wag his tail a little at the recognition of an old friend. Bob slid his hands and arms as gently as possible under Bert and lifted him up and walked out to his truck. Frances held the doors and followed him out with Max. After making sure that Bert was secure and Max was settled on the back seat of the cab Frances picked the bouquet up and locked the house.

It was almost an hour later when they arrived at the small wood. Lights from the farmhouse could be seen in the distance but Frances kept her head down and didn't look. Bob had already dug the whole which was under a Tulip tree.

"I thought this would be perfect here, next to the rest of his family with a view over the farm and valley."

"It's perfect, thank you." She struggled not to cry again. Bob opened the back of the truck up and gently lifted Bert out and carried him over to his final resting place. He lowered his little body into the ground and wrapped the blanket around him. Frances and Max stepped forward and said their silent farewells to Bert, Max peered into the hole and made small whimpering noises whilst Frances said nothing as the tears rolled down her face. Bob started to fill the hole in with his shovel, Max didn't move but watched intently. Soon the job was complete and they all stood looking at the small grave, Frances placed the bouquet of leaves gently on the fresh soil and stepped backwards.

"I'll make him a little wooden headstone tomorrow and we can put it on when your good and ready love. I know you are upset but I would just like to say some words if that's okay?" She nodded in agreement.

"Bert what can I say but thank you." Bob paused. "I remember the day that you and your brothers were born, six of the shiniest black Labradors that I had ever seen in a litter and all boys. Six whirlwinds of trouble we used to say. You, Max and my Jet all stayed on the farm and your brothers all lived a few miles away, and when you met up there was no mistaking that you were brothers." Bob laughed and Frances smiled. Thanks for looking after this girl, you and Max stood up and became all that she needed and all that she wanted. You were more than a dog, you were loyal, a friend and like Max here you were always there. Rest in peace Bert." Bob bowed his head and remained silent for a few moments before he spoke to Frances.

"I'll wait for you in the car lass, no rush, take all the time you need." He turned and walked away. Frances stayed a few more minutes at the grave with Max and whispered to her friend her final goodbyes. Max as always was by her side as she walked back to the truck. She helped him onto the back seat and settled herself in the front.

"Do you want to come back to the farm for a cup of tea, you look perished, I'd love it if you would?"

"Thank you, but I don't think I can today, maybe next time. Thank you for helping me I don't know what I would have done on my own." Bob just smiled at her, started the engine and drove away from the small wood.

Alone in the house with just Max felt very strange. She had put Bert's and Max's beds at the bottom of her own, she didn't think she wanted to be on her own tonight and she wanted Max to be with her. She had sent a quick text message to Esme on the way home explaining what had happened and asked if she could have the day off tomorrow to be with Max. Esme had replied with a kind reply agreeing to the day off and offered to come over which Frances had politely declined. Death she thought, it just keeps happening.

She had managed to eat a little bit of soup and some rich tea biscuits but she wasn't very hungry but she knew baby would need something. By nine 'o' clock she and Max were tucked up on her bed, she had to help him up but he seemed to need her as much as she definitely needed him. She felt exhausted and fell to sleep stroking Max and her little bump, all three of them were still and resting very quickly after such a long and difficult day.

The low winter sun fell into her bedroom just after nine in the morning. She looked at the clock in disbelief, she couldn't remember the last time she had slept so long. She turned over to wake Max with a little snuggle. He was still and cold. With sad realisation, she knew that Max had joined his brother in the middle of the night. She pulled him in her arms and held his little body close to her. She would need to call her uncle Bob again, but for now the tears flowed again and all she could do was hold her friend for the last time.

Chapter 7

The last few weeks had been really hard. She felt sad and lonely, she missed everyone and felt guilty that she felt so sad and worried if her unborn child would be affected by her malaise. Today was Friday 22nd December and she had two whole weeks off work to sort herself out and was due a well, deserved rest. She seemed to have slowed down over the past few weeks, struggled to wake up and struggled to sleep. Her little bump had grown and she could now feel it wriggling inside her. She wished she could tell someone, let someone feel it, it was amazing! She had decided that she would tell Esme today and Bella in a couple of weeks. If Bella knew then everyone would know including Marcus. She felt nervous and anxious but hopeful that they would both be pleased for her, and not sack her on the spot.

"Frances can you get me the stable accounts for daddy and can you get my horse and one of the mares ready for me and a friend at about 2.00, we fancy a last trek before all the festivities start and we are still sober enough to mount." Bella laughed at her own joke and then looked at Frances who had jumped up to act on Bella's commands without remembering to zip up her coat.

"Oh my god Frances!" Bella stared at Frances's stomach. "Are you pregnant, you bitch?" Esme ran into the stable's office from the kitchen with her mouth wide open and the shock obvious on her face. She just stared at Frances's stomach. Frances looked between Bella and Esme. All three women were silenced for a few moments.

"OMG Frances are you pregnant?" Shouted Esme who was still looking at Frances's tummy when she spoke. "Why didn't you tell me, OMG you must be 4 or 5 months, OMG Frances why didn't you tell me?"

Frances placed her hands on her tummy and slowly stroked her baby. "Yes, I'm pregnant, it wasn't planned and I've been trying to come to terms with it for a little while. Now I couldn't be happier or more excited. I was going to tell you today Esme but I thought I would put you in a really difficult position if I had told you earlier but I did want to tell you and I know if I had told you weeks ago you would have had to tell Bella and I would've lost my job. I'm so sorry I didn't mean not to tell you but I didn't want to put you in a difficult position. I was going to tell you tonight before I left."

"Too right you are going to lose your job you bitch, how can you work in my stables and ride horses when you are so very pregnant, I'm sure my insurance doesn't cover being pregnant. Get your stuff and just go, go now and never come back. You betrayed me, after all that I've done for you. I have bent over backwards to be a good employer and given you loads of extras and time off. Just go, get your things and go. Now I have to find a new groom and you did it to me just before Christmas as well, how am I going to manage? Esme give her what she is owed and one month's severance pay." The steam was almost visible out of Bella's ears as she spoke. "I'm going to see my father and tell him what a mess you have left me in, you'll never work in a stables around here again." With that Bella turned her back on the girls and stormed out of the office.

"I'm so sorry Esme, I knew that would happen and at least she now knows that you didn't know so your job is safe. I'm so sorry. I've worked really hard for her all the time I've been here and I have been loyal always, haven't I?"

"I can't believe you are pregnant, I can't believe you didn't tell me! I'm your friend. I'm your only friend I would have been there for you, helped you, supported you, I can't believe you didn't tell me." Esme looked utterly shocked and almost as if she was about to cry. Frances felt guilty and she suddenly felt her misplaced loyalty had somehow affected their friendship for ever.

"You have a family and a mortgage, I felt I couldn't put you in a difficult position. You know I need to work, you know how much I need the money. I was actually going to tell you at lunch, look." Frances fumbled in her coat pockets for a brown envelope which had the single word 'Esme' on the front. She handed the envelope to Esme. "Merry Christmas."

Esme took the envelope from Frances and slowly opened it. On the front of the card was a cute picture of a little girl opening a present under the Christmas tree. Esme looked blankly at Frances and opened the card. Inside was the black and white image of Frances's baby. She read aloud the words in the card. "To Esme, my friend and the best mum I know. This is my little one who is looking forward to meeting you and we would both love it if you would agree to be our Godmother, love Frances and baby."

Esme sat down at the office desk and just looked at the picture and didn't say a word, she just fiddled with the card and looked at the picture.

The silence and the stillness in the room were unbearable for Frances, the moment hadn't gone as she had planned in her head. Finally, Esme spoke.

"Yes, you have put me in a difficult position." She said without taking her eyes off the photo.

"Well I'm going to go and get my stuff together now and I'll be out of your hair in five minutes. All the stables have been cleaned out, all have had breakfast and vitamins. So, all morning jobs are done and new bedding put in all of the stables. Bella wants her horse and one of the mares ready for 2.00pm so she and a friend can go for a ride." Frances almost ran out of the room and went into the kitchen to get her coats, hats and riding equipment, she stuffed her mug in her pocket and grabbed her lunch out of the fridge. She left by the back kitchen door, so that she didn't have to pass Esme again and ran to her car and stuffed everything into the boot as quickly as she could. She had some riding boots in the office which she needed to collect and that was everything removed. She hesitated, she really didn't want to go back inside and have another confrontation with Esme. She gingerly walked back into the office to get her boots and saw that Esme had not moved at all. Esme looked up at her when she walked in but didn't speak.

"Well, okay then, I'll grab my boots and I'll be gone. Can I just say a quick bye to the horses when I leave? " Esme remained silent. "I'm really sorry Esme I didn't mean to upset you. Please say something, we've worked together for nearly two years, we are friends, aren't we? Please Esme!"

"Yes, you can go and see the horses when you leave but not too close. I will sort out your money and send it via BACs to your account later today. If you've got all your belongings then I think its best that you get going now."

Frances left the room as directed and walked to her car. She left moments later without saying good bye to her horses. She was able to get to the end of the estate drive before the tears engulfed her forcing her to stop in a nearby layby to deal with what had just happened.

Frances had been on automatic pilot for the last few hours. She had arrived home, emptied her car, eaten her lunch and had showered and changed out of her work clothes. She hated being in the house all on her own now, it was way too quiet. She had changed into her waitressing clothes ready for a shift at the restaurant tonight. Thank god she still had that job she thought, hopefully she could get a few extra shifts. Her shift started at 6.00pm so she left the empty house and walked down the road to the No 64. The minute she walked into the restaurant she knew something was wrong. Instead of the usual noise and loud greetings she was met with quietness and averted gazes. She instinctively knew not to take her coat off. She hadn't been expecting this at all.

"Err, hi Frances, can I have a quick word with you in the office please?" Gino spoke to her but he didn't look at her. He walked towards the small office at the back of the restaurant and waited for Frances to enter before he closed the door.

"Look Frances, I'm really sorry but I need to let you go, we are now fully staffed with the kids home and I'm sorry but I just need to let you go. I'll pay you for tonight," he handed her a brown envelope that was already lying on the desk.

"I'm happy to give you a reference and if there's anything I can do to help in the future please don't hesitate to let me know." He glanced at her stomach and quickly looked away. Frances had worked for Gino for nearly two years, he was her boss but she had always thought of Gino and his family as friends as well. She knew she was being sacked because she was pregnant. "Who told you I was pregnant Gino?"

"Look Frances, I don't want any trouble, you have worked for us for a long time and we think the world of you and you have always helped us out when we've asked but Bella.........." He pulled his fingers through his thick black Italian hair before he spoke again.

"She called to say that she had sacked you today because you hadn't told her you were pregnant. We didn't know you were! She and her family own this building and they are big clients of ours as are most of their friends. She said that it was 'advisable' to let you go. I'm really sorry Frances but she gave me no choice." Frances dropped onto the chair as if someone had pushed her down. She sat quietly for a few moments. She put the brown envelope back on the desk and forced herself to stand up. She cleared her throat before she spoke and tried to steady her voice "I haven't earned any money tonight Gino. I wouldn't want to put you and your family in a difficult position, and your loyalty is to your family. As we know now, I am not your family or even your friend." She slowly took off the white apron that she had been wearing under her coat and put it down knowing that she had worn it for the last time at No 64. Frances opened the door and walked out of the small office trying to stay standing even though her legs felt like buckling. She walked through the busy kitchen where everyone, people who she thought of as friends, kept their heads down and finally entered the restaurant. She reached the front door and slowly opened the door. No one in the room spoke to her and no one said goodbye. Laila stood quietly with her head bowed not watching the unfolding event in front of her. She knew that Frances was on her own, with no one to look after her and as far as she knew there was no boy on the scene. She wanted to rush after her to hold her, to say sorry but she didn't. She just stood still with her head bowed.

Frances left the restaurant and let the door close behind her. Twice in six hours she had lost her job and people who she thought were her friends had turned their backs on her. She couldn't argue with them, it was what it was. She started the walk up the hill to her house. Every limb in her body ached as she walked. She felt exhausted as if she couldn't take another step. But she had to, there was no one to help her. She opened the front door and closed it behind her leaving the rest of the world outside.

It had been a long, cold night. She had struggled to sleep and when she had finally fallen asleep in the early hours of the morning, she had woken up to nip to the toilet when Splodge had laid on her bladder. Finally, morning arrived much to her relief. She didn't need to get up as she had nowhere to go and nothing really to do. How she missed Bert and Max, they always gave her a reason to get up and start the day with a walk. Now she could just stay in bed and do nothing all day. The mantra running around in her head had been pretty constant for the last twelve hours, "two jobs in one day!" How was she going to cope with no money coming in and absolutely no one to help? She felt overwhelmed and let the tears start again.

"I'm so sorry my little one, life's a bit of a mess at the moment. But it will be better and I promise to be the best mummy in the world. You will want for nothing, I'll always be here for you and you are absolutely my first and only priority. If I'm careful and I can sell the Defender in the New Year we will be okay for money. I then need to find a little job where I can take you with me, I won't leave you with anyone, your mine and all mine. I love you so much and I can't wait to meet you." Frances felt calmed and better, it was amazing how just talking to her baby made her feel better and stronger. She lay back in the bed in the new silence which was now her new normal. She pulled the covers up around herself and let herself drift off into a world that wasn't real.

When she woke again it was 1.00pm. and she was feeling hungry. After a quick nip to the toilet and a shower to refresh herself she got ready and went down into the cold and quiet kitchen. She opened the fridge which had more than normal in it as she had just been shopping. It had extra christmas treats in it. She decided that it was going to be bacon sandwiches and brown sauce for lunch followed by a slab of homemade fruitcake. The smell of the bacon frying made her even more hungry, she decided that bacon cooking was one of her most favourite smells. She settled herself down on the sofa snuggling into the quilt to try and keep warm. Bacon sandwiches! Her absolute favourite thing in the world to eat, crispy bacon, brown sauce and thick bread. She smiled, was this her strange pregnancy craving? After lunch she decided to tidy her Defender up and removed all her personal belongings. She vacuumed the seats and the carpets and gave it a quick wash as Paul had said he would give her a lift home tonight as it was due to be icy. The wash wasn't the best she had ever done but it would have to do as it was too cold to do much more. She decided to brave the cold bedroom again and sort through which clothes still fitted her. The bedroom was always so cold now, the heating bills were a constant worry for her. She often slept downstairs on the sofa when she had had the wood burner on as it seemed silly to leave the warm room.

She made the decision there and then to move downstairs and sleep on the sofa until it was warmer again. She didn't need to heat the whole house just for her. She needed more wood as she only had enough for one more fire, she made a mental note to herself that she would do that tomorrow. She was due in tonight at 6.00pm and the ball started at 7.00. She had a nervous feeling in her stomach. Paul had asked her to work tonight and then the New Year's Eve Ball. Bella might have already told Paul that she was pregnant, would she keep her job, she so needed the £200.00 that she would earn over the two nights. Surely, she couldn't be sacked again, could she?

Winter had arrived and it was freezing outside, it was freezing inside. Frances had decided to only put the heating on once a day to try and keep control of the gas bill. She spent the rest of the afternoon cocooned in her quilt with a blanket around her head watching some DVDs that she had picked up at the charity shop in the summer. She had watched them so many times she knew the scripts off by heart. At 5.00 she got up and got ready to go to work, she pulled on her black work trousers which she had got from her favourite charity shop and secured the zip with a safety pin. The white shirt had been her grandads but it fitted perfectly and hid her expanding waistline. A black pinny and black trainers finished the look. She brushed her hair back into a ponytail and put on the smallest amount of lip gloss.

Five minutes later she was walking into the town to get the bus up to Scarr Point and then it would only be a five minute walk to the farm. She had put on a large felt coat which had been her grandpa's which she had found in one of the wardrobes and had exchanged the trainers for wellies. Paul had offered her a lift home after the ball so she didn't have to drive home on her own. She was grateful as she still didn't feel really confident driving in icy conditions. Just before the bus arrived she nipped into the newsagents to pick up some mints, she always seemed to be craving bacon and onions both of which left a taste in her mouth. As Frances waited in the queue to be served she noticed a job advert poster for a paper Boy/girl/person. She laughed.

'Wanted paper person, six early mornings a week and six afternoons a week. 45 minutes per session. £45 a week. Please apply inside.' It was her time to be served.

"Hi just these mints please and I wondered if I could apply for the position of paper person?" The man behind the counter stopped what he was doing and just stared at her for a moment. "It's for a child, it's a pocket money job for a child. It's not for an adult, I'm really sorry. That's 70p for the mints." Frances handed over the money and left without saying anything else to the shop keeper and hurried past the other people in the line. What was she thinking! She had just been turned down to be a paper person, she who had once had dreams of being a doctor. She felt crushed again. On leaving the shop she saw that the bus had just arrived so she jogged over and quickly paid for her fare to Scarr Point and tried to hide herself away from everyone and everything around her on the short journey. She weaved one of her hands through the layers of clothes and patted her tummy and instantly felt reassured by her little bump wriggling around inside her tummy. "It's okay, I'm okay, there's nothing I wouldn't do for you. I'll get another job soon and it will all be okay I promise." Suddenly she longed for her cold bed.

Ten minutes later Frances was walking up Barden Hall Farm drive towards the large marquee that had been put up for the Christmas Eve Ball and the New Year's Eve Ball. It looked amazing, glowing a pale orange in the darkness. Fairy lights lit the way from the temporary car park to the entrance of the marquee and also to the onsite toilets! It looked very Christmassy, lights had been put on all the trees in the garden and a Christmas themed photo booth had been placed at the entrance with a professional photographer getting ready to take photos of all the guests as they arrived. She walked past a small group of people and made her way to the kitchen so she could catch up with Paul.

"Hi Frances, I'm so glad you are here, two have called in sick so it's all hands to the decks, you don't mind taking on an extra table for me, thanks." Before she had chance to reply he had changed the subject and was addressing the whole group.

"Right, two tables each, twelve on a table. Starter, bread, red and white wine, water, mains, dessert and coffee are all your responsibilities. When they are all served and all cleared then you are free to go. Jo, Sarah, Pip and Frances will stay on and will clear all the tables and remove everything apart from the table cloth. There is no supper tonight and it finishes at 1.00am so an early finish for a change. All tables are numbered, so check the table plan, memorise which tables are yours. Go and check them, make sure they are properly set and check the wine and water glasses are sparkling. Now off with you all my darling Cinderellas."

Everyone left and either checked the table plans or made their way to the tables. Frances quickly took off her coat and wellies, tied on her pinny and left her belongings on an unoccupied chair at the back of the kitchen. Tables 1,2 and 3 had been allocated to her. She quickly went into the main room and found them. The theme was red and gold and copious amounts of christmas lights had been hung everywhere. The room looked amazing, very Christmassy, Paul had done a great job this year she thought . She started to check all the cutlery was set correctly before she started on polishing up all the glasses. It was nearly 7.00pm when the first guests started to arrive. The noise levels went up in the large marquee as people started to arrive and chat, the DJ started his music at the front of the room.

The men as usual all looked smart in their dinner jackets and some, as usual, arrived in their tweeds. The photographer was soon working hard taking photos of everyone as they arrived, single, couples, families and groups all happy to wait for their free photograph. By 7.15 the room was already full and thankfully it was also getting warmer. Her tables checked she had retreated back to the area outside of the kitchen and waited in line with the others to be called in.

She smiled at some of the regular girls and said hello but most were just watching the room and all the beautiful people who were arriving. A girl ran past her with a young man in tow, both laughing, both beautiful and she noticed how much the girl's dress resembled her dress. In an instant she felt sad, she wanted to be that happy carefree girl, pulling a laughing boyfriend behind her without a care in the world. She was only twenty but she felt much older. She'd never really had any days where she had felt like that girl, maybe her 16th birthday party and possibly the one night, at Marcus's Ball when she had worn that dress and had danced the night away but now that was all just a sad memory. She quickly cleared her mind and stared at Paul waiting for the cue to go in and get the trays of food.

At 7.30 the large crowd of people were asked to find their table and to check on the table plans if they didn't know where they were sitting. Gradually the crowd started to meander their way to their seats. Frances watched her tables to see who she was going to serve. She hoped and hoped she didn't know any of them. Paul eventually called the servers forward, Frances was first to go and get her tray. Bread basket and twelve plates of either melon or goat's cheese. Each plate had a number on which needed to be removed before serving but it was a much better system than usual ensuring everyone got the meal which they had ordered.

She took her tray to her first table, table one which was located on the front row to the left of the dance floor. Her heart sank, it was the Bucannons, Felicity and her family, Bella, Bill and her mum and dad. Everyone she had hoped not to see or speak to was on her table, her first table. Suddenly she felt sick and panicky. "Good evening," she said as she approached her table "I'm Frances and I will be your server for the night. If the new system works you will all get your correct orders straight away." Frances started to serve the now quiet table who all looked as if they had seen a ghost apart from Robert who was smirking and Marcus who was busily buttering a slice of bread. One by one she handed out the plates and no one spoke to her apart from number ten, Marcus who said a quiet thank you. Marcus's mum called her over. "Excuse me, can you fetch me a new water glass and a new red wine glass, they are both dirty."

"Mine too." Said Bella. Frances took the glasses and placed them on the empty tray knowing them all to be clean as she had checked them, she would be behind straight away now.

"Sorry, I'll bring clean ones back straight away." She rushed off to the kitchen and gave each glass a quick polish before returning to table one and replaced the missing glasses. No one spoke to her so she quickly left to pick up the tray for table 2 and then table 3. Some people said a small thank you or a small acknowledgment that she had actually served them but most said nothing. As soon as she had finished table 3 it was time to go and clear table 1, then 2 and then 3 again. Luckily no one had spoken to her on table 1 when she had gone to clear the table of plates. She retreated to the sanctuary of the kitchen and waited in line to be called to collect the mains for each table. The trays were much heavier this time and she struggled to lift it and walk. Roast beef, salmon or vegetarian nut roast were the three options on the tray. As a server they were always offered a meal around 9.00 when the dinners had all been served and she definitely would be having the beef. She hadn't eaten last night as she normally ate at No 64 on her break and hadn't felt much like eating when she had arrived home. Even though she had eaten today she was ravenous again and smiled to herself when she thought if it was actually possible that she could eat everything on the tray. She arrived at table 1 and everyone stopped talking and starred at her. Frances instantly felt very uncomfortable. Marcus played with his glass of wine, swirling it around and around. Robert just smirked at her, again.

"Okay here we go, beef, salmon and nut roast. The vegetables, Yorkshire puddings and chips will arrive in a few minutes." She quickly removed the numbers on the plates and served the meals as quickly as she could. Marcus said thank you. She quickly went back to the kitchen and picked up two bowls of chips, Yorkshire puddings, vegetables and two jugs of gravy. She walked quickly back to the table and placed the sides in the middle of the table.

"My dinner is cold," barked Mrs Bucannon. "You were too slow getting the rest of the meal, take everything back and bring out fresh again. Everyone, stop eating! Actually, bring Paul back with you and he can sort this out. The colour drained from Frances's face and she quickly ran back to the kitchen and found Paul and told him what had happened.

"That's so typical of her, she's a nasty one she is. Don't worry Frances I'll go and sort it out, I know it's not you. You keep doing your other tables and I'll do *that* table for the rest of the night, don't worry it's sorted, I dare her to say anything to me." With that, Frances got on with her job, delivering meals to the other tables, clearing the tables, ensuring the wine and the water flowed. Some people spoke to her but most didn't. Teas and coffees were eventually served and she had a chance for a quick glass of water. Paul walked over to her.

"Hi," he looked awkward. "Can I have a quick word with you in private Fran." Her heart sank as she followed him out of the marquee. She noticed that Marcus was watching her. He knows.

"Look I'm really sorry, I don't really know what to say to you but you do know that Mrs Bucannon is affectively my boss as she's the chairperson of the Hunt and this is their Ball." Paul looked very uncomfortable when he was speaking to her, not the usual Paul, happy, jolly and smiley Paul. He couldn't even look at her when he spoke.

"It's okay Paul, am I sacked again?"

"I'm sorry she said her meal was cold and that you were too slow because... because your pregnant and she doesn't want you working at the Hunt Ball again, not now, not on

New Year's Eve or ever again. I'm so sorry. I said you were my best worker and the person I trusted most, but it was very much a one sided conversation. I'm so sorry but I've got to let you go. He reached into his jacket pocket and took out a white envelope and tried to hand it to her. "It's tonight's salary, plus a tip and the money you would've got next week as well. I know monies tight for you and you work for food and stuff and not to buy silly stiletto's or make up. I'm really sorry." Paul still couldn't look at her as he spoke.

"Did everyone on the table hear that I'm pregnant?" Paul nodded. "Mmmm, so my secret is out." Frances felt totally numb and didn't really know what to say back to him, she decided in that brief moment she was finished here, it wasn't Paul's fault so it was best to make it easy on him.

"It's okay Paul, Bella sacked me yesterday morning, Gino at No 64 sacked me last night and I was even turned down for a paper boy's job this evening on the way to the bus stop." She sighed. "I'm getting really good at being sacked. I'll go and get my things and I'll be off. Thank you for always giving me the chance to work for you in the past and good luck Paul." She said with real sincerity. Paul said nothing in reply and continued to stare at the floor as she walked away. He felt angry and weak and powerless. He felt pathetic.

Frances walked back into the marquee and back to the kitchen to get her coat and wellies. She quickly changed and popped her trainers into her rucksack and was just walking out of the kitchen when Esme walked past her.

"Hi you okay? I'm sorry but I do think we need to talk, oh you've got your coat on, are you leaving early I thought you were working all of tonight?"

"Hi, how are you? Wow, you look beautiful, that dress is amazing you look stunning Esme." She hesitated not really wanting to have this conversation now. "Don't worry about me, I'm absolutely fine thanks. We've finished serving the meals and Paul had too many waitresses so I opted for the go home early, put my feet up option," she lied. "It will be gone ten 'o' clock by the time I get home and that's way past my bedtime as you know." She feigned a yawn. "We can catch up in the New Year but I hope you and your *lovely* family have a lovely christmas and don't worry about the godmother bit, it was only a stupid thought, could you imagine the christening, just you and me which would have been a bit sad really, it's alright honestly, I totally understand. So, I'll say my goodbyes and hopefully see you again, in the New Year or sometime. Okay bye." Before Esme had a chance to say anything Frances was gone. She tried not to look back or look into the room, she did not want to see anyone and there was no one that she needed to say goodbye too.

Outside the marquee the wind was cold and it was still snowing. She was glad that she had decided to wear wellies tonight, the snow was settling quite quickly on the ground now but regretted not coming in her car. She had cleaned it and it was now officially up for sale with a cardboard notice placed on the dashboard. She didn't want to get it dirty so had taken Paul up on his offer to drop her off. But now that plan had changed. She pulled her rucksack closer to her back, rolled down her hat down further and tightened the coat collar around her neck. Paul who had obviously been looking for her walked over to her. "Hi, I thought I'd missed you, I said I would give you a lift home tonight, come on I've got my keys. Who could have predicted how much snow has come down tonight, they'll be some cars stuck here tonight! I'm in my truck so we'll be okay, follow me I'm just over here."

"Paul, stop, it's fine. I can get myself home, I don't need a lift, your still in the middle of the Ball and the last thing you need to do is run me home. I'm absolutely fine just walking home and it is downhill all the way. Also, I think this belongs to you," she said handing him back the envelope which he took back without realising what it was. "I can only take what I earned tonight so the rest is in here." She smiled and walked away not allowing Paul time to reply, down the drive into the darkness.

Marcus was still in shock. She was pregnant and it was his. Bella had said that she was about four months pregnant but he had done the sums and he knew that she was at least six months. Why hadn't she told him? Why had she kept it a secret, maybe it wasn't his, maybe the father already knew. His poker face was still holding firm, it had to, he had to remain emotionless but inside he was shocked, crying, fuming and confused, all in one body all at the same time.

It had been nice to see her again, he hadn't seen her since the Hospital Ball. Even in just a white shirt, black trousers, her hair scrapped back, she was the most beautiful woman in the room. He couldn't believe his luck when he realised that she was the waitress at their table. But he knew something was wrong the minute they had all sat down. Bella and her bloody big mouth, the gossip, she was merciless and never ending. He had to listen to every little detail, just like everyone else had done. But he needed to hear everything and yet at the same time he didn't want to hear it. He felt ashamed that he was listening to Bella and all her nasty gossip and not actually sticking up for Franny.

"Well, I went down to the stables about 11.00 to ask her if I could have the accounts for daddy to look at and also to ask if she would get some horses saddled for Melissa and I to go for a final ride before christmas. Well, all of you who know her know that she always moans about being asked to do anything, she's always been difficult to manage at work, she never seems to want to work. You know about that Mrs B don't you, didn't she leave you once during your party and left you to do all the catering by yourself?" Mrs Bucannon nodded. "Yes, she did Bella, she left me in an awful mess and I paid her too, thankfully I was able to manage and my Robert helped me too, didn't you Robert." Robert smiled in agreement. Marcus just fumed at Bella and his mother who were both obviously just lying. He clenched his fists into white knuckled balls. Bella continued enjoying being the centre of attention.

"So, when she eventually did get up she had left her coat unzipped and I could see straight away that she was pregnant. OMG, I was so shocked. She tried to deny it initially but it was plain to see. Esme ran into the office and she couldn't believe it either, she obviously didn't know and I think Esme is not talking to Frances now for not telling her. Well, you can't be a groom and work with horses when you are pregnant so I sacked her on the spot, made it clear to her to get her stuff out and never ever set foot in the stables again. She did ask for money and to say goodbye to the horses but I told her to pack her things and just go. Eventually she just left. How rude is she, no thank you or goodbye. Good riddance I say. So, I called Gino at No 64 just to let him know what had happened and to warn him that she was quite pregnant and I thought he should know. No one wants to be served by a heavily pregnant woman and we go in there three or four times a month and well I didn't want to be served by her and mummy and daddy agreed didn't you." Both nodded in agreement. "So, Gino felt that it was best for him and his business that he let her go so Gino sacked her last night when she turned up for work. What a bitch she really is. Everyone thinks she's a quiet little thing who wouldn't hurt a fly but let me tell you all, I know the real Frances Tulip."

The table erupted into conversation, mostly disbelieve and disapproval of Frances. Name calling and nasty comments flew around with abundance. His own mother called her a slut, Felicity called her bitch, his own father called a whore, but said he wouldn't have said no to quick ride on her when he was younger which led to the table erupting into laughter. Marcus could stand it no longer, he excused himself to the table and said he needed to deal with a text from work. No one seemed to notice him when he walked away, they were all enjoying the gossip too much. On his way out, he was met by an unhappy looking Paul who was walking towards his table with a tray of coffees and teas.

"I'm just off to check dinner was hot enough and if there is any more arse licking I can do for your mum. Shitty thing your mum made me do, sacking that young girl you know, a real nasty thing I've done. I feel like shit."

"As far as I'm concerned you can shove those cups and saucers down their throats for all I care. Please tell me I'm adopted Paul." The two friends passed by each other with neither stopping. Paul noticed his friend was very angry and distressed. "You okay mate?" Marcus didn't answer him and continued to march out of the marquee and headed out into the blizzard to sit in his car. He clicked it open and just sat in the driver's seat watching the snow fall. Then he smashed his hands onto the steering wheel with such anger and force that he broke the BMW badge in the middle. And then he just started to cry.

He had just sat and listened to everything that those people had said, he had watched when they had all ignored and made fun of her and he did nothing. She was the mother of his child and he had just sat there, how pathetic was he. As soon as Bella had said she was pregnant his eyes had frantically searched for her in the crowd. He couldn't keep his eyes off her, he could see the bump when she leant forward to serve the other tables and he could see that she had lost weight in her face. She was having his baby, he was certain of it.

When he had found the condom in the bin six months ago, he thought it might have split but wasn't sure and when he hadn't heard from her he had assumed that everything was okay. The way she had left afterwards and the way he had treated her had affected him deeply. He felt he had bullied and abused her into something that he didn't think she was ready for. He hadn't called her to check that she was okay because he felt so ashamed of himself, how he had treated her, and how he had treated Felicity as well. He had received some texts from her in the summer but that was about eight weeks later when he was on holiday in the Med with Felicity and her family on the yacht. But she hadn't said anything, didn't say that she was expecting, only asked him to call her back. He suddenly felt really sick and had to jump out of the car quickly. When he had finished he got back into the driver's seat and wiped his mouth on his hankie. She had tried to talk to him. She had tried to tell him she was pregnant. OMG. She was twenty, six months pregnant, had no family or friends to support her. Everyone had turned on her on the day she had actually told them she was expecting and now she had been sacked from three jobs in one day! God no wonder she hadn't told anyone. OMG how was she feeling now, how was she going to manage with no job, no support? He needed to be there for her and he was going to help her and his baby as much as he could.

Marcus needed to find her and to find her quickly. He didn't want to go back into the marquee at all, he didn't want to see Felicity or his family or any of the others who he had sat down with earlier in the evening. He just wanted to talk to Frances. He figured that his mum had forced Paul to sack her on the spot, and she would threaten him appropriately to do so. Bitch. He really didn't like his mother sometimes. Suddenly the passenger door opened and Paul slipped into the leather seat.

"For god's sake it's freezing out there, turn my electric seat on." Marcus turned the engine on and the electric seats. Paul sat back in the seat removing snow from his face and hair with his hand.

"Well," he said eventually. "I thought you might need someone to talk to daddy." Marcus just looked ahead into the snow storm and told his friend what had happened and grateful to be able to confide in someone. He couldn't look at his childhood friend as he felt too ashamed of what he had done.

"What should I do? I must make it better for her. She's so nice, she is such a nice person, she doesn't deserve any of this. I've ruined her life, she was saving to be a doctor you know, she's got a place at University but couldn't afford to take it up. My mother is such a bitch and my father's just about unbearable. OMG Paul what should I do?"

"Marcus, you and I have been friends for a very long time and I think it's about time I was honest with you. I don't think you are going to like what I have to say but I am going to say it anyway. Your mother and father have always dictated to you your path in life even down to the job you do and the woman you are to marry. Don't get me wrong they have tried to do their best for you but it is always on their terms. 'Marcus, you will study medicine, Marcus you will be a Consultant, Marcus you will run the estate and farm when we tell you too, you will marry Felicity as it protects two old Northumberland estates and family names. You must drive a BMW because we do, you must go skiing every January to the same resort, to the same lodge because we do'. Do you get my point! And Frances? Well, she's nice, she works hard, keeps to herself, has a lovely little giggle which she always covers up with her hand. No make-up and no expensive dress and she was still the most beautiful, serene woman in that room tonight. I can see why you fell for her, she's such a nice girl and she has absolutely no expectation of you. She doesn't do what she doesn't need to do either my friend. If she slept with you, gave up her virginity to you and she wasn't off her head drunk then I would suspect that she cared about you, she let that constant guard down that she has around her for just a few moments, for you and you fucked it up big time. Now, my next suggestion is that you drive back down to her house and see if you can find her walking home, alone in the dark. She wouldn't take a lift off me even though I had offered one home after work. I really feel shitty that I let her walk home alone on such an awful night and in her condition as well. She's on her own walking home in a snow storm so I'll be on the end of my phone waiting to hear how it goes and that she's safe in your car. She left about 15 minutes ago." Paul patted his friend's arm and then was gone leaving floating snow to settle inside the car.

Marcus pushed the gear stick into first and drove off like a man possessed to find her. Visibility wasn't great but it didn't slow him down, after half a mile or so he slowed down and started to look on the pavements on the side of the lane to see if he could see her. The snow was falling faster now and the temperature had fallen to minus 1. Where the hell was she? He pulled up her number on the car phone and dialled it. No answer so he tried it again. Straight to answer phone. Suddenly he saw a lone figure about ten foot ahead of him walking slowly, bracing against the snow. Thank god, it was her.

Frances saw the car lights next to her before she heard the car pull up. Her first thought was complete panic and fear but then when she saw the BMW drive slowly past her and stop she quickly realised who it was. Marcus. In the whole of Northumberland, in the middle of a blizzard only one car had gone past her and the person driving it was the last person that she wanted to see. Slowly she approached the car and tried to decide what to do. The decision was actually really quick and easy to make. The snow storm had quickly developed into a blizzard and she was already exhausted and cold and she had only managed to get about a quarter of the way home! She stopped by the door and attempted to shake off some of the snow that had landed on her. Quickly she opened the door and slipped into the front seat of the BMW, and made sure before settling that it was actually Marcus who was driving. Once she was buckled in he started to drive down the road again. Marcus gave her a few minutes before he spoke to her.

"Are you Okay, I've put the heating on fully so you should start to feel the benefit soon and I've put your heated seat on too?"

"I'm fine thank you, I do appreciate you stopping to pick me up, it was only the odd flake of snow when I set off but this is awful now, so, thank you."

"You are very welcome. It's the absolute least I can do after my mother got you the sack and you had no lift home. My mother honestly, I just keep wishing I was adopted especially when I'm around you. She really does seem to have it in for you. I actually think she blames you for Robert being a homosexual and you failed in 'converting' him." They both smiled at each other.

"Will you be able to get back? The road will be very slippery and I presume that you are the designated driver since this is your car."

Marcus paused before he spoke. "I'm not sure that I actually want to go back to that stupid Ball, full of stupid, malicious peacocks with more money then sense. Every time I see you all I seem to do is apologise for the behaviour of my stupid family and friends and now I find that I have to apologise for the behaviour of a whole table including myself. I didn't say very much before Franny, at the ball, I was just taken by surprise. I only found out tonight when Bella told the whole table. I think we need to have a talk, don't you? A talk about our baby."

Frances bit her bottom lip, the conversation that she had been dreading for months was now about to happen, the father of her baby needed answers to questions. But she didn't really feel that she was in a position to chat about everything tonight. She was tired, exhausted and so cold and hungry. "I know that we need to talk but not tonight please, I'm cold and hungry and I just want to go to bed. I've had a really bad few days."

"I know." He hesitated before he spoke again. "I know that Bella sacked you, that Esme isn't talking to you, Bella persuaded Gino at No 64 to sack you, I know that my mother got you the sack again, tonight *and* forever and I know you didn't get the job as a paper girl. I think that covers your last 24 hours or so, you must be exhausted and in a state of shock to lose all your jobs just because you are pregnant. It is bonkers, disgusting and probably illegal. So, I know you have had a terrible few days, all just before christmas too. And I also realise that I must be the dad. I now know that you did phone me and tried to tell me. I'm sorry I just ignored your texts, I'm so sorry, I'm a complete shit, a typical Bucannon by all accounts." He stopped talking and waited for her reply.

Frances continued to look out of the window at the snow as it raced past. She loved snow normally, Bert and Max loved to play in the snow, playing with snow balls, trying to catch and eat them. Tonight, she didn't like the snow very much and she didn't have Max or Bert to play with anymore which broke her heart every day.

"It's sorted Marcus, everything is Okay, I'm feeling fine and my baby is doing really well." She gently stroked her bump and felt strangely very calm and serene. "Congratulations on your engagement, christmas day isn't it? You and Felicity will be busy planning your wedding, honeymoon and before you know it you will be having a family of your own. They arrived outside of her home. Well I am extremely grateful for the lift my feet are like two ice buckets."

She hesitated before she reached for the handle. " I'm fine honestly, I'm stronger than I look and I'm having a baby not you, just me. I won't be putting your name down on the register and I won't be telling anyone who the real father is. I promise you that I will be totally discreet always but.........thanks for the lift and drive carefully, the snow is settling fast now so you need to be off, bye." And with that she was gone from his car, running around the front and up the steps to her front door. She ran away from him quickly, not allowing him to answer or talk to her.

Marcus sat back in the seat and for once in his life he didn't know what to say or what to do but he did know that he didn't want to drive away and he still needed to talk to her. He knew that she was exhausted, cold, tired and upset but he needed to make things better for her as quick as possible. He turned the engine off and got out of the car and ran up the steps to the front door and knocked hard a few times. Within a few moments the door opened and Frances stood aside to let him in.

"I knew that you just wouldn't let things go Marcus, but honestly I'm okay and I don't expect anything from you at all." She closed the door and walked through to the kitchen knowing that Marcus would follow her. He quickly took off his shoes and jacket and as predicted followed her into the kitchen.

"Coffee or tea, I'm having a slice of toast too as I didn't get my supper after the ball tonight so I'm starving, again! He looked at the almost empty bag of bread and declined her offer with a shake of his head.

"No just a tea please. Look, I know you said that you are tired but I just want a quick chat to sort some things out. I'm really, really sorry that I got you pregnant, I thought we were good as we used a condom, and I'm really sorry when I freaked out when I realised it was your first time. Your first time should have been with someone much nicer, better, kinder and much less of a shit than me. It was all my fault and I take full responsibility for it, you are twenty with your whole life ahead of you and I'm just a fucked up mummies boy who apparently according to my best friend Paul, can't seem to make any decisions on my own." He pulled his hand through his hair and wiped the moisture off his face.

"I never meant for this to happen, the truth is that you are the nicest and most genuine person that I have met in a very long time. I like being with you, you made me feel like a better person, I felt that being close to you, some of 'you' may rub off on me, absurd I know. That night, the night we, you know...it just happened for me, I had no plan at all, honest. I just had this overwhelming need to be close to you, to hold you, care for you and in a way, I suppose...love you. I'm so sorry. I acted like a real shit. I'm due to get engaged in two days to Felicity which apparently is the right thing for me to do but I have let her down as well but mostly you. Honestly Franny, none of it was planned and I will make it better. I will take responsibility for my baby and I will arrange to transfer £1,500 a month into your account to look after you both and that means you won't have to find a job and hopefully at some point you will be able to study to be a doctor at Newcastle , before I messed it all up for you." Finally, he dropped down into one of the lounge chairs. He looked around the room which was empty of christmas decorations but he didn't say anything, he now knew better to comment on anything. The exhaustion and emotion now easily visible on his face. Frances watched him whilst she waited for her toast, he looked broken and felt so sorry and sad for him which was a feeling that she hadn't expected to feel tonight.

Frances picked up her tea and slice of toast she had prepared whilst he had talked to her. She followed him into the lounge and sat down on the sofa munching away at the slice of toast. When she had finished the toast, she took a few tentative sips of the hot tea.

"Your tea is on the counter, I couldn't remember if you wanted milk or not. I'm not sorry that I'm pregnant. It was a bit of a mess to begin with and I must confess that I was really scared and I felt really lost and alone when you didn't return my texts. It's funny but no one apart from my doctor and midwives knew that I was pregnant till yesterday and since then all I've had is trouble, name calling, sacked three times and my one and only......friend in the world didn't support me or even congratulate me. I asked her to be Godmother but I don't think she wants to be. Everyone has turned against me and so far only the doctor has congratulated me , which is really rather sad. Not bad going for 36 hours!" Marcus noticed that her eyes were brimming with tears, as he turned in the chair to face her fully.

"I didn't tell anyone that I was expecting as I actually had no one to tell but you. I didn't tell Esme because I knew that Bella would sack me straight away and as you know I need all of my jobs to survive. Esme thinks I betrayed her when actually all I thought I was doing was protecting her and not putting her in an awkward position. I feel sad about that but....." Frances was quickly lost in thought sipping her tea.

Marcus stood up and went into the kitchen to get his tea and put some milk in. It was Saturday the 23rd December and the only things in the fridge was milk, butter, bacon, some carrots, some potatoes, a very small chicken, some slices of ham and some eggs. Most people's fridges and freezers were rammed at this time of the year he thought to himself. There were no cheeses, cakes, sausage rolls, pork pies, jams or even tomato ketchup in the door. It didn't look like a festive fridge at all. He returned to the lounge and sat down.

"May I just say that you have the tidiest fridge in the world. Mum's fridge is full to the gunnels and getting anything else in it is an extreme art form and the utility fridge is full too, mainly with booze I'm afraid. Are you going food shopping for christmas or are you going out for christmas dinner?" He took a drink from the hot milky tea and noticed the fire wasn't on. Placed in front of it on the hearth were four holly wreaths stood up blocking the wood burner. "Still got the old TV I see, a sucker for antiques."

"I just need to nip to the loo again, sorry." Frances almost ran out of the room and upstairs to the toilet. She knew her cupboards were a little bit empty but she thought her fridge looked quite full for a change and suddenly felt really awkward and didn't really know what to say to him. He always seemed to have a comment about the contents of her fridge which she found annoying. She thought about saying she was going out for christmas dinner but he knew that she had nowhere to go. She did as she always did when she felt like this, placed her hands on her baby and just stroked her tummy. Presently she began to feel the calm that always seemed to come to her when she thought about her little baby. She sorted herself out and went back downstairs into the lounge only to find Marcus kneeling in front of the fire and the start of a little fire burning in the wood burner.

"Hi, it's so cold in here I thought I'd save you getting down and start the fire for you. A real fire is always so much cosier than a radiator, don't you think?"

Frances looked at the small fire just beginning to take hold and saw the last pieces of wood that she had saved for christmas day, go up in smoke. "Marcus, I've been saving that wood for weeks for christmas day, I'm going to bed now, I don't need a fire I need to sleep!"

He looked at the sofa and the pillow and quilt that were already laid out. "I figured that as the house is so cold you hadn't put the heating on to save money and you are obviously sleeping on the sofa so I just thought you were keeping one room warm for you and the boys. Hey, where are Bert and Max, are they asleep upstairs?"

She looked at the holly wreaths that she had made which he had tossed to the side and braced herself before she spoke. "Thank you for the lift tonight, it was much appreciated but I think it's time you got back to your family. I have everything I need and I am totally independent and I don't need any money from you which could actually be traceable and run the risk of Felicity or your family finding out about my baby. I'm sorry that I don't have much wood in for the fire or that my fridge and cupboards are not bulging with festive food, or that I don't have a massive christmas tree full of baubles and lights but it is what it is and I can't keep apologising to you for my circumstances. My nursery is nearly ready and I've started to get everything that my baby will need and I'm going to the sales in Newcastle to get the rest of the stuff I need next week. My Defender is going up for sale and that will give me enough money to live on for a while and to buy a cot and a pram. I don't really do christmas but I will next year and my baby will not want for anything. I don't have much wood in at the moment because I can't really bend down at the moment to pick up wood but I do have gas central heating which I can switch on at the push of a button. So, in short Marcus, you go back to your family, your fiancée and your life and let me carry on with my life and don't touch my wreaths again."

Frances stood back as he got up and allowed him to walk past her into the hall way but instead of leaving he turned and ran up the stairs. Frances shouted after him but soon he was standing at the door of the small bedroom with the light on looking at his child's nursery. Frances eventually made it to the top of the stairs and tried to switch the light off.

"This is private Marcus."

"This is our baby's room? You are due soon and so far, all that you have is a wardrobe and an old chair!" He walked over to the old mahogany wardrobe and opened the double doors. Hanging rail on one side and six shelves on the other side. Nothing was hanging but on the shelf side he could see packets of white baby vests, baby grows which still had their labels on and hand knitted tiny cardigans, booties, hats and mitts. Rolled on another shelf were a selection of knitted blankets and cot sheets. "Are you planning on having a carpet or are you leaving it as floorboards," he spoke with a hint of sarcasm creeping into his voice. "You are having a baby soon and you are not ready at all Frances."

"I am, the carpet is being laid on Wednesday and I have only just finished painting the walls and I wanted the paint to dry totally before the carpet was laid." Marcus looked at the walls, there she had done a great job. The walls were pale blue with a hand painted sea side mural, with a sea full of fish and smiling sharks, the beach filled with children playing in the sand with balls, buckets and kites. Dogs digging holes. This he had to admit was amazing. "You are really talented Franny but this doesn't make up for the fact that you are not ready for the baby at all, the house is cold, your food cupboards are empty and...... Where's the dogs?"

She leant back on the wall, sighed and cleared her throat before she spoke. "I lost Bert two weeks ago and then the next night Max died in his sleep, of a broken heart I think. So, it's just me now."

"Oh god Franny, I'm so sorry I didn't know. I know how much you loved those dogs. God you have had the worst few weeks ever. Please let me help you. I could help with our baby, be a part of its life and you could go to Medical School and I could help pay for it."

"Thank you but no I can manage. This was a shock initially but now I will have my own little family and I can bring my baby up on my own. Your fiancée, mum and dad would never forgive you or accept us or my baby and that would just be unbearable for everyone. Please just go and leave me alone from now on, please," she begged. She turned and as quickly as she could, went downstairs and waited for him at the front door with her hand placed on the door knob.

"I'm sorry but you can clearly see you are struggling here, I can help, please let me help." He put his shoes and jacket on and slowly left the house. He heard the door shut behind him. "Well that didn't go well at all." He got in the car and turned the engine on and the heaters waiting for the windows to clear. He had the overwhelming feeling that he had just made everything even worse for her now.

Chapter 8

The snow had settled on the ground but the blizzard had past thankfully. As he drove back to the Ball his mind was whirling with the events of the last few hours. He wasn't sure how he was feeling, he couldn't decide if he was sad, angry, frustrated or scared. The conversation with Paul was also reverberating around in his head. Everything that he had said was true. He did exactly what his mum and dad wanted him to do, he went to the School they told him to go to, the University to go to, the Speciality they had told him to do and for the whole of his life his parents had planned that he should take over the estate and marry Felicity. And Paul was absolutely right, he had done everything to please them as that's what a son and heir did, wasn't it? He tried to think what he would have done differently if he had had the chance, or the choices that he would have made if he had been given the opportunity. He loved being a doctor and the years at University had been the best years of his life, freedom, best friends and adventure, lots of adventures.

He had the best five years of his life whilst living away and he had loved every minute of that part of being a doctor but how did he feel now! The days were long and hard, some days were good and some days were bad. He liked helping people but it affected him when his patients died and he had to deal with grieving families asking him why? He didn't like surgery and he didn't like the gossip of the hospital and he didn't like knowing which doctor was sleeping with which nurse. He hated the feeling of walking into a building which he knew he would spend all day in, not see the sky or take a full breath of fresh air for another ten hours or so. Being indoors was the worst part of his job, he felt trapped most days, at the beck and call of other people constantly.

If he had ever really had been given a choice in his future he remembered he had thought about going to Agricultural College to learn how to be a 'real' farmer. He had ventured such an opinion to his dad at the time but he had just said that the Bucannons paid people to run the farm and not get their hands dirty. The Bucannons were educated men, he had said, his own father had been a Cardiac consultant but he was forced to leave the profession and run the estate when his father had died when his dad was only forty. It was bizarre that he couldn't decide what he really wanted to do with his life, not really, and he was so annoyed with himself for allowing his parents to have dictated so much of his life. He resolved that he needed to grow up and be more independent and not rely on his family so much. And then Felicity popped into his mind. Bang, the thought hit him like a freight train. Did he love Felicity? She was great, worked hard, lots of fun, reliable and his family liked her. They liked her so much that they had been planning their wedding for the last twenty five years in fact. Had he just fallen into line and kept everyone happy by being with her and then the thought hit him, what did she actually think of me? They had been a couple for about ten years now. They did everything together, went everywhere together, had their flats in Newcastle during the week but both came home to their parents houses most weekends. He was quieter than her, more of a home bird than her and calmer than her. She had wanted to go to New York for one year with her company but he hadn't wanted to go. He blamed his job but he knew that wasn't the only reason he had not gone with her.

Eventually he arrived back at the Marquee and was able to park up at the top near the entrance as some of the cars had already left. Someone had already been out with a tractor and cleared the drive so getting up the drive had been no problem at all. The perks of a farmer's Ball he laughed to himself. He secured the car and went inside to find his friend Paul who was leaning on the bar chatting to a group of people Marcus didn't know. He got to the bar, ordered a tonic water and waited for Paul to finish his conversation. He looked around the room and saw Felicity and his mother were dancing in a large group to the song 'I'm too sexy'. They were having fun and all the women were singing at the top of their voices and pretending to be sexy. Not a good look for his mother or most of the women really who all seemed too drunk to be anything let alone sexy. He was sure his mother would be totally embarrassed in the morning, once her hang over allowed her to be! He wondered if any of his family or Felicity had even noticed that he had been missing for just over an hour. Sadly, he thought not. He never danced anyway so they would think he was in a corner somewhere talking to someone or with his enduring friend Paul.

He was busy watching the dancefloor and his embarrassing family when he felt a tap on his shoulder, he turned expecting Paul but it was Esme, Franny's Esme.

"Hi Marcus, I am sorry to bother you but Paul said that you had taken Frances home and I was just wondering how she was, did she get home safely?"

Marcus was taken aback by her question as, apparently, she had fallen out with Franny according to Bella. Eventually he spoke to her.

"Hi, yes I found her walking down the hill in the blizzard, she'd been fired from here by my bloody mother just because she was pregnant," the anger crept into his voice. "She agreed to get into my car only because I guess, it was so cold and she couldn't keep going. I took her home. She did let me in and we had a little chat. Her house just seemed so sad. It was so cold and there's no christmas decorations up and there is hardly any food in the fridge, just enough for a few days or so, not the usual full christmas fridges and cupboards that most people have. She worries me Esme. Why does she live on her own and endure the hard life that she has chosen for herself? I feel awful for her, so sorry for her. Do you know that as well as being finished from the stables Bella phoned No 64 and she forced them to sack her as they owned the building. My mother has got her sacked from here too, pressured Paul and did you also know that on her way up here, she tried to get a job as a paper girl and even they said no. Can you imagine just how she's feeling now? The last thing she needed in the world was to be pregnant. God it is such a mess, OMG, I felt awful leaving her, I set her last wood on fire too, she was saving it for christmas day. Can you imagine that, picking twigs and bits up and saving them to burn on christmas day? Was she coming to you on christmas day or was she going somewhere else?"

Tears stung Esme's eyes as she listened to Marcus talk about her friend. What a complete bitch she had been to Fran. She knew how hard it was for her every day, it was a constant struggle for her to keep the house going, car and save for university. She had ignored and hurt her friend badly yesterday. She had just been in such a state of shock and hurt she had just stopped functioning or thinking. She had felt very hurt that Frances hadn't confided in her. Now in the light of day, she understood that Fran was only trying to protect her, and she had only kept working as she needed the money and the job for as long as she could. There was obviously no boyfriend or father of the baby in Frances's life. She was having a baby and she was doing it on her own. Esme suspected that Marcus was the father but she wasn't sure whether to say anything to him. When Fran had asked her to be the Godmother she had ignored her because in that moment she had just been hurt. Now she knew that Frances would never hurt her or her family. She had tried to speak to her earlier but she obviously didn't want to talk about the baby or what had happened at the stables. She didn't want to make things worse for herself but for me too. The word bitch just kept running through her mind, she had been such a bitch and had let Frances down when she needed her most.

"Marcus that is awful, I didn't know she was pregnant, I could have helped her and supported her but she needed to work and felt that if she told me then she would have put me in a position of having to be loyal to Bella and she may have lost her job. I'm such a bad friend. I was so shocked when I saw she was pregnant that I just didn't think! She asked me to be the godmother and all I did was ask her to leave. I think we were the first people she has told that she is pregnant and I ignored her and told her to go and Bella sacked her. I can't believe how she is feeling now, especially at christmas. You know that she doesn't celebrate christmas and why, don't you?

"No, no I didn't, she had some homemade holly wreaths on the fireplace but apart from that it didn't look christmassy at all. Why doesn't she do christmas?"

Esme picked up the courage to ask him a question. "I presume that you are the father Marcus, is that right?" He remained silent.

"If you care about her at all you can find out about her on Christmas morning, I can't tell you, I promised that I would never tell anyone about her past. I can't let her down again. I need to make things right with her, I need to be there for her again and support her. I'm not sure if she will let me in again, you probably know more than most, she is very careful about who she trusts." She looked around her before she spoke again. "She will be in the middle of Rothington at 11.00am on christmas day and that's all that I can say." Before Marcus had a chance to ask her any more she was gone, and back to her friends. Marcus watched her disappear onto the dancefloor consumed in the business of the crowd of revellers. He was re playing the conversation in his head when Paul came up behind her and slapped him on the back.

"Hi daddy, how's it going?"

"For god's sake shut up Paul, someone may hear you."

"Sorry, just trying to lighten the mood. You never guess what, I've just been asked to do by that family that I was just talking to. Well, they want me to organise their daughter's wedding, they are having a marquee on the back lawn in August and have asked me to arrange the caterers, bar and music. Just a thought but if you want me to organise yours, you need to ask quick, as I'm getting booked up fast." Paul smiled at his own joke. Marcus didn't say anything.

"You were right, she is pregnant and it is mine. Just the one time, at my flat in the summer. She is six months pregnant and not four or five months as everyone now thinks thanks to Bella. I feel so awful about it all. I was initially angry that she hadn't told me but she did try to contact me when I was on the yacht with Felicity. She asked me to call her twice but I just read the messages, deleted them and ignored her. When she needed me all I did was ignore her, what a shit I am"

"Well in all fairness to you, you didn't know and she didn't actually say that she was pregnant in the message, but I suppose she was just being careful in case Felicity read your messages. Didn't you use protection?"

"Yes we did but during doing it I realised that she was still a virgin and I just suddenly felt that I was in the wrong to be with her, to take her virginity, I was betraying Felicity and it just all ended........badly. I took the thing off and threw it in the bin, apologised, left her and went back to my own room. In the morning when I got up, I waited about an hour for her to wake up and come out. Eventually I knocked on the door and it was then that I realised that she had already gone and left all the clothes, shoes and bag and asked me to get rid of them for her. Apparently, she had walked to the bus station and got a bus back home. Her first time ever should have been with someone her own age, someone who loved her, and cradled her in their arms, telling her how wonderful and loved she was. And what did she get? Me! I completely let her down and walked out on her." Marcus hesitated before he spoke again. "I've offered to help her financially and be there for her and the baby and that I want to be in their lives but she just said no. She thinks that as I'm getting married it's best that no one knows that I'm the father. She was trying to put me before her and the baby. She thinks that no one will ever accept her so there is no point even trying."

Both men were quiet and reflective for a few moments, it was Paul who spoke next. "What about Felicity and your family? You are due to get married next summer and engaged in less than 48 hours, have you thought about what you are going to do?"

"I can't just walk away from her, she's carrying my baby. I can't let her deal with it on her own anymore, she has been dealing with it on her own for six months. She is completely worried about money and loosing all three jobs in 24 hours has made it all even worse for her. I know she's got savings as she was saving up to go to Medical school in Newcastle but knowing her she won't touch that. Christ, having a baby has messed that up for her too. I really have screwed up her life and she just dealt with it all not complaining and carrying on. I said I'd give her £1,500 a month to help her, she does not need to work anymore. She can be a full time mum till she goes to medical school, and they have a great creche at the hospital. I said I would fully support her Paul."

"What did she say?"

"She was very kind to me. She said that it wasn't my fault that she was pregnant and she had been a willing partner too. She said she was initially shocked but she was now used to it and was really excited about being a mum and having a family of her own. Yes, it changes things for her but she said it was best that there was no contact between us, the less chance that my family or Felicity would find out. She said none of them liked her anyway and that they wouldn't except the situation and she could not bare for her baby to be ignored by my family. It was best that her baby had no family at all than for my family to ignore *her* baby. She was also aware of Felicity in this whole awful mess too. She told me to marry her, have a family with her and in order for me to have a happy family life I couldn't tell anyone and that no money should pass between us as it would be traceable. Sensible or what!"

"The more you tell me mate the more I like her. She has nothing, doesn't seem to have any friends or family to support her but yet, she's still not asking for anything from you. She is a tough little thing really. I think she will be okay, a great mum and you, my friend, have been allowed to carry on with your life, just like before. She has given you a get out of jail for free card if you ask me but are you going to use it? If I was you I would take this, all of this, as an opportunity to reflect on what you want and where you are going in your life,...daddy!"

Marcus flinched. "Yes, I need to have a serious think about things and decide what I want to do and what I have to do. Funny but Esme, Franny's boss from the stables said that if I wanted to know everything about her I should go to Rothington on Christmas day at 11.00, which is a bit weird don't you think?"

"I think you have a problem then. Your christmas day is totally organised already, pressies with the family, big party, you on one knee and a massive engagement ring. Or, my friend, do you make an excuse to disappear for a few hours and then find out Frances's big secret. And if you choose to find out where she is on christmas day are you ready to find out the truth about Frances and why she has secrets. Paul put his arms around his friend and pulled him closer. "Marcus it's late, take your vile drunken mother home or at least take her outside and leave her somewhere cold and wet to sober up but it is time for the party to end and for me to go home to my beautiful wife and family, my very uncomplicated family I might add!"

Chapter 9

Frances had struggled to sleep and had woken up to go to the toilet at least twice. In the end she had got up, made a cup of tea and a hot water bottle for her feet. The heating was due to go on at 6 'o' clock but at 4 she had turned it on to try and warm the house up a little. The snow had settled and everywhere outside was still and white. She couldn't believe that she wasn't asleep as she felt totally exhausted. She had worked hard for days, cleaned the car walked miles in a blizzard and she was still wide awake. In the last few days she had fallen out with Bella, Esme, Marcus, Gino and his family . That may be the reason I can't sleep she told herself! She wasn't sure what reaction she had been expecting when she actually did tell people that she was going to be a mum, maybe a hug, maybe a few questions and definitely some questions about who was the father. But no, none of that had happened to her. A lot of shouting had occurred. Copious amounts of sacking had definitely happened. A little bit of shock and a lot of ignoring had absolutely happened, all wrapped up in a lot of condemnation. But as yet not one person had said "Congratulations, great news, wonderful news even."

No one had asked how many weeks she was, did she know if it was a girl or boy or names, or where the baby was going to be born or if they could help her! No nothing like she saw on TV had happened to her. No grandparents rushing out to buy cots and prams. No boyfriend over the moon that they were going to be a daddy, excitingly planning on the first football strip they were going to buy whether it was a boy or girl. Even when she had gone to see the doctor at the medical centre all he had said was, 'Congratulations' without even looking at her, "we need to get you booked in with a midwife quickly and get things started." No, it had been a strange couple of days in deed. She missed her mum and her family, especially her mum, uninvited tears escaped again.

She had been really hurt by Esme's reaction. The one person who she thought would be able to be her friend, support and understand her a little had turned her back on her. She had wanted Esme to be the godmother for two reasons. One, it meant that her baby had family, someone special in their life and two, someone who would be there for her child just in case anything, god forbid was to happen to her. Her baby needed one other significant person in their lives. She had thought about asking her to be her birthing partner but she had now opted for a home birth much against the midwife's advice. But now she was going to give birth on her own, unsupported but at least now she was in her own house. That way she didn't have to endure a stay in hospital watching all the other women and their babies being pampered and hugged and kissed by family members. She knew no one would visit her now, that no one would bring her baby a floating congratulations baby balloon, cards or flowers. No one would be thanking her for giving them a son or a daughter. She knew that all the other mums and babies would receive nice gifts but she just didn't want to see it or for her baby to be the only baby who didn't get any visitors or presents. It was best for everyone if she gave birth at home, on her own bed surrounded by all her little memories and photographs. The added bonus was that there would be no mad dash to the hospital to give birth and no problems with regards to how she was going to bring her new baby home from the hospital. The decision to sell her Defender had also solved the problem of the pushchair or pram dilemma, she didn't need a car seat now or a pushchair to collapse into the back of a car so now she could buy a nice big heavy duty, off-roading pram. It would have been nice to have wrapped her baby up, popped him or her in the Defender and driven to the coast for a nice long walk along the beach. She could still do that but she would need to catch a bus and go to the busier more touristy beaches and not her special beach. But as her mum always said, 'you can't cry over spilt milk'.

Now it was just her and her little Splodge. She had done okay on her own so far and she had so many plans for them both. The bedroom would be carpeted soon and she was going to the sales to get the cot and a new single bed. She needed to get a pram, the navy blue one with a giraffe on which she had seen on the internet was her favourite one. A baby carrier, a baby bath and a listening monitor were on her list and then she would have everything she needed. She hoped to buy baby clothes in the sales and also a pack of terry towelling nappies. She had decided to be an eco-friendly mum and not use disposable ones whenever she could. She would have some disposable ones in for emergencies or for days out ones when they were easier but the terries ones were so much cheaper and begrudgingly she thought her best option.

She had decided that she was going to feed her baby herself, which she wasn't quite sure how she felt about that yet. Initially she thought it wasn't for her but now it seemed a quicker, cleaner and cheaper option. Esme had once told her a story about one of her boys who was born with teeth and how shocked she was that he had been the best one to feed, always gentle and never ever bit her. It made Frances cringe! Today was a good day, decisions had been made and she knew what she needed to buy and where to buy them. Hardys department store in Newcastle was the only place to go to get everything in one go and if she spent over £500 they would deliver it all for free, which was a bonus as she planned to go into Newcastle on the bus! She tried not to think about any of the others, the stable, the restaurant, the Hunt Ball or even her family. "Yesterday was yesterday," she said to her bump. "Today is today and I'm so excited to see you. Tomorrow will be a sad day, and I may get a little upset but Boxing day is the first day of our new lives together and we can start to plan for our amazing life together just you and me."

Marcus's day hadn't got off to such a great start. It was christmas eve and both his mother and father were nursing a massive hangover. He needed to go into Newcastle urgently to do a bit of last minute christmas shopping and he also needed an engagement ring for Felicity which he had totally forgotten about until Paul had mentioned it last night.

"Right, I'm off. Do you think you are going to be alright if I'm gone for a few hours or so?" His mother and father were both in the kitchen drinking copious amounts of black coffee in a futile attempt to get over their hangovers.

"Yes darling," his mother spoke, "be back for around 6ish, I've prepared a small salmon supper just for the four of us, a chance to be a family once more before all the madness of tomorrow begins and six months of wedding preparations get started. Have fun and drive carefully as there is still a lot of snow around, bye." With a quick wave of her hand he was released and he was quickly on his way heading towards the shops. He knew he should be thinking about Felicity and the 'expensive' ring he needed to buy her from her favourite jewellers but he just couldn't seem to concentrate on that, all he could think about was Franny and his baby. Nearly an hour later he arrived in the Portland Road and Fintons. Everyone he knew had got their engagement rings, wedding rings, sorry rings and every other sort of rings you could imagine from here. He rang the bell to be allowed in. A gentleman quickly came to the door and asked if he had an appointment.

"What, I need an appointment to buy a ring!"

"Most people do sir but if you don't you are more than welcome to come in and look around but our Gemmologist isn't in today so if you need a custom-made ring I'm afraid we need to book an appointment in the New Year."

"No, No I know what I want. I'm getting engaged tomorrow and I need an engagement ring. My girlfriend wants a Fortesque one, a diamond solitaire and a big one. Do you have any in?"

"Yes sir, we have a wonderful selection of Fortesque rings at the moment. Come into one of our private viewing rooms and I'll bring the trays to you. All I need is a copy of your driving licence or passport and I will be with you shortly. Would you like a drink of coffee or tea or a glass of champagne?"

"Yes, a black coffee would be great, thanks." Marcus said as he handed over his driving licence and his hospital ID card too, which he thought showed he was a doctor and could afford the ring!

The salesman showed Marcus into a small room which was oak wood panelled. The desk was an old oak antique one which had been heavily used. The room was carpeted in a dark navy blue carpet, navy ceiling and gold accessories were scattered around the room. There was no window but spotlights on the ceiling and an ornate gold desk lamp gave the room its light.

"I'll be with you in just a moment, just take a seat and I'll send in your drink in a few moments." The salesman left Marcus alone in the room, He pulled out one of the gold ornate velvet covered chairs and sat down. The salesman was about fifty thought Marcus, tall and slim and very well dressed. Marcus wondered how long he had been doing this job for, he seemed very good at it.

The salesman entered carrying a wooden tray of rings, accompanied by a slightly younger woman carrying a tray with a coffee cup and small coffee pot on. Marcus nodded and smiled at the lady.

"Mr Bucannon, my name is James Finton and I have a wonderful selection of rings for you. Can I start by showing you the rings that I consider the best and then as we ascertain exactly what you are wanting I can go and get some more out for you if nothing is suitable."

One by one Mr Finton took the rings off the tray and talked about the settings and the diamond sizes. They all looked quite similar to Marcus but one caught his eye, a single square solitaire diamond, surrounded by smaller diamonds. "I like this one the most," he held it in his fingers as he looked at it with the magnifying glass.

"Yes, I think this is the one. How much is it?"

"That one is £15,985.00. Do you know the size of the ring you need sir?" Marcus shook his head.

"We currently have it in 2 sizes this being the larger of the two. I would advise that you take this one and if it needs reducing in size we can do that at no charge. I personally think it is more romantic to get a ring that is too big for the finger than trying to arrange the perfect ring. It is always more romantic if the bride- to- be has no choice regarding her ring, sometimes the best surprise is the not knowing, don't you agree. This way she gets the surprise of the ring and then she can come back into the shop and arrange the perfect fit for herself if she needs to." Marcus thanked him for his advice and the ring was swiftly boxed, wrapped and paid for and Marcus was on his way home.

The ring was stunning and he was really pleased with his choice and the price was about what he thought needed to be paid. His mum had said between £40,000 and £50,000 but there was no way he was going to pay that much for a ring, that was ridiculous! He hoped she liked it, she deserved a nice ring and a nice day. She hadn't deserved what he had done to her.

The salmon supper had been a quiet, low key affair in the kitchen with just the four of them. His mum didn't cook too often as she wasn't a natural cook. Marcus did appreciate that she had made a real effort for him and his family to be together, enjoying a family meal before everything changed. His mum and dad didn't drink at all whilst he shared a bottle of white wine with his brother.

"This time tomorrow your life will be over. You'll be at the beck and call of your 'wife' constantly and then you'll have a brood of screaming, snivelling kids hanging onto your ankles and for good measure, four doting grandparents who will turn up at your house whenever they choose. I have to say Marcus I don't envy you." Robert had a way of putting things that seemed to annoy everyone at the table. His mum was the first to bite. "Robert, my grandchildren will not snivel. They are Bucannons and they will act accordingly!" Everyone laughed at her typical comment. It would be the last fun night that Marcus would have with his family for a while.

Chapter 10

Christmas morning had arrived, the day Frances had dreaded for the previous 364 days. Yesterday had been a bit of a daze. Christmas eve was traditionally a busy day in most households, shopping, cooking, families getting together, getting ready for Santa. But, it had been a quiet day for Frances. She had spent most of the day on the sofa snuggled up in her quilt, finishing her book and trying to distract herself from her own thoughts. She had felt in danger of being crushed by those thoughts.

Marcus now knew her secret and she wasn't really sure how she felt about him and his reaction to the news that he was going to be a dad. He had discussed options with her. He had discussed all the problems and solutions with her. But he hadn't said he was happy or that he loved her or that it was wonderful, best ever news. He had offered money and he said he would support her but had said no nice comforting or kind words. He had dealt with their baby purely as a problem. She thought that she would be able to be a great independent mum, perfect mum with an enviable close bond with her baby but doubts had crept into her mind since speaking to Marcus. He had said that she wasn't ready or prepared for the responsibility of being a mum on her own. She felt uneasy that his words had stung. Would he want to take her baby away from her! He and his family were powerful, he could do it but would he do it. She cradled her bump and reassured her baby and herself that everything was going to work out as she planned. The last few days had been so hard for her losing her jobs, her friends, her routines and the things that she needed to continue. She had only just lost Max and Bert and suddenly she felt more alone than she had ever felt in her entire life and it was just too overwhelming for her to deal with today. It was very tempting to stay on the sofa all day but today she needed to go and see her family. She hadn't been since last christmas day and it was just something she needed to do. When her baby was in her arms, christmas next year would be a different one for her, full of excitement and hope for the future. Today she had to do what needed to be done.

It had been a few days since she had driven and she definitely appreciated the heater that her Defender had. On the hour drive the car had warmed up very nicely. Frances wondered if she should just move into her car for the next few weeks as it was definitely warmer but did lack the essential loo which she seemed to need all the time at the moment. Eventually she arrived at Rothington and drove into the Market Place and found a place to park near the church. The service in the church would be over soon and the brave patrons who had ventured out on such a cold and icy day would be leaving.

As predicted the large wooden doors of the church opened and the congregation left quickly wishing each other 'Merry Christmas' and 'Happy New Year'. Frances stayed in the warm watching everyone shuffling away, buttoning coats and collars up. Eventually there was only the vicar, a petite older woman and her uncle Bob left in the porch, all looking towards her sitting in the car. She turned the engine off and pulled on her hat and gloves and pulled her zip to the very top. She carefully got out of the car and walked round to the back of the Defender and opened the back door. She reached in and picked up the four holly wreaths that she had made. She secured the door and made her way up the path to the church to the three people who were all looking at her with strangely smiling faces. She breathed in and braced herself.

"Good morning Frances and how are you my dear? It seems ages since we last saw you. Don't be a stranger to us, we are always here for you my dear," said the elderly white haired vicar with a softness to his voice.

"Thank you, Mr Campbell. Next year I promise I won't be a stranger." She smiled at her uncle and the lady with the kind face. The four of them turned and walked into the cemetery together. They walked towards the back of the graveyard, an area where the old yew trees formed a canopy over the graves. They reached a row of graves, stopped and all turned to face the same way. The area was at the very back, next to the old stone perimeter wall. A low metal ornate fence about ten inches high surrounded the enclosed area where the new looking gravestones all stood proud next to each other. There were four headstones in total. All black granite with gold writing on them. Suddenly it was all too much and immense grief swept over Frances like a tidal wave, engulfing and consuming. Her uncle put his arm around her waist and gently supported her. Frances stepped over the fence and knelt down before the first gravestone. She lay one of the wreaths down just in front of the stone. She bowed her head and stayed still and silent. The tears began to fall immediately. She stretched out her hand and stroked the gold letters which gave names to the inhabitants of the graves. She cleared her throat and started to recite out loud.

"Here lies James and Eliza Tulip. James born 25th April 1965 and Eliza born 11th June 1965. Tragically taken from this world 25th December 2018. Loved and missed by their daughter Frances." She did not read it from the stone as she knew it off by heart. Next, she shuffled and knelt in front of the second stone. She paused, the burden almost unbearable. She lay the second holly wreath down.

"Here lies Barnabas Tulip. Born 12th June 2001. Tragically taken from this world 25th December 2018. Beloved Brother of Frances." She paused and wiped her nose. "Here lies Clara Jane Tulip. Born 4th November 1999. Tragically taken from this world 25th December 2018. Beloved Sister of Frances." Frances's voice broke as she moved to the next stone. "Here lies Edwin and Clara Tulip. Edwin born 20th August 1930 and Clara born 1st August 1930. Tragically taken from this world 25th December 2018. Beloved grandpa and nana to Frances." She bowed her head and lay down the third wreath. Eventually, she moved to the last head stone and turned and looked at her uncle who joined her, kneeling on the ground next to the final headstone.

"Here lies Rosie Graham. Born 12th May 1967. Tragically taken from this world 25th December 2018. Loved and missed by her loving husband Bob and Frances. Till we meet in heaven, may the angels watch over you." Frances lay down her wreath and Bob lay down a single white rose, the stem carefully wrapped in foil.

The group remained silent for a few minutes all lost in their thoughts. It was the vicar who broke the silence.

"May god keep them safe and always watch over their beloved family Frances and Bob, Amen." Bob stood up and kissed the top of the gravestone, gently but with heartfelt emotion in such a small act. He stepped back over the small fence and put his hat back on. He held out a hand to help his young niece.

"Come on lass, come home with me and our Aggie. She has prepared so much to eat you need to come home and help us out or we will be eating christmas food till Easter." His sister laughed and punched his arm.

"Frances my love, you are very welcome to come home to our mad house, all the family will be there and now I have ten grandchildren you won't be bored or left alone for one minute." She laughed. Frances liked Aggie, she had been a great friend after the accident, she had taken control, organised everything and held her and Bob together. She liked her very much and she would take her up on the offer next year but not this year, it just felt a bit too soon.

"I'm sorry to interrupt," said the vicar." I need to be off as I said that I would call in at the nursing home to conduct a small christmas service for them. Take care dear Frances, you are always in my thoughts and prayers and I do so hope that we will see more of you next year." He blew her a kiss, knowing not to embrace her. After brief goodbyes he was gone.

"Thank you so much for inviting me Aggie, next year I promise I will spend christmas with you and uncle Bob but today I just need to be here, then go home. Today, I think I need to have one last day remembering the past and then from tomorrow I will start a new life where I only look forward. And if I'm not being to presumptuous Aggie, I'd like to invite myself to yours on New Year's Day. I don't think that I can cope with coming up to the farm just yet but hopefully soon. But today I hope you both don't mind, I just want to stay with mum and dad, I have something I need to tell them about."

"Absolutely lass, New Year's Day dinner is beef this year with all the family as well. Come over whenever suits and we will have the kettle on and a good catch up. You are such a lovely, lovely girl," She cupped her hand under

Frances's chin. "Your mam and dad would be so proud of you and we are always here for you whenever you are ready. Everything at your pace lass and soon it will all fall into place." She pulled Frances into her and gave her a tight hug before turning and walking away trying to ensure that her tears were not seen.

"Any time lass you need me you know where I am. I know you needed to be on your own, sick of the hugging and the sympathy and sad looks you got from everyone but you do seem stronger and hopefully you will feel able soon to be part of this family again. You know lass, I do understand that you couldn't be here anymore but I also need you to always know that I need to look after you, your mam, dad and my Rosie and the whole family would want me to look after you." She embraced her uncle for a few moments. They held on to each other not saying anything but just content in each other's embrace. Then he was gone and she was alone in the graveyard. It was time for her to tell her family her good news and how she would never be on her own anymore.

Marcus had woken early from a bad night's sleep. He had chosen to stay with his mum and dad for Christmas eve and Felicity had chosen to stay at her mum and dad's as they usually did! He had struggled with his conscience all night. He was having a baby with one woman and buying an expensive engagement ring for another. One wanted for nothing and the other could hardly afford the basics in life and he was well aware of fact that he had just made her life incomprehensively more difficult. He hadn't meant too but he had spent most of the night comparing the two women. Felicity, smart, intelligent, confrontational, loud, powerful, beautiful, manicured, popular, strong, hard and selfish. He was trying to be honest with himself inside his head and definitely selfish had to be at the top of his list. Always her way or no way! And Frances. Well what could he say about her. He didn't really know her that well, he didn't know her favourite film or song or colour. The only thing he really did know about her was that he liked her and he wanted to get to know her and be with her and find out everything about her he could! He thought about her most of the time over the last six months if he was honest. He watched a programme on the TV and wondered if she was watching it on her antique TV or new TV. Horses always reminded him of her as well as Defenders! He thought he was being stupid though, his future was planned, she was so young.

He eventually got out of bed, showered, dressed and meandered his way down stairs to get a much, much needed coffee.

"Morning darling, Merry Christmas." His mum came over to him and kissed him on his forehead. "I'm so glad you are up, it's been so hard to stay quiet this morning, I do love christmas morning and you boys opening all of your presents and playing with them. Well maybe not playing with them but you know what I mean darling." Marcus knew exactly what she meant. One thing for sure was that christmas was always a big thing in his house and his mum relished every minute of it. Six or seven real trees were always put up and overly decorated and there were decorations in every room in the house including the estate office which always annoyed his father.

"Morning mum and a very Merry Christmas to you too. Can you get me a coffee, I just need to nip back to my room to get my presents?" Marcus ran up to his bedroom and picked up a Christmas sack full of presents. It was 8.00am and he had decided during the night that he did need to go to Rothington to see what happened there at 11.00am. What was he going to say to his mum, how was he going to go missing for two hours on christmas day?

Eventually his father and brother got up, Robert a bit worse for wear. They breakfasted together, bacon filled croissants and Bucks Fizz. Coffee only for Marcus as he announced that he needed to nip out to get something for Felicity. After breakfast they made their way into the large drawing room and Marcus had to admit his mother had done a wonderful job and the room looked stunning. In the family, this room was known as the first room. It was the best room and only used on special occasions. It was full of antiques and portraits of Family members from the last 100 years or so. His grandfather's portrait dominated the room as it was the largest and hung majestically on the chimney breast over the fire. The christmas tree was at least twelve feet tall and six feet wide and it was covered in gold and red ornaments. It looked like it belonged in a castle somewhere. His favourite tree was the one in the kitchen. It was always full of the homemade ornaments and school made hanging 'things' from his and Robert's younger days. It had plastic baubles filled with stars and glitter and a photo of him mounted on card, surrounded by cotton wool snow. He knew it was his mothers least favourite tree but it was traditional so it always went up anyway.

They settled down and started to open their 'Santa' presents, his mum always gave them a sack of presents form 'Santa' and the sack was always on the same seat on the sofa so they all knew where to sit instinctively. The family's gifts to each other where placed under the tree and were always opened after dinner and with the friends who came to join the celebrations. Today it would be quite different as his mother had invited about twenty for christmas dinner and for the official engagement celebrations. The party was due to start at 4.00pm with dinner at 5.00, engagement officially at 6.00 at the dinner table in front of everyone, and presents etc at 7.00pm and then party fun. His mother and Felicity had organised everything to the last minute so that it would be perfect and he was sure it would be. His perfect christmas would be spent in his joggers, watching junk TV and definitely no working clocks! He joined in opening the presents which was always fun. His mum always made such a big effort to get them great presents. He loved the pale blue jumper and new ties but wasn't too sure about the empty silver photo frame for his engagement photograph. He loved the new blue bedding set and all the chocolates and alcoholic drinks. His dad had wrapped up some ear plugs and slipped them in the sack without his wife knowing. "You will need those when you are married, you will thank me for them son." Everyone laughed. The mood in the house was good and everyone was getting on well. It was nearly 10.00 and if Marcus was to get to Rothington in time he would need to leave soon. He had to say something now!

"Right, thank you for all my amazing presents they are brilliant as usual and so very thoughtful. I'm going to pop out for a while as I need to go and pick something up, so I'll be back about 12.00 for lunch. I'll just take these to my room as I go."

"Marcus, it's christmas day you can't go out today. Where do you need to go?"

"Sorry mum," he smiled. "I have my secrets today, but good ones," he almost ran out of the room and ran upstairs to the sanctuary of his room. Ten minutes later he was in his car driving to Rothington. His phone connected to the car.

"Morning, Merry Christmas to you and yours. Looking forward to seeing you later."

"Morning to you too, thanks for all the presents, they are great. A Mulberry handbag for my missus, should I be worried?"

"Definitely, Felicity bought it and she may teach your wife some expensive shopping habits!" The friends laughed.

"Paul, I'm sorry to ask but I need to find out what happens at 11.00 in Rothington. I'm driving there this morning. I just said I needed to nip out for something. My plan is that I'll tell them if pushed that I have left the engagement ring at my flat in Newcastle to ensure that no one saw it before the big moment. I don't think anyone will ask but just in case they do, that's my thinking, is that okay."

"Sounds feasible. You be on your best behaviour today my friend. Make sure no one sees you and no one finds out what is going on. At some point and very soon you need to make some decisions. Let me know how it goes and don't be late for your own engagement party or christmas dinner, your mother, Felicity and probably my wife will kill you if you are late. Wifey can't wait to come to yours for dinner and see inside your house at christmas. Felicity is making a real effort to be friends with her and she is totally into having her as a friend at last. See you at 4.00, be careful."

When Marcus arrived at the market place, it was quite busy. He decided to park up on Bank Road. It gave him a great view of the Market Place and the church which looked pretty in the remains of the snow. He had scanned the car park to see if Franny had arrived yet but he couldn't see her car. He settled down in his seat and pulled his collar up.

He didn't have long to wait before she arrived in her Defender. She drove straight into the car park and parked up in front of the church. The church opened its doors and let out its congregation who swiftly disbursed on such a cold morning. Soon the car park was empty apart from three cars and Frances. Marcus noticed that the vicar and a couple hovered in the door way and seemed to be watching Frances. She sat in the car for about a few moments before she got out and walked around to the back of her vehicle. She opened the back door and reached in and took out the four wreaths that Marcus had previously seen on the fireplace in her house. She held them by the red ribbon loops on the top. She secured her car and walked up the path to the small group who seemed to be waiting for her. The group chatted for a moment and then walked away together into the graveyard. They stopped at the back of the yard and gathered around some graves. Marcus saw Frances lay the first of her wreaths down. He noticed that she had slumped over the first grave. No one went to help her. Whoever was in that grave was important to her, very important to her and he could feel his own emotions starting to change as he watched Frances.

Slowly she made her way along the four graves and placed the wreaths down on them. She hesitated at each grave and was joined by the man at the last one who seemed to put something on the grave as well. The group then chatted, some embraced and then they left leaving Frances alone at the graves. She knelt in front of them and sat like that for about fifteen minutes, in the cold, kneeling in the snow. Marcus wondered who was in the graves. Some questions had been answered but more questions had launched in his head. Eventually she stood up and steadied herself. She touched the top of the stones and slowly walked away turning back occasionally to look at the graves. She reached her car, got in it and started the engine up. Marcus saw the lights of the car come on but she didn't drive away immediately, she just sat there, with the engine running. The reversing lights came on a few moments later, she reversed and then drove away slowly in the direction of home.

Marcus waited before he got out of the car to ensure that she had left the area. He walked down the road and went into the church yard and over to the graves where Frances had laid the holly wreaths. He read the epitaphs one by one. With horror and shock he realised who the graves belonged to, her whole family. Her mother, father, brother, sister, grandparents and auntie all died on christmas day, three years ago, today. He suddenly felt sick. He knew that she had secrets but never had he envisaged such a terrible and immensely sad reason. He too knelt on the ground and stared at the gravestones and his heart absolutely broke for her. He didn't know what to think or what he was going to say to her when he saw her. He couldn't believe that she had lost her whole family, he couldn't image losing his family, especially all on one day, Christmas Day.

He walked back to his car and collapsed into the driver's seat. He cradled his head in his hands and just cried. Frances must have been only seventeen when it happened, it was so young to have lost them and to be on her own. There seemed to be an uncle but she had never mentioned him to Marcus. He needed to speak to her to tell her that he now knew her secret. Why she needed to work so hard, to be so careful around people, her quietness and why she was on her own. She had let him into her lonely world, only very briefly and he had absolutely blown it and let her down so badly. No wonder she would not let him back in. He suddenly felt immense shame and sadness as the tears started again. He needed to be there for her. He needed to support her and be loyal to her and his baby no matter the cost. It was all too much for Marcus to deal with, he needed to talk to Paul. He needed to talk to Frances and he needed to be home as quick as possible to deal with his family and the day ahead.

Frances drove home on automatic pilot. She arrived outside her home, parked up and turned the engine off. The trip home had been a strange one as she was definitely parked up outside of her house but could not remember the drive at all. She didn't like that feeling. After she had left the graveyard she had called in at the farm and laid some holly bunches on Max and Bert's graves. She remembered doing that, she remembered her tears and the feeling of overwhelming sadness but she could not remember the walk back to the car.

The snow started to fall and the temperature had suddenly dropped. Frances got out and made her way up to the house and let herself in slowly closing the door on the world outside. She took off her coat and boots and nipped upstairs to change out of her wet trousers and put on her comfy joggers and baggy jumper. She went into the kitchen and put the oven on and started to prepare herself a hot chocolate and toast. She turned the heating up full and put the radio on. She loved to listen to the radio and wondered if the show was recorded or live on christmas day. Alex Noble played a mixture of classical and modern and he always had funny little stories and lots of phone-in guests. He was her favourite presenter. She sat down to drink the last of her hot chocolate and cradled her growing tummy.

"Well my little one, I told my family about you today and I think they would have been really excited about meeting you. Your grandparents would have loved you and spoiled you. My brother and sister, who could be annoying would have been great, a brilliant uncle and auntie but one thing for sure is that they are all up there, in heaven watching over you and making sure that we are loved every minute of every day. I have cried my last tears today and I'm going to try and be the best mum in the world. In a few days we are going to Uncle Bob's and Aggies house for dinner and I will introduce you to them. Aggie will be so excited, she is lovely, such a family person. Uncle Bob is a little on the quiet side but we can always rely on uncle Bob, he is such a solid and reliable man. I've kept my distance for a little while. It wasn't their fault it was me, I just couldn't cope with it any more. Everyone was so kind to me, they all tried to help, to hug me and offer help and support but I just needed to hide and not have people look at me with sadness and pity in their eyes. It was the pity that made me come and live in this house, my grandparent's house, your great- grandparent's house. I know its old and cold but I could cope in here better and I needed somewhere away from the farm, somewhere that I could cope with the memories. I had the boys, Bert and Max and I couldn't leave them at the farm without me and go off to Medical school could I? They had lost their family too. So, the three of us came here and started again. I got a job and it was going fine, I was managing. I managed until I met the Bucannons and in particular Marcus." She hesitated before she carried on talking to her baby, almost afraid to say who Marcus was.

"Marcus, he's your daddy, he got into my world, I let him into to my life. I liked him I really did. He's a nice man but the timing just isn't great at the moment for him or for me. So, things are going to change around here for us. Uncle Bob and Aggie will be there for us and hopefully Esme, my friend, will be around occasionally too. I'll sell my car which will make money a little easier for us and if not, I always have my Medical School savings to fall back on. Things need to change. A warm house from now on and a little more in the cupboards. If I don't go mad I'm sure we will have everything we need for a year or two. I will make you a promise my little one," she bent her head down talking directly to her tummy.

"I will be the best mum in the world that I can be, I won't let money be such a big part of our lives anymore and we will be part of uncle Bob's and Aggie's family. I think you will need that and I think that it's time for me too. And I will love you more than anything, you have the same blood running through your veins as me and having blood family is the most important thing in the world to me. And your daddy, well we will just have to see what happens there my little one." Frances noticed that she didn't call her baby 'Splodge' any more, suddenly it just didn't seem to suit. She drank the rest of the chocolate as she peeled the potatoes and thought about names for her baby. Today she felt positive. Today was now the first day of her new life.

Chapter 11

Marcus felt like he had run a marathon when he arrived back at the farm. He was twenty minutes late getting back and he knew that there would be a hundred questions from his mother. He braced himself and got his story straight in his head. He hated lying to his family but he needed to put himself first for one day. He got out of the car and picked up the Fintons bag that he had put in the glove compartment earlier when he had left the farm. Hopefully this would help distract his mother and father. He walked into the kitchen and found his family.

"Hello everyone, I see that you have started without me." He spoke to his family who were all seated around the dining table tucking into a light lunch.

"Where have you been darling, we were getting quite worried about you?" Marcus held up the bag and waved it around. "I'm sorry but I had to go back to the flat to pick this up."

"OMG Marcus that is so funny, you forgot the engagement ring, that's so..." Before Robert had a chance to finish his sentence Marcus butted in. "I didn't forget the ring I deliberately kept it hidden from all prying eyes, especially Felicity's."

"Marcus you bought it from Finton's, clever boy, Felicity and her family will be very pleased. Can we have a quick look. I know we shouldn't, but can we?" asked his excited mother who had thankfully forgotten that he had gone missing for over two hours on christmas day! He got the box out of the bag and opened it. The single solitaire surrounded by smaller diamonds sat majestically in the turquoise box. It was a beautiful ring.

"Marcus, it is beautiful and it looks very expensive. She will absolutely love it. Well done. Did you choose it on your own or did Felicity choose it?"

"No, I choose it, and bought it on my own, hopefully it will fit but they can change the size if it doesn't fit."

"The size doesn't matter son, you know that she will change the whole ring if she doesn't like it anyway!" said his father. They all laughed. Marcus put the box back into the bag and put it on the side and settled down to eat the meal. He felt sick and far from settled but today he just needed to pretend that everything was normal. It was far from a normal day in so many ways.

After lunch Marcus stayed in the kitchen with his mum. He washed and she dried, they didn't use the dish washer as it needed to be kept empty for later. Washing the pots reminded him of when he was boy and he had done it with his mum before the dishwasher had arrived in their home. He washed as he could stand the water being hotter and his mum dried the pots so that they were done properly, as she would say. His mum chatted away happily talking about how nice it was to have snow at christmas, their presents and how happy she was that he was eventually going to settle down with Felicity and give them grandchildren. She seemed happy and content. She had a nice home, two children whom she was very proud of and she had actually managed to marry someone she loved and cared about. They had met at university and got married very quickly. They had both always said it was love at first sight, she didn't know about his wealth and he hadn't cared about her past. It was love and it had worked, they had been happy.

Today was supposed to be a happy day. He was due to get engaged to the wonderful Felicity whom he had been with, for what felt like, a lifetime. He knew everything about her and her family and he had been told most of his life what a wonderful couple they were and how perfect it would be if they were to get married. He did love her. They had a very long and colourful relationship together. They had stayed together during university which had been hard and a little bit frustrating at times.

He remembered that he had shared a flat with two friends at uni, good mates who he was still friends with. After university they had gone off back packing around the world for a year, seeing and doing some of the most amazing things ever. Frazer boasted when he got back that he had slept with a girl on every continent and a different girl in every country and most states in America. Marcus wasn't convinced. They had bungee jumped in Australia, scuba diving in New Zealand, swum with sharks in South Africa, trekked through Peru and so much more. He had been asked to go. He had wanted to go so badly that he had actually sold his car to raise finances to actually go with them. But, Felicity hadn't wanted him to go with them, she had wanted him to go back packing around the world with her. His dad said that if he went with Felicity he would fund the whole trip, he had genuinely been nervous for his son being let off the lead after such a long and hard time in university that he had begged him not to go with his friends. Marcus had agreed eventually not to go. They ended up on a multi-centre holiday, 5 star resorts in Dubai, Hong Kong, Australia, New York and South Africa. Yes, it was an amazing holiday, a trip of a life time but it wasn't the experience that he had been after. He felt so annoyed at himself for being persuaded by them all to give up on his dream and ashamed as he had partly done it for the money. He shook his head in frustration.

"Are you alright darling you look a little annoyed."

"No mum, I'm fine I'm just trying to get my speech right for tonight and it just keeps coming out as 'hey you, do you want to get married or what', so not very romantic." She laughed.

"It's easy darling, just say what is in your heart, say you love her and need her to be your wife and the mother of your children. Say that you need her to be by your side always and you will always walk through this life with her by your side. Short and sweet but honest and sincere, that should do it darling. Now darling the caterers are due here at 1.30 to get dinner ready for tonight so I'm off to get some rest before its time for the festivities to start." She walked over to him and reached up and touched his cheek with her hand.

"My darling boy, I am so very proud of you. You are a most brilliant man and you are the man that I had hoped you would be. You are an obedient and loyal son who has never ever caused us one day of worry. You have worked hard and now have an amazing career and you will be a fabulous husband, father and eventually we will leave all of this, our life's work in your very capable hands." She kissed him gently and left the kitchen without waiting for her son to say anything. Marcus left the kitchen and meandered his way up to his room, closed the door and lay on his bed. His phone buzzed in his pocket.

'Can't wait to see you later, you will love my new dress, perfect to get engaged to such a wonderful man in. Fx.'

He rolled onto his back and stared up at the ceiling. He shouldn't be feeling like this he thought. He should be happy and excited after all he was getting engaged to an amazing woman and making two families very happy. Isn't this what men do, work, get married have families, run family business's, pass them on to the next generation and then die! He tossed and turned on the bed and failed to relax or come up with any successful solutions in his mind. All he could think about was Frances. It just all seemed too much at the moment. He decided to analyse it in stages and see if that process helped. What did he want in life? That was a hard question and one he wasn't sure if he could answer. Paul had been right when they had chatted in his car the other night. His life had been organised by his family and Felicity for so long he wasn't sure what he actually did want. He had wanted to go to medical school and he did like being a doctor.

He did love Felicity and he never really minded doing what she wanted. He did love Hudson Hall Farm and the Estate but what would he choose for himself if he could choose now, today, lying on this bed. He lay quiet on the bed as thoughts raced in and out of his mind. He sat up and shuffled back on the bed and rested his head on the headboard. He got out his phone, sent a quick message to Felicity saying he was looking forward to tonight and that she would love the ring.

Next, he sent a text to Paul saying that he had some news to tell him later. Then he picked up his lap top which was next to his bed and started to investigate some ideas that he had about his future. He had heard the caters arrive and soon the activities and the noises from downstairs forced him to leave what he was doing and go and start the process of getting ready for tonight. He put his laptop down and got showered and dressed for his *big* night. The pale blue suit looked smart and so different from the ones he wore everyday at work. He decided not to wear a tie as he thought it was too formal for this occasion. He tidied his bed up as he left the room and by 3.30pm he was caught up in the kitchen in the middle of the busyness of the caterers and the anxieties of his mother. His mother was in a beautiful red crepe dress with a short matching red bolero jacket and patent black kitten healed shoes. He did have to admit that she looked her usual stunning self with perfect hair and make-up.

"Darling out of the kitchen, you don't want to smell of cooking do you. Daddy and Robert are in the drawing room having drinks and I'll be there in a minute with a tray of coffee."

Marcus did as he was told and left the kitchen and went to find his dad. He popped his head into the dining room as he passed by. The dining room looked amazing, garlands of holly and fir tree cones festooned the room. The very large table which seated 30 when fully extended was full of greenery, christmas ornaments and little red and gold hearts. Each place setting had numerous glasses and the fine china dinner settings were white and silver and silver cutlery to complete the look. All the candle sticks in the house appeared to had been placed along the full length of the table and fitted with new candles. The table did look amazing and he was sure when all the candles where lit it would look even better. His mum had made such a monumental effort for him and he was very touched.

"Hi dad, I've come to join you in the calm before everyone gets here."

"Come in and join us, we are having a little dram of the hard stuff before it all kicks off, want one?"

"No, thanks, I need to keep a clear head until later, mum is bringing me a coffee."

Robert joined in the conversation. "Last night of freedom and happiness, how are you feeling? Looking forward to the ball and chain?" Marcus reacted quickly. "I am looking forward to getting engaged and married. Do you think you and Miles will ever get married or just spend the next ten years sneaking around behind mum and dad's back?" Roberts face flushed red as he glared at his brother and just before he had time to explode into a retort his father spoke.

"Today is not about Robert or his friendship with Miles. Do you think that we didn't know what our son was doing and who he was doing it with? It is his choice and his mother and I are fully aware. We had hoped that he would come to us to talk about his choices but he didn't and we didn't want to interfere. Miles has been invited tonight as your brother's guest and we do not need to discuss it further now. Tonight, is all about you Marcus and your future. At some point I will have a chat with Robert, but today is not the time or the place."

Both brothers glared at each other and finally sat back in their chairs. Robert looked in shock when he turned his head way from his brother, his parents knew. He was in for it now. Marcus was fuming with both of them and his mother. Everyone knew what was going on and his father had said that they had accepted Robert's lifestyle choices. God damn it, he had never been allowed to have choices. His mother arrived carrying the coffee tray and poured a cup out for herself and then one for Marcus. She passed his over to him, he didn't say thank you.

"Finally, that's everything sorted out and we are ready to go. Everyone will be arriving soon and I want best behaviour boys and not getting too drunk daddy." The men all remained quiet but she didn't notice the atmosphere in the room as she was too high on the events of the day.

Felicity and her family were the first to arrive accompanied by her grandma and younger sister India. They all arrived at the back door, into the back hall and hung their coats up as they were met by all of the Bucannon family. Marcus walked forward and took Felicity by the hand and encouraged her to twirl around. She was wearing a figure hugging, pale pink short cocktail dress which was covered in shiny sparkling stones. "You look amazing, that is a beautiful dress, you look beautiful." He pulled her into him and gently kissed her being careful not to smudge her pink lipstick.

"Thank you," she whispered into his ear. "I think it's time you ran upstairs and got ready too, everyone will be arriving soon." Without a moment's hesitation Marcus pulled her in again to him and whispered into her ear. "I am ready, this is what I'm wearing."

The party of friends left the hall and went into the drawing room. Drinks were served, corks popped and canopies offered. By ten past four all the guests had arrived. Marcus was very pleased to see his friend Paul and his family. Sometime during the evening Marcus planned on spending some time alone outside with Paul and tell him about the morning's events. Bella, her boyfriend and parents had also now arrived. Most of the other guests at the party were friends of his parents and Felicity's parents. Marcus did like most of the people who were there but if it had been up to him he wouldn't have had a party or invited any guests from outside of the families. He decided that engagements should be quiet things, not elaborate public occasions.

Tonight, was going to happen and there was nothing he could do realistically to change it or stop it. He would enjoy the dinner and he would get down on one knee in front of a room full of people and he would ask her to marry him, *again.* Then they would all talk about the wedding and babies. He would join in. He would put a smile on his face but his mind would be elsewhere, they didn't control his thoughts . He would be thinking about Frances. His future plans would, somehow include her and his baby. Now, this evening, was the last night that he would give himself totally to the will of his family and Felicity. He had told her that he wasn't prepared to change his suit and he was proud that he had stood up to her, it marked a change in their relationship. It was going to be a more equal relationship from now on. Tomorrow would be the first day of his new life.

Chapter 12

Finally, Christmas day and Boxing day were in the past and today was a good day. She loved the days that she went to see the midwife at the local Medical Centre. Today she would hear her baby's heart beat and know how well it was growing. She liked all the midwives that she had met so far and none of them had been judgemental about her having no partner, they had probably seen it all before she thought. The surgery was only a short walk away from her home and she arrived early for her 10.00am appointment. She booked herself in with the receptionist and sat and waited to be called. After a few moments the midwife came and called her through. As they walked down the corridor the midwife asked her if she was okay with a doctor being in the room who was looking to gain some experience. Frances happily agreed. They walked into the room and to her horror Marcus was stood in the room leaning against the window. Frances stopped in her tracks and he stood bolt upright.

"Frances, this is Dr Bucannon and he is with us today just observing. I will be doing everything just as normal and he will just be observing me," said the midwife who was totally unaware of the unfolding scene. "You know the drill, pop on the bed, just pull down your trousers a bit, roll up your top and be ready for the gel, it seems really cold today, sorry." Frances did as she was asked and got on the bed and exposed her tummy ready for the gel to be applied. She was careful and slow in her actions but in her mind her thoughts were racing. She didn't want him to be here, she didn't want him to be part of her baby's life, he had his own life, his own babies would come soon enough. She felt cornered. She couldn't say no or ask him to leave as she had already agreed to allow him to stay. What was he doing there? Had he asked one of the doctors at the medical centre to let him know when she had appointments with the midwives? She was confused and angry that he had taken her choices away from her. But he was the baby's father and maybe she should just let him be there, just this once.

The midwife prepared the ultrasound machine and popped the gel on the scanner probe. Frances watched the screen intently. Marcus tried to make eye contact with her but she continued to watch the screen. He hadn't seen or spoken to her since the night of the Christmas Ball. He now knew all about her past and her family and she didn't know that he had followed her. It made him feel like a stalker! He needed to talk to her, to support her but he had decided to give her some time and distance until after the New Year. He was very aware of how awkward this was for her but as soon as he heard the baby's heart beat on the screen he walked towards Frances and apologetically started to watch the screen as well. He needed her to nod to him to confirm that it was alright for him to see his baby but she continued to watch the screen. She was smiling. She could hear and see her baby and she smiled the biggest, most beautiful and honest smile that he had ever seen. She gave him eye contact for the briefest moment, just enough he thought to give him permission to be there.

He heard his baby for the first time. The heart beat was strong and fast. He then saw his baby for the first time, just a hazy black and white image, the heart was beating strongly. That was his baby, his son or daughter, their baby, Frances's and his! Emotion threatened to overwhelm him and he forced the urge to say something to her. Thankfully the midwife spoke and shattered the intensity of the moment.

"Well, Frances your baby is doing really well, it has a lovely healthy heartbeat and the measurements show that it's a big baby for twenty six weeks. I can tell if it's a girl or boy better today. Do you want to know?"

Frances's eyes flashed to Marcus's as if she wanted to know what he thought but just as quickly she said no to the midwife without any conversation with him. He smiled in affirmation to her.

"I think I would like to wait until my baby is born, it's the bit I'm most looking forward to and meeting my son or daughter for the first time."

"I didn't want to know the sex of mine either but most women do now so that they can get the baby's room ready and buy all the right coloured 'things' for the baby. How are you doing, have you bought much for the baby yet, got your bag packed?" Asked the midwife. Marcus remained silent.

"Yes, the room is painted now and the carpet goes down later today, I've knitted some coats and cardigans and some baby blankets too. I just need one trip down to Newcastle tomorrow and hopefully I will get the pram and the cot in the sales and maybe some other bits I need. I don't need to pack a bag as Dr Ray agreed that I could have a home birth as long as everything continued to be alright."

Marcus was shocked on hearing that she was planning a home birth and spoke before he thought. "I don't think a home birth is a good idea for someone who is having their first baby. I thought that was only an option for women who had already had one?"

"No, anyone can request a home birth if the pregnancy is progressing well and we agreed that Frances could plan for one as she is doing really well and we don't have many other women due on or around her dates so we can offer her a home birth."

"Most women in hospital are surrounded by midwives, staff, doctors and partners who are all able to offer advice and support to a new mum, I was thinking about the feeding side and breast care aspect. Wouldn't it be better for a young first mum to be surrounded by an experienced support team?"

"Ultimately it is the mum's choice where she has her baby and who supports her. You need to remember Dr Bucannon that women have been giving birth independently for thousands of years quite successfully. It's a natural process and we as midwives respect the mum's choices. We monitor and support our women and we build up relationships based on mutual trust. If we didn't think that a home birth was suitable then we advise the mothers accordingly."

Frances had remained quiet during Marcus's and the midwife's conversation but she had listened intently. Marcus was not happy about her having her baby at home. She felt very uncomfortable knowing this and also annoyed that he had passed comment. Why was it of any concern to him where she chose to have her baby?

"I'll just wipe that gel off your tummy Frances. It's all looking good for you both, do you have any questions, has that sickness finally gone?"

"Yes, thank you, I'm starting to eat normally at last, well I say normal I think I'm starting to eat more than I used to, who knew I loved bacon sandwiches so much? I've no questions really but is it still alright for me to have a home birth even after what Dr Bucannon has just said?"

"Of course, don't you worry about that. If we had any concerns we would let you know and discuss any change of plans with you. A home birth is booked in for you around the 27th March. Here is your next appointment card, you are booked in again in four weeks and then we will start to see you a little more often, usually every two weeks just to check the baby's size. Okay, I'll see you in a month's time."

Frances rearranged her clothing and sat up and got off the bed. She put her coat on and grabbed her bag and said goodbye to the midwife. She did not look at Marcus as she left the room. He shouldn't have been there, he should have left and he should not have said anything. He had spoiled the morning for her, it was such a precious time, a time to see and hear her baby and to check that it's okay and confirmation that she was doing a good job, being a good mum. She left the surgery. It was snowing now and the temperature had dropped again, she didn't feel cold, she felt too angry to feel cold. She zipped her coat up to the top and pulled up and secured her hood. It would now be a colder and a more treacherous walk up the hill back to the sanctuary of her home.

Just after five 'o' clock there was a knock at the door. It startled Frances as no one ever really came to her home. She opened the door with caution. To her instant annoyance she saw that it was Marcus, she opened the door wider.

"What do you want?" The emotion clear in her voice.

"I think we need to have a chat, don't you?"

She knew that they did need to talk about a few things, to sort things out and to set a few boundaries so with a little remorse she let him in. He took off his boots and put his coat on the bannister post.

"I'm really sorry about this morning, I had no idea that you would be there. I know you were shocked when you saw me and I should have told the midwife that it was inappropriate for me to stay. I'm sorry but in that split second when I should have done the right thing all I wanted to do was see our baby."

"My baby," she corrected him. "You are right we do need to talk. We can't change what happened this morning but it can't happen again. Congratulations on your engagement by the way." Marcus ignored her congratulatory wishes and followed her once again towards the kitchen and stood awkwardly in the doorway watching her prepare a pot of tea. They didn't speak. She got the cups and saucers down and the milk out of the fridge, she warmed the pot just like his nana had done when he was a boy. Two cups of hot tea were carried through into the lounge and placed on the coffee table. Marcus sat down and waited for her to talk.

"Marcus, what happened last summer shouldn't have happened, we are not a couple or even friends. I don't know why it happened, it was so not like me but I'm not sorry that I am pregnant or that I've decided that I'm having a baby. You are getting married soon, Felicity has been your partner for years and she is a beautiful, strong intelligent woman who you will spend the rest of your life with. You will be able to start a family with her and hopefully you will be blessed with lots of children of your own. But we are not a couple, this baby is mine. If we put your name on the birth certificate and you were at the birth, can you imagine the problems that it would cause in your life? You are the son and heir of a well- known and powerful local family and you stand to inherit not just your family's Estate but hers as well. You are a respected Doctor and a popular man locally. I can not see what benefit you would get from being in our lives? We don't need your money and being part of our lives would put the rest of your life in jeopardy. People would look at you differently, your family, your friends and would Felicity even stay with you. Your parents and brother dislike me and look down on me and you would spend the rest of your life being in conflict with the two sides of your life. I don't want that for you. You didn't plan this anymore than I did and I don't want you to suffer for something that wasn't your fault and you don't deserve to suffer any backlash from what we did. I need my baby and I want my baby. I need family and to have someone in this world who has the same blood as me. You have family, you must understand that. We can talk, you can ask about your child but I do think it is best that I bring up my baby on my own and that our child doesn't know who their father is. My baby will be brought up in a very different financial situation than yours and I don't want my child to long for the things that your children would have. Am I explaining myself to you, do you understand that I appreciate all your offers but I think in the long run its best this way?"

Marcus had listened to everything that she had to say. She had obviously thought about the situation a lot and prepared her speech. He did actually agree with every word. His family did not like her, it would be easier and definitely cheaper if he did not insist on being part of his baby's life. But he wanted his baby and even more now that he had seen it and heard its heartbeat. He wanted to be part of both of their lives but he wasn't sure if that was possible now. He picked up his cup and took a sip of the hot strong tea before he spoke. "I don't think you should have the baby at home Frances, I know you don't want me to be there and I understand that but as a doctor I wish you would reconsider and have your baby in hospital surrounded by people and appropriate machinery !"

"I know what you are saying Marcus and I honestly do appreciate your concern but it was a very easy decision for me to make. I am healthy and the pregnancy is going well and they gave me the choice so I jumped at it. You need to understand why I want my baby at home." She stood up and paced around the room before she spoke again. "I will give birth on my own, I won't have a birthing partner to support me. I had hoped that Esme would be there for me but I think that is not an option for me anymore. I am a little scared about giving birth and I think I would feel better in my own home, surrounded by my things and photos. In my mind I am planning a quick and easy birth and the midwives will be here for an hour or two after the birth. I will have the obligatory cup of tea and then I will be left alone with my baby and everything will be calm and normal. No worrying about how I'm going to get to the hospital on my own or how I'm going to get home on my own with my baby. I don't want to give birth in a strange place surrounded by people I don't know or be on a ward with other women who are surrounded by boyfriends, husbands, parents and family. It's a small maternity unit and I have had a look around it and it looks great but I don't want to see those other babies being given cards, balloons and teddy bears and being picked up and shown off when my baby will get none of that. I know you won't understand me Marcus but I do think that my way is the best way for me." She wiped away the tears that had begun to fall when she was talking.

Marcus hesitated before he spoke ensuring that he didn't mess up what he was about to say. "I do understand everything that you have just said and I understand why you feel this way and I don't want you to be on your own when you have your baby. I want to do the right thing by you, I need to help you." He fiddled with his cup and drank the last of the tea before he spoke again. He looked directly at her as he spoke. "I also need to tell you that I followed you Christmas Day and after you left the graveyard, at Rothington, I went down and read the epitaphs on the four graves that you had visited and I am so sorry, I just didn't know, I am totally lost for words really but now I know about.........your family. I will be here for you and your baby always. I want to be your birthing partner, I want to be there for my baby from day one. I want my name on his or her birth certificate. I don't want my baby to wonder who their dad is, ever."

Frances sank into one of the seats, the tears began to flow and her body shook with each sob. She didn't speak or respond in any way. Marcus did not know what to do, he sat quietly and let her cry. He wanted to pull her into his arms and tell her everything was going to be okay but he wasn't sure if that would help her or upset her more. The crying steadied and she got up and walked back into the kitchen. Marcus thought he might have got things wrong again and that she was going to throw him out. She returned with a tissue and sat down again on the sofa.

"You didn't need to follow me, I would have told you everything if you had asked. Only Esme knows about my family over there and I would appreciate it if you didn't tell anyone about it, just until I'm ready to deal with it all again." Marcus nodded his head. "I have been on my own for a long time, three years now. It was Christmas Day and we had all been invited to Aggies house for Christmas lunch. Aggie is uncle Bobs sister and had been mum's best friend from school. I wasn't feeling very well so I stayed at home and persuaded them all to still go. Uncle Bob stayed behind to finish milking the cattle and he was going to go over later. The car hit some black ice and came off the bridge at Deansway and fell over the edge and down the steep embankment and the car exploded." She hesitated. "All of them died instantly according to the coroner."

She wiped the tears away before she spoke again. Her voice was almost a whisper. "It was my decision to leave home and come here to my grandparent's house. Everyone was very kind but no one really knew what to say to me. My friends at school who I had known most of my life slowly stopped coming to see me or contacting me on the phone. My boyfriend at the time gradually stopped coming to the farm using the excuse that our 'A' levels were beginning to swamp us and needed our full attention, which was true really. Everywhere I went people would say little comments, pitying me, feeling sorry for me and I found it all too much. I eventually stopped going out and the school sent me work home. I sat my 'A' levels and did really well, 3 A*s which I think mum and dad would've been really proud of me for getting, especially under the circumstances," she wiped away the tears and blew her nose. Marcus didn't interrupt and sat quietly watching her. "I hated being around the farm. Three bedrooms were empty and it was just so quiet. My uncle Bob moved in from his cottage to look after me and the farm. He is a very quiet man, a lovely man but he had lost his wife and he was struggling too.

He took over running dad's farm and kept himself busy but eventually I couldn't stand to be in the house or even out of the house. This was my grandparent's house but they spent so much time at our house we didn't come here too often. I felt that here I could start again without people feeling constantly sorry for me. I couldn't take my place at medical school as I didn't want to leave Bert and Max alone, they had lost their family too. Uncle Bob agreed to take on the farm and I would re-invent myself here and start a new life eventually. I knew the boys were old and when something eventually happened to them my plan was to go to University and become a doctor. I had thought about selling this house and going back to the farm whilst I studied but I felt I needed a home here for just a bit longer. But now, as we both know, things have changed for me and I have decided not to train for a while. I may stay here or I may try living back at the farm with Bob, I'm not sure yet. Selling this place would give me the money to have choices but I'm afraid the farmhouse is still too painful a place for me to return to. It was a happy home once, a really happy home." She stopped talking for a moment before she spoke again. "Decisions, decisions. And that Marcus is the end of my story and the main reason why I don't want to go into hospital to have my baby, hopefully you understand everything now."

Marcus sat forward in his armchair and perched on the edge. "I'm so sorry Frances, you have suffered so much in such a short life. I am really sorry about your family, you lost so much. I cannot say anything to make things better for you but I do want to say that I admire and respect you more than you will ever know. Your strength of character is something that you should be very proud of and I'm absolutely sure that if your family were here today they would be beyond proud of you. You are the most amazing person I know."

He stood up and walked towards the hall. "I think that I have upset you more than I thought I ever would today and I am so truly sorry, I never meant to hurt you. I have been selfish trying to find out about you behind your back and I honestly don't know what to say, I don't know how I would have coped at your age. But knowing you and your story has changed me. I need to be a better man who follows his own path and his own heart. I will always put you and our little baby before myself, that is the very least that I owe you. I am the person who has made you change your plans and I need to make amends. I am prepared to tell Felicity and my family and hopefully things will stay the same for us but I will be prepared for whatever happens as long as I have my baby. Think about what you want and I promise I will do what you want. Now, I think it's time I left you in peace and stopped talking." He walked into the hall and pushed on his boots and pulled on his coat. Frances joined him as he was opening the door.

"Why were you at the doctors today really?"

"I need to change, I need to do the things that I want to do and not do the things that I am told to do. Like you, my life is going to change."

Chapter 13

"Marcus, Marcus wake up, it's nearly 8.30. We need to be in the car for nine if we want to get to Newcastle by ten. Quick, grab a shower and be dressed and downstairs as quick as you can." Felicity almost ran out of the room in her haste to get downstairs. She wanted to get into Newcastle as quickly as possible and start to get the wedding together. She had to put the Wedding Gift List into Hardy's today and she needed to order the stationary as well. She had picked up the stationary choices weeks ago but had decided on the pale grey ones with silver writing on them. She knew that Marcus wouldn't really be interested in choosing them so she had asked her mother to help. The Wedding Gift list was long, over two hundred items . She had found it difficult to cut the list down any further, it gave people choices, how much they wanted to spend and they had a choice of how many of the items on the list they wanted to buy. She had made sure that there was a large price range as some of Marcus's friends only had limited budgets. She had decided that anything that wasn't on the list she would buy anyway. Her mum had suggested that she should check the list over with Marcus just to see if he liked everything on the list as well but she had decided that Marcus was too busy to look at it.

The day had been planned out by her and the two mums. Both dads had agreed to come too! They would be going straight to Hardys, then coffee at Mateo's in the basement, then up to the top floor to look at Bridesmaids dresses, suits and maybe wedding dresses. She thought that she might plan a quick shopping trip to New York to get a wedding dress and her honeymoon clothes. Honeymoon, where did she want to go on her honeymoon? In the car she'd ask Marcus if he had any ideas? Her mum and dad had gone to Florence and then toured Italy for a week. The honeymoon had been a surprise wedding present from her mum's parents. She did not want to have a surprise honeymoon, she hated not being in control of everything. She wanted a perfect romantic honeymoon somewhere like the Maldives or the Seychelles. Only the very best for her. The honeymoon was one part of the wedding plans that she wasn't prepared to leave to anyone else.

They had spent the night at Hudson Hall Farm. She loved the house, it was more like a small stately home really and she couldn't wait to call it home. They still both had their flats in Newcastle but this was going to be the home, where they started their family. One of the flats would need to be sold, hopefully Marcus would agree to sell his as hers was in a much better location down by the Quay. Marcus's mum and dad had agreed to her moving in permanently after the wedding and had even offered them the top floor of the house which they could convert into a luxury 2 bedroomed apartment which, of course, she had jumped at. In the new year she would start to put out some feelers for a good architect who would help her design the flat of her dreams. The flat for now was her second priority, she had a wedding to plan and her head was just full of amazing ideas.

Marcus appeared in the kitchen just before the allocated time suitably dressed in dark jeans, a pale blue jumper and a navy jacket.

"Do I have time to grab a quick coffee before we go or...." Five sets of eyes stared at him but it was his father that spoke.

"Son you are going wedding shopping and the first thing that you must learn is that your wedding is the only thing that matters now. Every conversation for the next six months will include the word 'wedding'. Except it and don't fight it, that is the only advice that I can give to you." He lifted up a thermos beaker and handed it to his son as they all walked out of the kitchen.

The drive down was noisy. The two dads had gone down in Mr Bucannon's car and Marcus had Felicity and the two mums with him. From the minute they left the house to the minute they arrived in the car park next to Hardys the only topic of conversation had been the wedding, the honeymoon and the suggestion by Felicity that she would need to go to Fintons to get the ring size changed and that whilst there she might just have a quick look at the other ones to see if there were any other 'lovely' rings. That meant in Felicity language, 'I'm going to see if there is a much better and a much bigger ring which I want and not the one that you chose for me'. Marcus didn't pass comment and just continued to listen to the three overpowering women. His dad had parked up already when he arrived and he pulled into the space next to him. Hardys was a very old shop in Newcastle, it had been established over a hundred years ago. He liked the fact that it looked old and imposing on the outside but super modern and luxurious inside. Only the old lifts that clanked their way up and down each day and the ornate staircase gave away the true age of the building. Soon they were all walking through the front doors of Hardys, chattering noisily, walking towards the set of lifts at the back of the luxury department store.

"First stop is the top floor, I need to drop off our choice of stationary and then I need to hand in the Wedding Gift

List so that it can go online as soon as possible. Then I thought it would be a good time for a coffee break at Mateo's in the basement and then back up to look at wedding dresses and suits. This is just so exciting guys." She grabbed hold of Marcus and squeezed his arm and kissed his cheek. Marcus was not expecting either from her and both actions immediately incensed him but he held his tongue and just smiled at her. What was wrong with him. He felt like an alien in this group today yet he had known them all of his life. He waited for the lift that he had called to arrive. Moments later the bell rang and the brass doors opened. Stood, alone at the back of the lift was Frances. Everyone in the group stood and stared at her for a few seconds before they went into the lift.

"Hello Frances, how are you?" Marcus was the first to speak. Frances smiled at him in response. The others all turned their backs on her as they found their positions in the lift. Marcus pressed the button for the top floor.

"I am very surprised to see you here, in Hardys Frances, I didn't think here was your sort of shop at all." Said his mother. Before Frances had a chance to respond Felicity spoke. "I heard that some of the supermarkets do some amazing baby products now, cots, pushchairs, clothing especially designed for the people with very low incomes or no incomes at all. Have you managed to find another job yet, it was strange how you lost all three jobs in just two days." She smiled still looking forward at the brass doors. Both mothers and fathers laughed at her comments. Frances continued to stare at the floor and did not speak or respond to the comments. Her heart was beginning to race and she was suddenly feeling very trapped and claustrophobic in the lift.

Marcus's father turned around and then spoke directly to her. "I'd offer you a job on my estate or in the kitchen but sadly I'm unable to take on anyone who has been sacked." He laughed out loud at his own joke and the others joined in apart from Marcus who continued to stare at the lift control buttons. He could feel his heart thumping in his chest now, his hands had fisted and he felt like he was just about to explode when the lift stopped, the bell rang and the doors opened allowing Frances to escape.

She pushed her way out of the lift and ignored the sarcastic farewell comments that were aimed at her. She paced away from the lift as fast as she could towards the Mother and Baby section. She felt sick and a little faint, she needed to sit down and quickly. She saw the sign for the toilets and quickly made a detour to them pushing open the door before locating the cubicles and locked herself in. Her heart was pounding and she felt sick, really sick. She concentrated on slowing her breathing down, she closed her eyes and rested back against the door. Her mind was racing and the tears began to flow uncontrollably. She needed to stop crying every five minutes, she had no time for gestational emotions. What had she done to deserve that from them or anybody, they were such a horrible, mean group of people. She stood with her back to the door for a few minutes more. Eventually the tears stopped and her heart slowed down. She was suddenly feeling exhausted. It had been a long day already and it was only 10.30.

The bus trip had been longer and more arduous than she had envisaged. She didn't feel like shopping now for the things for her baby. Today was supposed to have been a happy day for her, the exciting day that she had waited for when she was going to buy the cot, pram set and all the other bits she needed for her baby. And that group of nasty people had spoiled it for her! She decided that it was best if she found somewhere to have a sit down, have a drink and see how she felt in another hour or so. She composed herself and opened the cubicle door and walked around the corner to wash her hands and to splash some water on her face. A grey haired lady, who wore a Hardys uniform dress stood up from one of the comfort chairs and spoke to Frances.

"I'm sorry to intrude, but I did notice you run from the lift to the ladies and I noticed that you seemed....upset and you were on your own. Tell me to go away if you want but you looked like you were coming to see me in the Mother and Baby department and wondered if you were unwell or needed help?" The kind lady's eyes fell to Frances's tummy.

"Thank you, that is so kind of you but I'm Okay, really. The bus trip in was long and I felt quite hot and claustrophobic in the lift but I'm fine now. I think I need to find a little café somewhere and have something to eat before I carry on."

"Absolutely, I remember when I was pregnant over the summer with my first one, it felt like I had a permanent hot water bottle strapped to my tummy and I constantly felt hot and bothered. Go and eat, get a sit down and hopefully I will see you later. We have some lovely things in the department and in about an hour I'll be putting some of it in the sale." The kind lady held the door open for Frances and she headed back to her department. Frances decided to use the stairs and not risk the lift again. She walked carefully down holding the thick metal bannister and went out of the shop. She decided that she needed some fresh air for a while before she found a café so stopped and sat down on a bench that was on the same street as Hardys. The lady had been very kind to her, so different from Marcus's family in the lift, she reflected on how different people could be, some kind and some mean. She was beginning to feel better already.

The lift stopped at the top floor , the bell rang and the doors opened. The noisy mothers and loud Felicity left first and walked towards the Bridal Boutique followed by the fathers. Marcus felt as if his feet had been glued to the floor and he just couldn't lift his feet to walk out of the lift. Not that he wanted to follow them. He was angry and disgusted in each and every one of them, he knew immediately he could not marry Felicity and he was finally going to stand up to his parents and tell them his new future plans. The lift doors closed on their own and the lift started to go down stopping at the third floor where Frances had got out. The Mother and Baby floor. Without thinking and with no real plan in his head he got out of the lift and went to look for Franny. He searched for her but couldn't find her.

"Can I help you sir," said an elderly assistant. "You look like you are looking for something in particular?"

"Hi, yes I am. I'm looking for a friend who I think just came in here, she was wearing a black coat, small petite, quite pregnant..."

"Yes, sir she did come in briefly but she decided she needed some refreshments before she started to have a look around."

"Great, thank you, has she gone down to the basement?"

"I don't know sir, sorry"

"Marcus ran to the lifts and pushed the call buttons for all of them. They didn't come fast enough for him so he rushed to the stairs and ran down them to the basement level as quickly as he could. His eyes scanned the café and the food hall but he couldn't see her. He walked around checking that she wasn't hidden away on a table out of view, his body panicked when he couldn't see her. His heart was thumping in his chest and sweat was forming on his forehead. God, where was she? He had so let her down this morning. He should have said something, stood up for her, shut them down, made them apologise to the mother of this baby. Christ he was such an idiot. She was more to him than all of the others put together. He needed her and he absolutely wanted her. Sleeping with her hadn't been a mistake he absolutely wanted her, needed her just like he needed air. He absolutely had to find her.

He took his phone out of his pocket and quickly found her number and rang her. It rang and rang but she didn't answer the phone. He ran upstairs to the ground floor and ran towards the main doors. Quickly he was outside on the street looking up and down it frantically searching for her, for his Franny. He desperately needed to find her, to tell her how he felt, his plans and his dreams and he wanted her to be the biggest part of it. Left or right, which way should he go? He turned left towards the quieter end of the street, he thought that would be the way that she would go. He started to run up the street and then just as he thought his heart could take no more he saw her sitting alone on one of the benches. The relief was instant and so too were the tears. He stood and looked at her and let the tears gradually stop. He took a deep breath and walked towards her.

"Hi Franny, I have been looking for you everywhere. The lady in Hardys said that you had gone off to get a drink. I have been frantic trying to find you to apologise to you, I let you down, again, and I am so very sorry. Are you alright?" He didn't sit down next to her but perched at the other end of the bench to her. He waited for her answer.

"I'm alright, I'm always alright." She said quietly.

The silence between them seemed relentless to Marcus.

"What my parents said to you was unforgivable and I am so very sorry. Felicity doesn't know it yet but that's us finished, I can't take one more day of her or her family. Stupidly I've let these people plan and organise my life and even worse, I didn't know what they were doing until it was too late. And I am so ashamed of myself too. In the lift I should have said something, I should have told them to stop being so nasty to you, to shut up but I felt like I was going to explode myself. If the lift hadn't stopped when it had and let you out, I honestly don't know what I would have said or done. I am so sorry, are you sure you are okay, I was so worried?"

"I was just thinking to myself about your family. I am not sure what is worse really. To have lost all your family in a tragic car accident, a loving, caring, brilliant family or to have a selfish, nasty, living family who don't seem to care about who you are or what makes you the person you are. What do you think?"

Marcus snorted. "I think that may be a question for another time because at the moment my answer would be too emotional." He smiled and sat back on the bench. This time the silence seemed calmer and mutual.

"I think we need a coffee and something to eat before I go home. There is a lovely little coffee shop just down the street, would you like to join us?" Frances shocked herself when she asked him to join her but it did seem the right thing to do. Marcus stood up and held out a hand to Franny to help her stand up. They walked up the street and eventually came to a little café. It was much quieter than the others they had passed. A tiny bell rang when they opened the door. They were directed to sit in one of the booths on the back wall. A waitress came over to greet them and to hand out the menus. They settled into their seats and removed their coats and scarves. Marcus ordered just a coffee and Frances ordered a pot of tea and a bacon sandwich.

"Sorry but I do seem to be hungry all the time now and bacon sandwiches do appear to have become my secret craving." Marcus noticed just how her eyes danced and smiled when she spoke, he could watch her talk all day. He knew she was the most stunning woman he had ever met and he seemed to be falling in love with her more and more with every passing by second. He was now free of his past and little by little he seemed to be allowing himself to fall in love with his future.

The waitress brought their hot drinks to the table first and quickly returned with the bacon sandwich for Frances.

"Snap," she said in a broad northern accent. "When are you due, I'm due in 8 weeks now, can't wait, I'm having a little girl, Lilybeth after the queen, what about you?"

The smile on France's face was instant. Someone who didn't know her was asking her about her baby, it was the first time that someone had just asked her about her baby and she suddenly felt excited.

"I do like Lilybeth, such a pretty name. I have 12 weeks to go and I agree, I can't wait to have my baby it's just so exciting. I'm here to buy a pram and cot today, but I don't know if I'm having a girl or a boy yet which adds to the excitement but it also limits me because I just cannot decide what colour pram to buy. Have you got yours yet?" She asked eagerly.

"I have, I went for a white cot and bed set and a red pram from M and D's. Have you been there, it's an amazing shop, it sells everything you could possibly want for your baby, you should go and have a look."

"Where is it, is it the one near the football stadium?"

"Yes, that's the place, they have a great sale on now so it is worth a look and they are online too. Sorry, I am keeping you chatting and your breakfast is getting cold. Enjoy and good luck." The waitress left Frances to enjoy her breakfast.

"That was nice, that was the first conversation that I have had about my baby that wasn't medical or without conflict. I like talking like that, about being a mum!"

Marcus realised the magnitude of such a simple statement, here she was, over 6 months pregnant and she had just had her first honest and open conversation with someone about her baby. He felt so sad for her, he was the cause of that, he had made her hide it away from people. The smile on her face showed that she was happy and had enjoyed that brief interaction with another expectant mum and that made him feel positive too.

"Have you thought about names yet or which you would prefer a girl or a boy?"

Frances finished the last bit of her sandwich before she spoke. "I want a healthy and a happy baby and preferably a baby that sleeps a lot too," she smiled. "I'm honestly not bothered if I have a girl or a boy but I have chosen my boys name and I am struggling with the girls, I've got three that I like."

"Do you want to tell me them or are you keeping them to yourself until the very last minute" Marcus smiled, happy that she was letting him join in the conversation.

Frances suddenly gushed with excitement. "For a boy I like Bertie Maximus James Barnabas Tulip and the girl names I think I like are Eliza and Clara after my family but when I was a little girl I always liked the names Fleur and Florence, Fleur means flower in French. I sometimes think it may be better if I give her a new name and use the family names as her other names, like Fleur Florence Eliza Clara or Fleur Clara Eliza Tulip." She smiled at her own excitable voice. "Sorry." Marcus could instantly see her closing down and withdrawing back into being her usual self and he needed to act quickly.

"I absolutely love all those names, both unusual, personal and chosen with thought and love. I remember you once saying that you liked the name Jet. I love that name. I don't think it really matters if you have a boy or a girl now as either would be guaranteed a really good strong name. Well done you, good choices." He did not comment on the surname which he did hear as Tulip , he wanted it to be Bucannon but after the events of today he understood why and could almost be tempted to change his own name. "Have you finished? I think we need to get going and start to buy lots of nice things for you and your baby. I would love to join you if I may?" The phone in his pocket began to buzz. He grabbed the phone and saw instantly that it was Felicity calling. He noticed that he had been absent for nearly an hour and they had only just phoned him to ask where he was. He answered the phone and put it to his ear.

"For god's sake Marcus where the hell are you? Our fathers have chosen the suits that they want to wear and I have seen a few nice bridesmaid's dresses but no bridal gowns are suitable for me here. You need to get back here now, we need to sort out the wedding stationary and the

Wedding List. Where are you anyway?" He briefly looked at Frances before he spoke, she sat quietly in her coat watching him. "I'm sitting in a lovely little café and I have just finished a lovely cup of filter coffee enjoying myself. I'm not coming back to Hardys." Before he had a chance to say anything Felicity angrily started to speak again.

"What the hell Marcus, get back here straight away, weddings don't plan themselves and you know I had booked a table at Mateo's for us. Get back here now!" She shouted.

"Sorry but I'm not coming back now or ever." He felt heat develop in his face and the anger rise in his body. "The wedding is off, we are off and tell my mother and father that I will be in contact with them when I have eventually calmed down enough to talk to them. Tell my dear mother that I will also arrange a suitable time to call round to pick up the rest of my belongings, a time to suit me. Now I must go, I have new plans." He kept his eyes on Frances when he spoke watching for the smallest reaction. There was none. He turned his phone off. And put it back in his pocket.

"Would it be alright if I came with you to M and Ds and Hardys to look for baby things. I really would like to be part of our baby's life now and always. I know it's a big ask but I promise that I will never let you down again. I now know what is important and what I want to do with the rest of my life thanks to you." He added.

Marcus stood up and pulled his coat on and grabbed the receipt read it and put some money down on the plate. Frances stood up and thanked him for paying, she didn't feel it was an appropriate time to ask if he wanted to go dutch! She followed him to the door which he opened and pulled back to allow her to leave first, he shouted bye to the waitress who was busy serving her next customer. "Where to now then, if your family are still at Hardys? I for one really don't want to run into them again." Frances felt uncomfortable at the thought of meeting any of them now or even in the future.

"It is funny how quickly it has turned into them and us isn't it. I think if we were to go back to the car park now dad's car will have gone and mine will be left, probably with a long scratch down the side." They smiled. As predicted when they reached the car park his dad's car had gone and luckily there was no scratch down the side of his. "I am sorry Marcus about today, its just so sad that you have fallen out with your family and fiancée. I don't think you are anything like them but they are your family and you must love them?"

Marcus took her arm and guided her back towards the entrance to the Shop.

"I love my mother, brother and father very much but I have to accept that things are different now. I will talk to them and things will be sorted out but this time they will have to listen to me like they have always apparently done with my brother. I found out on Christmas day that they knew that Robert and Miles were in a relationship together and they didn't mind one bit. They had just been waiting for Robert to tell them in person before they said anything. They accept that Miles and Robert live together, will probably get married and both live as two *happy* vets somewhere, happily ever after. For me it was always very different. I was brought up as the older son and alot of expectations have been placed on me always. Felicity, medical school and the Estate to say just a few. But recently things have changed for me. I want a life that I chose, do things that I want to do and be with people that I want to be with. That definitely includes you and Bertie or Fleur. My family need to accept that I want different things for myself than the things that they have wanted for me. Felicity will be happier in the long run too. I think she will go and live in New York or Sydney without me tying her down. I think she has been trapped too, her family have always pushed and moulded her. I think she is more suited to a fast life in a city with a penthouse apartment, a flash car in her parking bay and a large group of girl friends who she can go shopping with. I'm not really sure that she wanted to get married or start a family herself or if it was just something expected of her and she did just what her parents asked her to do. Just like me."

"Maybe. Well, after that very long speech I need to go in and find the loo again." Frances was not sure what to say or think. Marcus seemed to have turned his whole life upside down and even though he had tried to explain why he had done it, she wasn't really sure that she did understand.

After a short ride in the lift and a quick trip to the toilet she joined him in the Mother and Baby department looking at the prams. With him was the nice lady whom she had spoken to earlier. "Hello again, are you ready to have a look around now?" Frances smiled and followed the lady to the start of the row of pushchairs and prams, escorted by Marcus.

Chapter 14

They didn't go to M and Ds baby superstore as they had managed to get everything they needed at Hardys. They had so much fun looking at all the different things and making decisions. Marcus had made all the assistants laugh when he asked if there was an electric pram option yet on the market. At first both Frances and Marcus were awkward in the department, tip toeing around each other and Marcus had been really careful not to say too much or too little. Frances had cleared the air a little when she had pulled him to one side away from the assistant and spoke to him. She had said that if they were going to do this together then they needed to do this together. Marcus had agreed that they needed to be a team and that included paying for everything together. He didn't think it was the right time to offer to pay for everything. That had cleared the air and from then on, they just had a lot of fun choosing, planning, discussing and laughing.

They had bought a pram, cot, car seat, pushchair, more bedding, mobile, toys, bath, baby towels, bottles, baby monitor and some baby clothes by the time they had left. Marcus had persuaded her to let him pay for everything on his credit card now and that they would sort it out later which she did agree too. The bigger items would be delivered in a few days but all of the smaller items were packed in lots of bags and to be taken home directly. She was thankful that Marcus had brought his car, she had not been looking forward to the trip home on the bus. They quickly loaded up the boot and the back seat with all the bags and purchases, Frances couldn't believe how much they had bought.

"That was so much fun, thank you so much for letting me come and join in. I will stand by my invention though, I do plan to invent an electric pram, I think we would make a killing!"

"You are so funny, the assistants didn't know what to say to you, I think they all had a great time laughing at your jokes and impressions of babies." She smiled and shuffled down in the car seat, she felt relaxed and happy in his car. Looking out of the window as they drove home she saw the night had drawn in and the lights had started to switch on.

"What time is it please?" Marcus looked at the car clock. "Wow, its nearly 3.30. I can't believe we spent so long in there. Are you okay, are you hungry?"

"Yes and I'm really sorry but I think I may need the loo as well!"

Marcus put his indicator on and gracefully pulled the car off the road and headed out into the darkness of the country side. "There is a lovely little Inn up here, St Mary's Rose, we can grab a meal, my treat and you can go and nip to the ladies." They pulled up into the car park. Marcus dropped her off at the door, parked the car up and went into the inn. He spoke to the bar tender who grabbed some menus and took Marcus over to a small table by the window. Frances joined him a few minutes later.

"Better?" Marcus asked.

"Much better, thank you." Replied Frances. They each read the menu and placed their orders with the waitress.

"This is all very exciting, we have never been out for a meal together before and today we have manged to go to a café and a pub and we have spent most of the day buying everything possible 'to buy' for your baby. Not a bad second date?" He cringed as the words came out of his mouth. "Sorry I didn't mean that it just came out, I wasn't thinking, I was trying to make you laugh."

Frances sat back in her chair and let the waiter place the drinks on the table before she spoke. "I think the word I would use is unbelievable! This morning I dragged myself out of bed at 7, forced myself to endure an hour on the bumpiest bus in the word, had an unpleasant episode in a lift with your mother, father and fiancée, cried in a toilet cubicle and cried on a public bench in the middle of Newcastle. And here I am now in a posh pub, having spent most of the day with you choosing everything our baby would ever need and probably will never need. I don't really know what to say apart from thank you. I know we need to sort things out further but thanks for today, for being with me and helping me choose things. It was more fun with you." They smiled at each other and settled into eating their meals which the waiter had just brought over. The conversation remained cheerful while they ate, talking about school, holidays and sport. They finished their meal, Marcus paid without an argument from Frances and they were soon on the road home.

Twenty minutes later they had pulled up outside Frances's house. She walked up the steps to open the door and to put the lights on. Marcus opened the boot and started to unload the car. He declined her offer to help him, happy in this fatherly role. He kicked his boots off and then took all the bags up to the baby's room and put them on the new carpet. He looked around the room and felt contentment. He ran down the stairs where she was waiting for him in the hall.

"I love the carpet, it looks great. I've just left everything on the floor so you can sort it out at your leisure. You look tired. I think its best if I left you to put your feet up and get some rest."

"Thank you so much for doing that for me, it would have taken me about a day to go up and down those stairs. Thank you, I think I do need to put my feet up and have a little sleep now. Who knew that shopping could be such hard work. Thank you again for today, for breakfast and dinner and for taxiing me around."

"Any time, your chauffeur awaits. Right I think I need to get back to my flat now." He picked his phone up out of his pocket whilst talking to her and turned it back on. Eventually it burst into life. Ten voicemails and thirty six text messages. He put the phone away but knew that the next few hours were going to be busy on his phone. He would wait till he got back to his flat in Newcastle before he contacted anyone. He wanted to enjoy today for just a little bit longer. Frances saw his face change when he looked at his phone.

"Everything alright?"

"It will be, I think I need to make a few phone calls when I get back to my flat and start to sort a few things out. Look." he hesitated. "I'm coming back up here tomorrow for a few hours, there is something I need to do and if you are not doing anything I would really appreciate your advice. It's a plan I have in my head and I'd love it if you would come with me?" Without any hesitation Frances agreed.

"I'll pick you up at twelve, prompt, see you tomorrow. Thanks for today, I can't tell you how much it means to me." He thought about kissing her on the cheek or another small show of his feelings but decided against doing either. And then he was gone.

Frances was exhausted. It had been such a very strange unpredictable day indeed. She ran herself a nice hot bath and then changed into her pyjamas and dressing gown. She settled down on the sofa with a hot chocolate night cap and watched the end of a DVD she had started yesterday. Her mind kept wondering and she struggled to concentrate on the film. What a strange day! It had started badly but it had ended well. Marcus had been so kind to her all day despite the obvious problems that were mounting for him. She wondered what he was doing now. She hoped that he wouldn't be persuaded to go back to Felicity, she really was a horrible person, so rude and cruel. He deserved to be happy, to do what he wanted to do. As her mum had always said to her 'you only get one life so use it well'. It was so true. Her mum and dad had always been great together. She remembered them being happy, kissing and dancing in the kitchen after the washing up was finished. Her dad always took her mum out, bought her flowers and they always had date nights. He always put her before him . She was lucky, she had been brought up in a happy home, full of laughter, music, large family gatherings and love. She deserved that and wanted that for herself and she wanted it for Marcus too. She had agreed to let him be part of her baby's life now. He had given up so much, lost so much to be part of her baby's life. He had said he had done it all willingly, wanted to change his own life and be happy but she worried about how much the changes would affect him.

As Marcus drove home he felt nothing but relief and happiness. He was sorry that his parents would be hurt and angry at him but hopefully they would in time forgive him and understand him. If they didn't, couldn't forgive him, then he would totally understand and accept their decision. They loved Robert unconditionally and the decisions that he had made and he was sure, eventually, that they would forgive and accept him too. He also hoped that they would understand about Frances and his baby and come to love and care for their first grandchild. The baby was now a big part of his life. The relationship between them and Frances would always be a difficult one sadly, his mother and father were set in their ways and he couldn't see future big family occasions together at Christmas or Easter.

He wasn't sure what Frances thought about them as she said very little to him but he thought that she was far more accommodating than any of his family were. He needed to spend some time with Felicity to explain everything that had happened to him and why he had changed so much and so quickly. She would give him a hard time he knew that, the big throw the ring at him, shout at him but he knew that it was something that just needed to be dealt with. Luckily, they had both decided to keep their own flats in Newcastle, so no dividing up of a home. He had wanted her to move into his flat when she first talked about buying her own flat but she was adamant that she had a place of her own, just for a short time in between living at home with her parents and living with him. He always thought that she may have had other reasons for having her own flat but looking back now, he was happy to have his own space as well so hadn't asked any questions. Tonight, he would call his parents, he wasn't quite sure what he was going to say to them yet! And then he would call Paul. He would tell his parents in person about Frances and his baby, their grandchild and tell them about his other plans. He thought he would do that tomorrow afternoon if Frances agreed to his plan. Paul was the person he needed to talk to at the moment, he wanted to tell him everything about the day's events. He was so happy and he just wanted to share it with him, to talk about being a dad. He wanted to talk to him about Frances, to say how he felt and to ask for some final advice.

When he arrived back at his flat it was early evening and the flat was in darkness. He unlocked the door and found that Felicity had already been there. Cupboards and drawers had been left open and everything that she had left in the flat had gone. He went into the bedroom which had been stripped of almost all belongings including the curtains and bedding. All her clothes and shoes had been emptied out of the wardrobe. She had left a mess behind her in the kitchen too. Presents from friends and keep sakes from holidays had been smashed all over the kitchen. Marcus ignored the mess and grabbed a bottle of beer, pulled off the top and found a space on the sofa. The lounge was the least affected room and so the most normal place to sit to phone Paul. As the call connected he wondered if he would ever get his clothes back from her flat or if he even wanted them back. It was time to redecorate this place in a fashion to suit him.

Paul had been his closest friend for years and the one person who Marcus totally trusted. He was honest, blunt and always loyal. He was a very important person in Marcus's life and his opinions did matter. An hour later they finished their phone call. He had told him everything that had happened and they had laughed and he had to admit he had cried. He couldn't wait to be a dad and today for the first time, he truly felt that he was going to be a real, hands on daddy. She had let him in again, she had trusted him. She had laughed and teased him and been honest with him. Marcus had asked Paul if he thought that there was any chance for them to be together, be a couple as well as being parents together. Paul being Paul had told him that there was only one sure way to find out. He ended the phone call feeling positive and enthusiastic about tomorrow.

Chapter 15

Frances tossed and turned all night. Two cups of tea and some biscuits had been consumed in the early hours of the morning when the sky outside was still dark and full of stars. Frances often stood at the open back door of her home looking up at the stars, wondering if her family were up there, maybe somewhere. She hoped that they were up there, looking down over her and keeping an eye on her. She wondered what they would think of her right now, this very minute and what advise her mum and dad would give her. Yesterday had been a strange day in so many ways and lots of decisions had been made without her realising. She definitely wasn't going to sell her dad's car, she needed it and missed it so much when she was on the bus. She had spent so much money yesterday and she had enjoyed every minute of spending it on her baby. She had enjoyed being with her baby's father. He was a good man, he had been as trapped as she had been, in a life that he hadn't planned for himself and to break free from it he had hurt lots of people. He had proved beyond anything to her that he wanted to be a father and be part of his child's life. She smiled.

Her baby was going to have a mummy and a daddy and she was pleased that her baby would have him around. She could have managed on her own, helped by uncle Bob and Aggie but now she would have them and Marcus. She had struggled to sleep for a number of reasons. She couldn't get comfortable in the bed, she had slept on the sofa for so long the bed felt alien to her. She needed the toilet all the time even when she limited what she drank. And she could not stop worrying about Marcus. He seemed happy with her, he had enjoyed the shopping trip and the meal at the pub but she had a feeling that he wasn't being totally honest with her. He had tried not to speak about his fall out with Felicity and his family all day but he must be hurting and suffering.

Morning arrived eventually and she had managed to grab some sleep and felt a lot better. She had a lovely long shower and dressed carefully, drying her long hair straight with the hairdryer. She thought long and hard what to wear but the choice was ultimately made by what she could actually fit into. Her maternity jeans and a baby pink jumper were quickly put on. She felt excited about going out today, with him! Perfume applied she went down to have breakfast and to do some tasks in the kitchen. It seemed strange to her how quickly things had changed. Her future didn't look quite as dark as it had before. Later in the morning she sat on the chair in the baby's room and looked at all the bags of goodies for her and her baby which she had left in the middle of the floor. There was so much and more was due to be delivered. She wanted to unpack the bags and cut the labels off and start to sort them out but she hesitated in doing that. She wanted Marcus to be there when they put the cot up and put the bedding on for the first time. She wanted him to help put the pram together and assemble the baby mobile above the cot. She sat back in the chair and was surprised at herself for suddenly wanting Marcus to be such a big part of her life now.

With her perfume re-applied and a hint of lip gloss on she was ready and waiting for him when he knocked on the door. Marcus looked at her before he spoke. He stopped and stared at her. She looked stunning. Her hair was so long and straight, it touched the top of her hips and moved gently when she walked.

"Morning, sorry I just, well, wow, I love your hair and it is just so, well beautiful. You have such beautiful hair, you are beautiful. Sorry, err, are you ready?"

Frances laughed as she had never seen him lost for words before. She noticed that he had tried to look his best too. He had dark denim jeans on, a dark blue shirt and dark blue quilted jacket, with dark brown brogues. He smelt wonderful. He leant forward and gave her a quick peck on the cheek. Frances blushed slightly.

"Hi, it isn't often I get a chance to let my hair down," she laughed at her own joke. "I wear it up for work and so it's usually just up or plaited down the back. How are you? Did you have a tough time last night after you left me, I was worried about you?" All Marcus seemed to hear was that she was worried about him, that meant she cared about him even just a little.

"It was alright. I spoke to Paul for about an hour or so and I told him everything that happened yesterday. He has been my best friend for years and I trust and respect him totally. I did tell him that I was your baby's dad and to keep it quiet, which he will. But I was just so excited yesterday, being with you, talking about our baby, names, shopping and our meal together, friends at last I was just so happy, high on life. He did tell me to call my parents which I did and I'm going over to see them later on today to try and sort things out."

"It is your decision who you tell. If you really want to be on the birth certificate then you can tell anyone you want. I like Paul, he was always very kind and generous to me."

"I really want my name on the birth certificate Frances. I want our baby to have two parents who care and love it. I want it more than I could ever tell you," he said with genuine sincerity. "Paul really likes you, he really does. He honestly had so many nice things to say about you that I was almost feeling a little jealous and annoyed at him. He was so mad at my mum for forcing him to let you go and said that he felt like throttling her at the Christmas Ball. She wouldn't have felt his hands though as she was so drunk! He has asked if he could be a godfather now that he isn't being a best man, he said he has free time." Marcus smiled enthusiastically.

"He also said that being a dad is the absolute best thing that has ever happened to him and I promised that I will be the best dad in the world." He stopped talking for a moment before he spoke again. "Sorry, I'm going on and on again. I know it is very quick but I wondered what your thoughts are regarding telling my parents?"

Frances picked her coat up off the peg, put it on and pulled up the zip. She sat down on the step and pulled on her boots before she spoke. "It is up to you and I do respect that they are your parents but I don't think that they will ever accept us and even if they did I think it would take a long time for things to settle down. I think that it's up to you but I am happy for you to tell them especially if you are going to put your name on the birth certificate. Have you heard from Felicity?"

"Thank you, I think you are probably right but I have an overwhelming desire to tell the world and I think it's best if it comes from me today. We do have three months before we need to say anything, enough time for us to leave the country! Felicity left a lot of angry voicemails on my mobile yesterday which I will respond to when she's calmed down a bit. She went to my flat yesterday and emptied it, her stuff and a lot of mine. She had a smashing time in the kitchen, literally, she smashed loads of stuff on the floor but that can all be replaced at some point. I suppose she was allowed to be angry, I did finish with her whilst she was in the middle of wedding dress shopping". Frances pulled a face but said nothing.

Twenty minutes later they were driving up the coast road towards a small village called Limoton. It was a pretty little village that was on the coast. A few fishing boats sat in the harbour bobbing up and down on the gentle waves. Baskets and nets piled high against the sea wall, occasional fishermen trying their luck. Frances had always liked coming here, it was quaint and very picturesque. There was a small pub which she remembered going to with her family for Sunday lunch, a small Methodist church and small shop.

"Are we going for lunch at the pub?" She still didn't know why he had picked her up or where they were going or why he had asked her to bring her wellies. She was intrigued. Maybe it was lunch at the pub and a walk along the beach.

"Maybe later but I have an appointment at 12.30 and I would love it if you could be there with me. Here we are." He drove down the small lane for about a quarter of a mile before he stopped next to some old farm buildings. He looked at her by his side, she looked confused. He laughed as he observed her confusion. Another car arrived at almost the same time and pulled up next to them.

"Come on, it's time to go and have a look. Now you know why you need your wellies." He grinned.

Marcus got out of the car and walked over to the other gentleman who was just getting out of his car. They shook hands and both chatted for a few minutes before returning to their own car boots and getting their wellies out. Marcus got Franny's out and walked round to the passenger door, opened it and handed the wellies to her.

"You will need your wellies on now," he grinned.

"Mr Glover, this is Frances, Frances this is Mr Glover from Glover Forbes and Mayhew, Land agents." They both said hello to each other and then Mr Glover offered to show them the way allowing the couple to follow him to the old farmhouse which was found behind all the farm buildings. He opened the tired front door with an old metal key then pushed the door open with his shoulder and walked into the dark and tired porch.

"Welcome to **Southlands**. You are the first people who have had the opportunity to have a look around this wonderful old family farm. It is unusual to put a property up for sale like this at christmas but as you can see it has been empty, for quite a while. The family have decided that it is the right time for them to sell and they now want a quick sale, hence the attractive price. The main farmhouse dates back to the 1890's we believe. The sale includes the farmhouse, four outbuilding, one corrugated barn used to store the farm machinery which is also available to buy separately with the vendors, and the fifty acres of prime agricultural land. The property sits on the beautiful Northumberland coast and you have direct access to the beach. There is a small half acre pond at the north of the farm and shooting rights are also included. The track is also included in the sale. It is approximately a third of a mile long and the responsibility of maintenance falls to this property with another property having legal usage of part of the track. There is an ample sized hallway, a kitchen, utility room, boot room, drawing and dining room on the ground floor and the five large bedrooms and a bathroom are found on the first floor. It has been empty, for almost two years and now requires extensive refurbishment. If you would like to follow me I will show you around the main house and then we can go outside to look at the outbuildings and the rest of the farm. I have some extra brochures for you and if you have any questions please do not hesitate to ask me and I will try to answer them. Let's start in the kitchen, the room that is the most important room in the house, especially to the ladies."

Marcus smiled at Frances, he knew that she had no idea what was going on but she seemed to enjoy playing along with him. She smiled back at him. The house was beautiful. It still had all its original wooden doors throughout and the cast iron fireplaces were all in great condition. The kitchen needed to be extended and totally rearranged before any units could be fitted. Marcus was falling in love with the house as he walked around it. He had decided to buy the farm by the time he stood by the window in the largest bedroom. The view was amazing, uninterrupted views over the beach and coast. It was stunning and it had stolen his heart totally. He looked down at Frances who also looked lost in the amazing view. Mr Glover moved into the next room unaware of what was happening between Frances and Marcus. He invited them to follow him.

"What do you think Franny, do you think it has potential?"

"It is a beautiful house and the views are amazing. Can you imagine waking up to that view every day? It's mesmerising. But I don't understand, are you thinking of buying it?" He smiled like a Cheshire cat and beckoned her playfully to follow him with his finger, he knew that she loved it too. She obliged.

The outbuildings were all in good order, still with roofs and still standing but full of junk. It didn't look like any animals had been on the farm in years.

"The vendors parents used to mix farm here years ago but let the farm fall into ruin when it became too much for them. They had been in a home locally but the children chose not to sell the farm until their parents had passed away. It needs a lot of hard work and a lot of money to be allocated to this property but I am sure that it will be a wonderful family home again. You are free to walk the full extent of the acreage on your own and look at the lake and the coastline, and take in those amazing views. Do you have any questions before I go?"

"No, I think that I'm good, how about you Franny, do you have any questions?"

She shook her head and spoke to Mr Glover. "Thank you for showing us around the farm. It is absolutely beautiful and has so much potential, goodbye." Marcus walked Mr Glover back to his car and talked to him whilst the older man changed his boots. Frances looked at the front of the house as the two men talked. It had a pretty frontage. The oak front door had seen much better days and sat lopsided on the hinges. The door was at the top of millstone steps in the middle of the house surrounded by overgrown wisteria. Two wooden windows sat either side of the front door and three more windows sat on the top floor, all the same size and all an equal distance from each other. It was such a lovely building. It reminded her of a child's drawing of their perfect house. The setting was amazing and the views were to die for. This farmstead would make a fabulous family home for someone. She just couldn't understand why Marcus was looking to buy it and why he had brought her with him to view it. He was due to inherit Hudson Hall and he had his flat in Newcastle near the hospital. She was totally confused.

The car started up behind her and Mr Glover gave her a big smile and a wave as he left. Marcus walked back up to where she was standing and looked at the house again.

"Do you fancy a walk around the land with me, see if we can find the lake and the paths down to the beach? Do you need a rest or are you ready to keep exploring?" Perplexed she smiled at him and said that she would love to see the rest of the property with him. He resisted the urge to take hold of her hand and walk around the property with her at his side. He could wait to do that another day. He was still smiling. They walked in silence for a few moments both occasionally turning back to look at the property to view it from different aspects. They smiled at each other as they walked. He knew what was happening and she didn't. He wanted to talk to her to tell her but he wanted her to see everything before he spoke to her.

They meandered around the farm for about an hour before they made their way back to his car. They had found the small lake and a rather dilapidated jetty and boat which were at the north end of the farm. They had walked back along the path that ran next to the beach and watched the birds playing on the shoreline. Paths that crossed over the public footpath to the beautiful beach were found eventually, they were now overgrown and almost absorbed back into the natural hedge.

They eventually arrived back at his car. Marcus led her by the hand to sit in the front passenger seat and took off her muddy wellies for her before placing her boots on her feet and then lacing them up. He said he felt like her knight looking after his lady, Frances giggled. He took off his own very muddy wellies and changed back into his normal shoes. Marcus closed the boot and instead of getting back into the car he walked up to the front door of the house again and sat down on the top step and waited for Frances to join him . She noticed that he was grinning like a Cheshire cat as she walked up to him. She joined in and sat down next to him, smiling too.

"What do you think, do you like it, do you see the potential for a family home, a new farm, a place for Fleur or Bertie?" Frances was now shocked and confused.

"It is absolutely beautiful and a fabulous location. Farms like this never come on the market. How did you find it and more to the point why?"

"I know the owners, I went to school with them. I always loved this farm and said that if his parents ever decided to sell it I would definitely be in the market to buy it. Glover is dealing with the sale but they phoned me and invited me along to come and view it. I've got first refusal. It's a lovely house, I love it. It has so much potential. I remember it being such a great house to play in when we were kids, full of life and lots of noise. No rules or being told to be quiet in case we upset his dad, good memories here Frances really good happy family memories. The house needs a new life and I think that I do too."

"I'm still not really sure why you need it. It really is beautiful; the location is just the best on the coast and who would say no to such an opportunity. Are you thinking of living here and not at the flat or Hall? It's a long way from Newcastle so you couldn't commute every day, could you? What's going on in your little head Mr Bucannon?"

Marcus turned and pulled her forward to look at him. He suddenly felt incredibly nervous and not as smug as he had felt most of the morning. His mouth was dry and his mind was racing. He had planned this conversation over and over in his head. What he said next would be the most important thing that he would probably say in the whole of his life and he desperately needed to get it right.

"Frances." He cleared his throat and instinctively reached out to stroke one of her hands. "I want a new life. I like being a doctor but I don't love being a doctor in a hospital, it's all too busy for me. I don't like living in a city either. My parents wanted me to be a Cardiac Consultant like dad but I wanted to be a GP, living in a local community where everyone knew me and my patients were my *own* community. I want to walk into the pub and people just say hi to me. I've applied to train to be a GP, I did that a few days ago. That was why I was at the Medical Centre when you had your midwife's appointment. I honestly didn't know that you would be there I had just arranged with one of the partners to shadow his staff for the day. I want to be in charge of my own life and build up my own farm and not just inherit one. One day in the future, I may leave here and go and live at the Hall but I want to achieve something for myself before I do. And I want my baby, our baby to have a home, a real daddy and all this will be just for him or her." He looked directly into her eyes before he spoke again, his heart was thumping in his chest . "And most importantly of all I want you." He stopped and looked for some reaction in her face. There was none.

"I love you and I think I have since I the day that I gave you a lift home in the car on the very first day that we ever met. You are all that I have thought about, dreamt about. I love you so much and that night, at the Hospital Ball, I'm so sorry that I messed it up for you. It wasn't a mistake honestly. I wanted you so much I just didn't realise that you were so inexperienced and I felt like I had taken advantage of you. I was so mad at myself and so ashamed of what I had done and how I had handled it. I was a complete coward. I was stuck in a relationship which made everyone happy but me and stuck in job which I didn't really want but I was too afraid to say anything to my parents. It wasn't until I met you that I knew exactly what I wanted and needed. I know I have let you down so much but I promise I will be the best husband in the world, the best father and hopefully the best GP that I can possibly be. I know you will let me be there for our baby now but I want you too, I really want you." She hadn't changed the expression on her face or more reassuringly, run away in fear yet! He felt braver so he carried on. "Please will you marry me because I desperately need to marry you, be with you, support you to achieve your dreams. I love you so much. I really don't think I can live another day without telling you how very much you mean to me." He stopped speaking, suddenly able to control himself again. "Franny, please will you marry me and build a family home here for the three of us, a new start for both of us. Not at my family farm or your family's farm. One day we may choose to go back to them but just for now, this would be our new home, our new start. Please say yes."

The tears started to flow, confusion flowed through her head. She wasn't sure what to say or what to think. She had not been expecting any of that at all. He said that he loved her. He said that he wanted to marry her. She was confused. She did not know how to respond to him or what to say. Last June seemed a long time ago and things had changed so much for both of them. When she had slept with him it had been perfect, full of emotions and love. She hadn't planned any of this but neither had he. Both of them seemed to have been trapped in lives that they hadn't planned or wanted but making the best of things.

She now realised that he had been planning a new life to be able to break free and make a new life for himself anyway. A life where he planned to be happy and he had asked her to be part of it with him. She had felt trapped in a life that she hadn't wanted too. She had wanted to go to medical school and had dreams of becoming a GP as well. They were so similar in many ways. She still didn't want to go back to her family farm at Rothington, the house was so full of many sad memories. Maybe in the future she would go back there to live but at the moment she was happy to let her uncle live there and run the farm.

A new life with the father of her baby, was it possible, it would be best for all three of them. A baby needs a father, she needed the support and he seemed to need her just as much as he needed the baby. He said that he loved her, really loved her. He needed her just as much as she wanted and needed him. She turned to face him, the anxiety in his face clear to see. She lifted her hands and placed them softly on either side of his face.

"Yes Marcus, I would love to marry you and build a life here with you and our baby. I think that I love you too."

Marcus pulled her into his arms and kissed her gently at first and then with all the passion that he felt. She quickly responded and fell into the comfort of his arms. Gradually they parted and he looked into her face. "I'm so glad you said yes as I had already agreed to buy the farm for us. We need to plan a wedding and then we need to get the builders in as quickly as possible if you are going to have our baby at home."

… The End